The Aristocratic Eavesdropper

Lord Andrew Tyson shamelessly leaned forward to listen to the young lady's voice coming from the terrace.

"Husbands, it appears to me, are boring, demanding, autocratic, restricting, and in my view, completely unnecessary. I cannot conceive in the slightest of what use one of them would be to me. As for love . . . if falling in love is anywhere near as painful and consuming and uncomfortable as it appears from my reading of it, I shall do without it very nicely."

Lord Andrew's eyes gleamed. Here was the woman he was looking for. A woman who believed in cool reason rather than warm passion. A woman who could be his partner in a plan that would give them both the freedom to be free . . .

Now if only he could trust her not to change her mind and lose her heart . . . if only he could trust himself . . .

THE SINGULAR MISS CARRINGTON

More Regency Romances from SIGNET

Barbara Hazard
The Singular Miss Carrington

A SIGNET BOOK

NEW AMERICAN LIBRARY

For Jo—
Another "dreamer of the day"
with love—BWH

NAL BOOKS ARE AVAILABLE AT QUANTITY DISCOUNTS WHEN USED
TO PROMOTE PRODUCTS OR SERVICES. FOR INFORMATION PLEASE
WRITE TO PREMIUM MARKETING DIVISION, NEW AMERICAN LIBRARY,
1633 BROADWAY, NEW YORK, NEW YORK 10019.

SIGNET TRADEMARK REG. U.S. PAT. OFF. AND FOREIGN COUNTRIES
REGISTERED TRADEMARK—MARCA REGISTRADA
HECHO EN CHICAGO, U.S.A.

SIGNET, SIGNET CLASSIC, MENTOR, PLUME, MERIDIAN AND NAL BOOKS
are published by
New American Library,
1633 Broadway,
New York, New York 10019

First Printing, August, 1984

1 2 3 4 5 6 7 8 9

PRINTED IN THE UNITED STATES OF AMERICA

I grant I am a woman, *but* . . .

—William Shakespeare (1564–1616)
Julius Caesar

Chapter One

"No, Wilfred. I would not marry you if you were the last man on earth, and if you ask me one more time, I shall scream. For heaven's sake, get up off your knee and take that idiotic expression from your face. You look just like a puppy who has been caught disgracing himself in the drawing room."

"Well, I like that," a young tenor voice declared indignantly. "Have you no sense of propriety at all, Claire? No lady refuses a gentleman in such a rude, vulgar way."

"I was not rude or vulgar when you asked me the first time, nor the second or third either, but since my ladylike refusals have all been ignored, I see that only the most arrogant setdown will register in that bacon brain of yours. Give over, Wilfred, do! I will not marry you, I will *never* marry you, and furthermore, it is not very flattering to know I am being asked only because of my fortune. I promise to throw any number of heiresses your way if you will but cease harassing me in this ridiculous manner."

"The trouble with you, Claire, is that your inheritance has gone to your head," the young gentleman said hotly, and then he cleared his throat and added in quite a different tone of voice, "Assure you, my love, I adore you! All of you! Your lovely face, your black curls, your gray eyes, your shapely . . . er . . ." He stopped for a moment in some confusion and then hurried on, "Eternal devotion pledged, endless concern for your well-being, say you will grant me the wish of my heart and let me make you mine—"

"Bah!"

Andrew Tyson, the Marquess of Blagdon, leaned against the balustrade of the terrace, shamelessly eavesdropping on what was quite the most interesting conversation he had heard all evening, which wasn't saying much, since his sister, Lady Peakes, had invited to her musicale what appeared to be the dullest set of bores in the *ton*. Below him in the garden, the proposal raged on.

"*Bah*, you say? Try for a little more conduct, Claire! If you continue in this care-for-nobody, eccentric way, not even your fortune will win you a husband."

"And who says I want one?" the young lady was quick to retort in her rich contralto. The marquess could almost picture the head tossing and look of scorn that surely must accompany this airy statement, and his lips curled in a grin.

"But every young lady wishes to marry," the hapless Wilfred persisted. Above him, the marquess nodded his head in agreement.

"This one doesn't. And now that Aunt Flora has left me all her money, why should I have to, just because 'everyone' does? I have quite another scheme in mind, and a husband would only complicate it."

"I have never heard the like! Come, dearest, darling Claire, stop funning and say you will marry me. You will make me the happiest of men."

"I would make you the most miserable of men, and in a very short time, too," the ruthless yet honest young lady replied. "Admit it is just the fortune, Wilfred, and your mama's pushing. You know you don't want to marry anyone just yet, and especially not me at any time. Surely you have not forgotten all the trouble I have always been to you. Remember the burs I put under your pony's saddle, the time he tossed you off so hard you broke both your arms? Or the time I made such a terrible face in church that you laughed right out loud during one of the vicar's gloomiest sermons? I have been leading you into mischief since we were children, and you have always hated it. And when you consider the time I . . . But no, I do not think you realize I was behind that escapade even to this day. I shall say no more."

"I do so want to marry you—you, and no one else in the world," the gentleman persisted, and then he ruined this fervent plea by adding, "What escapade? Tell me at once!"

The marquess folded his arms and grinned. No doubt his sister would castigate his behavior in listening to a private conversation as ungentlemanly, but he had no intention of either making his presence known or going away. He was enjoying himself too much. Although he had never felt the least urge to propose to any lady of his acquaintance, he could not help but feel that the hapless Wilfred was going

8

about things entirely in the wrong manner. Why didn't the boy just sweep her into his arms and kiss her? Then at least she would not be able to argue and dispute everything he said. Some sympathetic masculine brain wave must have wafted over the balustrade, for suddenly he heard the young lady squeak.

"Now I know you are mad! Let me go, Wilfred, before I am forced to scream the house down. And how would you explain that to your mother and Lady Peakes?"

"One kiss, dearest Claire," a panting voice exclaimed, and the marquess could hear very plainly the sounds of a struggle beneath him. He wondered if he should go to the young lady's assistance, but somehow he was sure she was capable of handling the situation without his intervention. Only a moment later he congratulated himself for his astuteness, as he heard the young man howl in pain.

"You devil, Claire! Now, why did you do that?" his indignant voice demanded. "I think—no, I know—I am bleeding."

"I detest being pawed, Wilfred. Besides, it is all your own fault. I warned you, and if you had let me go I would never have had to hit you. Here, take my handkerchief. Your nose is dripping all over your cravat. Do go put a key down your back, or go home and lie down."

"Someday, Claire, when you meet your match and get your comeuppance, I hope I will be there to see it. I cannot tell you how happy I shall be when that day arrives," Wilfred said somewhat thickly from behind her handkerchief, all loverlike accents gone from his voice.

"But I told you I am not going to make any matches. Husbands, it appears to me, are boring, demanding, autocratic, restricting, and, in my view, completely unnecessary. I cannot conceive in the slightest of what use one of them would be to me."

The marquess's grin widened as he wondered what this singular young lady looked like. Her point of view was refreshingly different from that of most girls her age, whose only ambition in life appeared to be matrimony to a wealthy, titled gentleman as soon as they and their mamas could contrive it.

"But . . . but," Wilfred persisted, "what about love? Children? Companionship? Someone to shield you from the tempests of life?"

Claire laughed, a silvery cascade of complete enjoyment. "And to walk into the sunset hand in hand with, my dear? Come, Wilfred! I can face the 'tempests of life,' as you so poetically put it, O my Byron, by myself. Companionship I can have without marrying, with the added satisfaction that if the companion of the moment begins to pall, I shall be free to move on to others. I don't know anything about children, and since, unlike men, I do not have to produce heirs for Aunt Flora's illustrious line, why should I even consider them? As for love . . . if falling in love is anywhere near as painful and consuming and uncomfortable as it appears from my reading of it, I shall do without it very nicely."

"*Claire!*" The young man drew in his breath sharply. "You cannot mean . . . You do not understand . . . I beg you to moderate your conversation . . ."

Again she laughed, and the marquess, who had leaned nearer in astonishment at this forthright speech, frowned a little.

"I have shocked you, Wilfred, as I always manage to do. But why does what I say surprise you? You know the way I was brought up."

"Yes, I know, and if your Aunt Flora is not even now being brought to book in heaven, if indeed she is even there after the way she raised you, I would be astounded. You cannot mean what you say, admit it, Claire."

There was silence for a moment, and then the young lady said in a quieter voice, "Perhaps not. But since the desire for love seems to have been left out of my makeup, I do not fear its dire consequences. Men may be necessary for some women, but I have never met one I could spend my life with, and that includes you, my old friend."

Andrew Tyson heard someone come out on the terrace and moved away, a little disappointed that his enjoyment in the drama being enacted below him must cease. Whatever would the young lady say next? he wondered as he strolled back to the drawing room. The trio of musicians was just finishing a selection, and his sister came toward him from across the room.

"Wherever have you been for so long, Drew?" she asked in a petulant, scolding voice as she took his arm. "I have even had Percy searching, for Lady Greeley has been asking for you this age."

The marquess looked down at his older sister and an

impatient look came over his face. Anyone could see that they were brother and sister, although at forty the lady was older, and since her marriage, had become very proud. She was a tall, handsome woman with blond hair and icy blue eyes, and the only difference between them was that the marquess had a warmer expression and did not sport such a superior air. Now he raised an eyebrow and said in his deep voice, "Do me the kindness, Marion, to somehow inform Lady Greeley that I have no intention of proposing to her daughter. Perhaps if the matter was made plain to her, she would stop pursuing me so relentlessly. It would be such a relief to me, and to your dear husband as well, for then he could cease dogging my footsteps at every turn."

Lady Peakes looked more petulant than ever. "You are being ridiculous, Drew. Besides, you know Mama and I have made up our minds that your bachelor days are over. Pamela Greeley is perfect for you; why can't you like her? She is pretty—nay, beautiful—with that golden hair so like your own, and those melting blue eyes and lovely figure. What handsome children you will have! Her conversation and demeanor are such as must always earn approbation; she thinks just as she ought. Besides, her lineage is impeccable. It is too tiresome of you, Drew, and I, for one, do not understand why you have taken her in such dislike."

The marquess stifled a sigh. "I have not taken her in dislike; I have no intention of taking her anywhere, most certainly not up a church aisle. Perhaps it is because I cannot recall a single occasion on which the young lady had anything of interest to say."

"Why should that concern you? You are not marrying her to *talk* to her."

One of the marquess's blond eyebrows quirked and an unholy light came into his eyes, and his sister added quickly, "You must admit she is beautiful."

"Her beauty does not tempt me, but perhaps that is because I remember that your blue eyes were once called 'melting' too."

"Indeed? What has that to say to anything?" his sister persisted, continuing to nod and smile at her guests as she did so. "Remember, you were thirty-four in March."

"I realize that, my dear, but when the time comes, I shall choose the lady myself. I will not be badgered and bothered by the likes of Lady Greeley, or even by you and Mama. It is too bad of me, I know—you need not point out my failings one more time."

Lady Peakes glanced sideways and saw from the militant look on his face that he was determined to have his own way. She thought to herself that it was a pity that Drew had always been so stubborn, even as she changed the subject, knowing from long experience it would be useless to continue to press him now.

As they strolled around the large room, the marquess asked idly, "Do you know a young lady named Claire who is here this evening? And a young man named Wilfred?"

His sister looked puzzled for a moment, and then her face brightened. "You must mean the Wilfred who is Lord Wilson. He is here with his mother, and they brought a Miss Carrington with them. I am not personally acquainted with her, for she is new-come to town, but I believe Lady Wilson has her in her eye for her son. Of course he is only twenty-two and the girl somewhat older, but she is a great heiress. There was something else about her that was unusual, as I recall, but at the moment it escapes me."

"For someone you have never met before this evening, you are well-informed," the marquess observed, taking two glasses of champagne from a footman's tray and giving one to his sister.

Marion sipped and shrugged her shoulders. "One hears things, as you know, Drew. Sometimes I think there is nothing kept secret from the *beau monde*. And that reminds me, I have heard the most diverting thing and must find Percy at once and tell him of it. Do go and at least speak to Lady Greeley, for she must know I have told you she wishes your attendance. She is over there on that sofa."

The marquess looked across the room and saw the lady in question smiling and beckoning, her lovely blond daughter blushing beside her, and he sighed at his entrapment.

As he was making his way to their sides, a young lady coming in the opposite direction sidestepped a group of people and brushed against his arm.

"Your pardon, sir," she said, and the marquess had no difficulty in recognizing the low voice of Wilfred's determined spinster. He smiled at her and bowed, observing her carefully. He saw at a glance that she was not beautiful in the conventional sense: her forehead was too high and her nose too aquiline, but there was such an alive expression on her oval face, such intelligence in her large gray eyes, and such a vulnerability to her soft, full lips that were now curved in a tentative smile, that he could not help but be attracted in spite of her strange coiffure of cropped black curls. He judged her to be in her middle twenties. She was of medium height with a lithe, slender body, and she wore a plain blue silk gown that would arouse no envy in any female breast, although she held herself with grace and poise.

Suddenly she raised one black eyebrow at his scrutiny, and a warm smile broke out on his face and crinkled his eyes as he said, "You were quite right. Wilfred would not do for you at all."

"I beg your pardon?" she asked, her eyes now intent and puzzled. "Have we met, sir?"

The marquess bowed and she continued to stare at him, subjecting him to the same examination she had just received. She saw a man over thirty, who from the look of him was a complete town beau from the top of his faultlessly arranged blond hair down his elegant evening attire to his polished pumps. He had a rather long face with strong bones and dark blue eyes, and he was tall and somewhat lean in build, but he had a good pair of shoulders, and no valet would ever have to add sawdust to his silk stockings to improve his calves.

"I have not had the pleasure of a formal introduction, but I hope to remedy that in short order," he said, his deep voice as warm and intimate as if they were old friends who shared a secret.

She shrugged and would have moved away, except he tapped a woman nearby on the shoulder and said, "My dear Lady Hartley, be so good as to introduce me to this young lady, if you please, and assure her I am sober, trustworthy, and harmless."

Lady Hartley turned and smiled. "I shall warn her, rather, Drew, that you are incorrigible! Miss Carrington, let me make you known to Andrew Tyson, Marquess of Blagdon."

The marquess bowed and took the lady's hand, noticing she had neglected to curtsy, and wondering at it. "How delightful to meet you, Miss Carrington," he said, leading her over to a sofa somewhat removed from the others. The trio was tuning their instruments again as he seated her. Miss Carrington did not appear to be flustered by his singling her out this way. For himself, he was careful not to look in Lady Greeley's direction.

"And now we must become better acquainted," he said as he took the seat beside her.

"Why?" Miss Carrington asked in a cool voice.

The marquess checked for a moment. That was not quite the response he was used to receiving when he showed any interest in the opposite sex.

"Why, because I have a proposition to make to you, Miss Carrington," he replied just as coolly. Her eyebrows rose again, but he noticed her hands were folded serenely in her lap, and she sat quietly with no sign of disquiet as she waited to hear him out.

"First I must admit that I overheard you just now in the garden with someone called Wilfred. I inferred that he was an old childhood friend who was now desirous of a warmer relationship with you. Am I correct?"

He paused, and Miss Carrington inclined her head, her huge gray eyes never leaving his face. When she did not speak, the marquess went on, "When I saw you just now, it occurred to me that we might be of mutual benefit to each other. You see, Miss Carrington, I too am being pursued, and like you, want no part of it."

"But as a man, you do not have to play a passive role." She spoke at last, as calmly as if they were discussing the weather. He was delighted that she did not blush or stammer or act at all offended by this unusual conversational topic. "Even if you are being pursued, surely it is easy for you to avoid the lady? And no one can force you to ask for her hand. How lucky men are! Now, I have to listen to all kinds of silly flirting and passionate speeches without a weapon in my arsenal."

"What you say is true. On the other hand, I do not think you have any idea how helpless a man can feel when he is being stalked not only by the young lady and her mama but also by his own determined female relatives."

Miss Carrington's soft, mobile lips curved in a broad smile. "*En garde,* sir. Formidable opponents, to be sure."

"Most formidable," Lord Blagdon agreed with a small shudder. "I am not a coward, but after successfully defending my single state for some years now, I suddenly feel them all closing in on me. I should dislike leaving London during the Season, but I was beginning to feel that was my only recourse until I overheard you in the garden."

He paused and waited, and Miss Carrington looked down at her clasped hands for a moment before she remarked, "That

14

was not the act of a gentleman, was it, sir? To eavesdrop on another's proposal?''

"I admit to frequent lapses from that state," he said without a bit of regret.

To his surprise, she laughed, the silvery scale he had heard before. "So do I," she said, nodding her head. "Admit I am not always a lady, as the world defines one, I mean.''

"Shall we keep that information to ourselves?" Lord Blagdon grinned.

"Very well. And now, what is this proposition you want to make to me? I admit I am intrigued.''

She seemed so much older than he knew she must be, almost as old as he was himself, that he had to remind himself to go gently, so as not to frighten her.

"Miss Carrington, since *you* do not want to marry, and *I* do not want to marry, it occurred to me that we might band together for our mutual benefit. If it were suddenly noticed that I have formed a definite *tendre* for you, and you encourage my attentions, all our pursuers will be forced to retreat, and we may be comfortable.''

As Miss Carrington's eyes widened, he added, "I have not shocked you, I hope.''

She smiled again. "I think you would find it very difficult to do so, sir. I have never been missish.''

"What do you think of my scheme?" he asked.

Miss Carrington appeared to give it serious thought, her head tilted to one side as she pondered. "I see only one flaw, and one condition that I must make as well," she said at last. At his questioning look, she added, "It will mean we must spend a great deal of time together, will it not? There is no sense in pretending an attraction if we do not do so, for no one would believe us.''

"True. But why is that a flaw?" the marquess asked, completely bewildered.

"Suppose we find we do not care for each other's company? And even to avoid the pleas of Wilfred and M'lord . . . er . . . some others, I would not like to be bored.''

Lord Blagdon stiffened and raised a haughty eyebrow. "I shall do my best not to be boring, Miss Carrington," he said. If he had not heard her before, he would have been completely nonplussed at her frankness, and displeased at the unconventional freedom with which she addressed him. No one had ever considered him boring, and after having his company sought for so many years, his lightest *bon mot* greeted with laughter all around, and his pronouncements listened to so attentively, he could not like the thought that she might find him less than amusing.

She seemed to sense his withdrawal, for she leaned toward him. "I am sure you will not," she said, her voice kind, "but then, a bore is always the last to know he is one, isn't that so? Then too, you might find my open ways insupportable, my conversation insipid, and my interests of no interest to you at all. What do we do then?"

Somewhat mollified, the marquess took her hand. "Why, then, Miss Carrington, we decide we do not suit, and part. However, I hope we do not discover that for over two months at least. The Greeleys leave for Brighton July 1. But tell me, what is the condition you must insist on?"

"That at no time you will fall in love with me," she said, her expression earnest.

The marquess looked dumbfounded, and dropped her hand. "My dear Miss Carrington! I have no intention of doing so, my promise on it!" He paused and added, a new light in his dark blue eyes, "I should also require the selfsame promise from you, should I not? But how to phrase it without appearing insufferably conceited, I do not know."

"Why should you trouble yourself? I do not consider myself conceited in making the condition, just cautious. But you need not fear, sir, for I have no intention of falling in love with you or any other man."

She did not seem to notice that the marquess looked less than pleased as she continued, "Very well, let us try your scheme. You have my agreement—that is, if you are still desirous of going on with it."

The marquess collected himself and nodded. "Of course! And you may be assured I shall be on my mettle not to bore you or succumb to your considerable charms."

"What do we do now?" the lady asked, looking about her for the first time to see several pairs of eyes intent on their particular sofa, as she completely ignored his polished compliment.

"We remain here awhile longer, talking and laughing, and then I take you to my sister and introduce you, hovering close to your side. Eventually we part, and I call on you tomorrow. Perhaps a ride in the park will give us visibility. You do ride, don't you?"

"Indifferently. I would prefer to walk or be driven," she told him. He said he would be delighted to oblige her with a drive in his phaeton, and a time was set and her direction given.

"Will this cause any trouble for you with Wilfred or his mother?" he asked next.

"They will not be pleased. Oh, Wilfred will be, ridiculous boy! But his mother has set her heart on attaining my fortune and my estate. It marches with theirs, and she knows a good thing when she sees it, even to overlooking the unconventionality of my upbringing."

"I shall look forward to hearing all about it," Lord Blagdon told her, and then, as the music ended to applause, he rose and held out his arm to escort her to the group around his sister.

He noticed that Marion had on her most haughty we-are-not-amused look, and hoped she would not try to give the unusual Miss Carrington a setdown, for he was sure that young lady would be much too accomplished an opponent. But Lady Peakes was annoyed only with her brother for not going to Lady Greeley, and this new girl he had on his arm was of interest only because Drew had spent so much time at her side.

By careful questioning, she discovered Miss Carrington was twenty-four, resided in Berkshire, and had been brought up by a spinster aunt, a Lady Flora Dawson, after the untimely deaths of her parents when she was an infant.

"I believe I have heard of Lady Dawson," Lady Peakes said, her brow furrowed in thought. "But in what context escapes me now. No matter. You are here in London for the Season, Miss Carrington?"

Claire admitted she was, and volunteered the information that she was staying with a distant relative, General Archibald Banks, and his wife in Belgrave Square. The marquess hoped Marion would not notice the gleam of amusement in Miss Carrington's large gray eyes at the quizzing she was receiving, but his sister seemed oblivious of it.

"The dear old general, of course," she said, her cold voice managing a slight degree of warmth. "Quite a pet of mine, although it is too bad you must make your home with such an elderly couple during the Season. It cannot be amusing for you."

"It is true they live a retired life now, but there is so much to see and do in London, I do not miss a household full of activity. And Belgrave Square is so central, I can walk anywhere I wish in only a few minutes."

Lady Peakes, who had been known to call for her carriage for a visit to friends across St. James's Square, looked a little surprised at this, but before she could comment, Claire saw the Wilsons beckoning and excused herself. "My escorts are ready to leave. Thank you for a pleasant evening, ma'am. The flautist was especially talented. Sir."

She held out her hand first to her hostess and then to Lord Blagdon and smiled. Again she did not curtsy, but he distracted Marion's attention from this by reminding Miss Carrington that he would call for her at three the following afternoon.

As she moved gracefully away, his sister took his arm. "And what are you about now, Drew? You are up to something, for I know that look! And why did you avoid Lady Greeley when I told you she wished to see you?"

"But Lady Greeley's overabundant middle-aged charm cannot compete with Miss Carrington's elegant grace, my dear," he teased. When he saw she was about to argue, he put up a detaining hand. "Very well, I shall go over and do the pretty for a moment, but I don't mind telling you, I found that young lady intriguing. Who knows? Perhaps I have met my fate at last."

His sister watched his retreat with narrowed eyes for a moment, but then she was drawn away to say good night to several of her guests, and she resolved to speak to her mother as soon as she could manage it. There was something about the Dawson-Carrington connection—now, what could it be? But Mama will know, she told herself as she smiled and chatted.

The marquess was not kept long by Lady Greeley, for she was distinctly miffed, and her beauteous daughter was pouting in her disappointment. He smiled and chatted for a moment, as if nothing was wrong, before he said he looked forward to seeing them soon again, and bowed with loose-limbed grace to take his leave. Already Miss Carrington's presence by his side had been of great benefit, and he hoped for her sake that Wilfred's mother had also noticed the time they had spent together *tête-à-tête*.

Lady Wilson had certainly done so, and Claire was questioned at great length for the amount of time it took their carriage to return her to the general's town house.

"I have heard that Andrew Tyson is an incorrigible flirt, dear Claire," Lady Wilson warned her. "I would not like to think you had been taken in by any of his courtesy tonight. Quite likely he will give you the cut direct when next you meet."

"How awkward that would be, ma'am, especially when you consider that he is taking me driving tomorrow. Perhaps I should bring a book?"

Lady Wilson gasped, her pouter-pigeon breast swelling and her fat little hands aflutter. "Taking you driving? Now, how can this be, Claire? I distinctly heard you refuse Wilfred's escort earlier today, did I not, dear son?"

Her son squirmed as he peered into Claire's face with concern from his seat facing the ladies, and she smiled at him.

"Perhaps I knew Lord Blagdon was going to ask me, ma'am. You know I look forward to making a great many new friends in town, and although I am of course grateful for your escort, I would not think of troubling you or Wilfred for any length of time."

She was assured in fervent accents that it was no trouble at all, but their great delight, and on Lady Wilson's kicking her son in the shin, Wilfred chimed in and vowed that being by her side was his only pleasure in life.

As they drew up before the general's house, Lady Wilson remarked that old friends were the best friends after all, and Claire took her leave of them with her warm smile, but with no further comment. That Wilfred would be treated to a lecture on the way to their lodgings, she would be willing to wager any amount.

She greeted the elderly butler and scolded him for waiting up for her before she went to her room, thinking over her meeting with Andrew Tyson. There were those, she knew, who would condemn the course they planned to take, and those who would say she was foolish to agree so quickly without knowing more about the man. He might be a rake and a libertine, a card sharp or even a man on the lookout for a wealthy heiress himself, but somehow she did not think so. She had liked the way his dark blue eyes crinkled shut when he was amused, and the way he held his gleaming blond head so proudly, as well as the boldness of his proposal and his unconcern for the proprieties. Small things to base your trust on, she knew, but she was used to relying on her intuition and it had seldom led her astray. Besides, it would be an easy matter to question Martha Banks in the morning. Her hostess might live retired from the world, but she kept abreast of the *ton* from an assiduous reading of the court news in the newspapers, and innumerable sessions over the teacups with her friends.

Claire undressed without summoning a maid, as was her custom, and was soon fast asleep.

The following morning she joined her hostess in the breakfast room and in the course of the conversation mentioned that she was engaged to drive in the park with Andrew Tyson, whom she had met at Lady Peakes's musicale. Lady Banks opened her little round eyes wide in astonishment and clapped her hands in delight.

"Oh, my dear," she gurgled, all her gray curls bobbing under her lace morning cap, "how delightful! The Marquess of Blagdon, my, my! He will be a feather for your cap, for you must know he is one of London's premier beaux. Such wealth, such wit, such a handsome face and figger!" Lady Banks sighed.

"And so sought after, dear ma'am?" Claire asked, smiling at her elderly hostess as she took another muffin.

"For years, my dear," Lady Banks assured her. "He has never come up to scratch, and there are those who say he never will, but I have heard that his sister and his mother, the dowager marchioness, have taken a hand in the matter this Season. My cousin Lizzie tells me that his capitulation to Pamela Greeley is only a matter of time. How surprised she will be to learn you have caught his eye."

Claire knew that Lady Banks was delighted to have a piece of news that her cousin did not possess, for they were in constant rivalry, and she smiled as she realized she had made Lady Banks's day. After asking about the Tyson family and learning where in the country their estates were located, she could gain no further information, for Lady Banks had no idea what the man's main interests were.

"Do you mean what he does to amuse himself, dear Claire?" the old lady asked, looking bewildered. "Why, I assume he rides and hunts and attends balls and parties as all men do. He does not gamble or imbibe overmuch, or it would have come to my ears, and his *affaires de coeur* have all been conducted with discretion."

"No, I did not mean his amusements precisely, ma'am. Do you know what he finds to do with himself at other times? Does he care for any of the arts or for travel? Is he a music lover, or perhaps a scholar of anthropology or antiquity or literature?"

Lady Banks looked puzzled, as though she didn't understand the question, but she gallantly offered to investigate. Claire denied her with a smile of thanks.

"I shall find out myself, ma'am, never fear. I do hope, however, that hunting and parties are not the entire scope of his life. If that is so, it will be a long time until July, if indeed I am able to keep my part of the bargain that long."

Lady Banks did not understand her, but by this time she was used to dear Claire's incomprehensible remarks, and since she was not a clever woman, had ceased trying to understand them. She knew Claire was endowed with all kinds of gifts, from intelligence and health and looks to wealth and education and good birth, but she had never felt so sorry for anyone in her entire life as she did for her young relation. She was careful to keep this feeling from Claire, however. She knew the girl would hate pity, and if the reason for it was explained, would laugh out loud to think that anyone deplored her life and background.

Lady Banks went away to get ready for a morning's shopping trip after asking Claire if she could drop her anywhere, knowing all the while that her guest would choose to walk, as she always did.

Chapter Two

In another part of town, Lady Peakes, with her husband in
attendance, was making a morning call on the Dowager
Marchioness of Blagdon, for she felt her mama's counsel on
such an important subject as Drew's latest start should not be
delayed.

As they waited in the cold, formal drawing room for this lady
to make an appearance, she wondered out loud again about
Miss Carrington and her aunt, Lady Dawson.

"I am sure I have heard some rumors, Percy," she said,
frown lines coming between her brows, "but what they can
be continues elusive. Are you sure you know nothing of the
family?"

She looked to her tall, thin husband, his bald pate gleaming
in the light from the fire as he warmed his hands against the
chill of the early-May morning. At his wife's question, he
frowned as well. " 'Fraid not, old gel," he said finally.
"Never seen in town, not part of the social whirl, don't
y'know."

"Think, Percy, think! She is from Berkshire, she said so
last night."

Thus ordered, Percy frowned again, his usual expression
when he set his brain cells in motion, but fortunately for his
mental prowess, his mother-in-law came in then. After greeting them formally, she took her customary seat in the high-
backed wing chair that one wag had designated "the throne."
The dowager marchioness was even prouder and more haughty
than her daughter. She found many things in life regrettable,
but her major disappointment was that her late husband had
been so remiss as not to have been born heir to a dukedom.
She considered the rank of duchess much more appropriate to
one of her exalted quality.

"I am surprised to see you, daughter," she said as she
arranged her skirts, and Percy hastened to adjust her footstool.

"There was something of great importance about which you wished to consult me?"

In her frigid tone was more than a hint of displeasure, for her daughter knew very well that she was supposed to make prior arrangements before calling on her. The dowager deplored the casual modern custom of dropping in without an exchange of formal notes, even going so far one afternoon as to refuse to readmit Lady Jersey when she returned to get the gloves she had left behind her on her morning call, because she had not written to say she was coming again. Lord Peakes, remembering this, adjusted the lace at his cuffs while he eyed his mama-in-law with some trepidation. He was very much under the cat's foot in his own home, but the combination of his wife and her mother completely cowed him.

"I must ask you, Mama, if you know anything of a Lady Flora Dawson," Marion began, getting straight to the matter at hand.

Lady Blagdon inclined her gray head a fraction of an inch. "I do," she said, and her daughter noticed how her thin lips tightened, her pinched nose rose in the air, and an even more disdainful expression came into her hard blue eyes. "I do not choose to speak of the woman, however. You notice I did not call her a lady? Just so."

Very unusually, after such a declaration, Lady Peakes persisted. "But we must speak of her, Mama. Her niece, a Miss Claire Carrington, came to my musicale last evening as a guest of Lady Wilson, and Drew was very taken with her. In fact, he spent over half an hour at her side in animated conversation *à deux*. If you had not spent so much time in the card room, you might have seen him for yourself."

Her voice was a little tart, for it was a bone of contention with her that her mother insisted on playing whist with her cronies everywhere she went, no matter what entertainment had been planned by her hostess. The dowager ignored the comment, as she always did, and remarked with considerable scorn, "I have never thought Lady Wilson had even a modicum of sense."

It was obvious she thought it was all that lady's fault for bringing an unsuitable female with her, and where the marquess's roving eye might light on her as well, and she shook her head at such folly. Her only son had always been a sore problem to her, refusing to take her advice and follow her instructions as to the way his life should be lived, his affairs conducted, and his dignity upheld, and as he grew older, he became less and less malleable.

"But, Mama, who was Lady Dawson? And why do you speak of her with such aversion?" Lady Peakes persisted.

Lady Blagdon's thin shoulders stiffened. "It is not unusual that you, daughter, and your husband as well, are ignorant of the woman. Although she made a great scandal, it was many years ago. She was an only child, and when her father died and left her one of the estates and a truly munificent amount of money, she announced she had no intention of conforming to the mores of society, and meant to travel and study and conduct herself as if she were a man. Hmmph! I was in town then for my first Season, for we were almost the same age, and when a relative brought her to London hoping to marry her to some worthy peer, she scandalized society by her behavior and *outré* opinions. Opinions, my dear Marion, no lady would ever have entertained for a moment, much less voiced, but Lady Dawson was known to say whatever came into her head, even in mixed company. I remember one evening when she informed the Duchess of Devonshire that she thought our matrimonial system was a barbaric custom which treated women as mindless chattels, and that she for one would never consent to throwing herself away on some man who probably did not have the brains she did, nor the education or wit. Well! You can imagine the uproar. But that was not the worst of it. Lady Dawson concluded by saying the world was overpopulated already, and she did not intend to contribute to the problem herself, just because—in her words—some stupid man wanted an heir to perpetuate a line that would be better left to die out."

Lady Peakes gasped, her husband coughed, and the dowager nodded. "Fortunately, she left the country shortly thereafter, for otherwise she would have been ostracized by anyone of the slightest refinement. I believe she lived in an African village for a while and at one time joined an expedition of male explorers in northern Canada."

The dowager's disapproving voice as she concluded this strange tale hinted of unseemly bacchanals in torrid jungles and on frozen ice caps, and her face was white with her distaste, which unfortunately her son-in-law failed to notice.

"Rather like that old gel who hung about with the bedouins, traveling by camel and sleeping in tents, what?" he remarked brightly, pleased to be able to contribute to the conversation.

"If you please, Lord Peakes," the dowager said in icy disgust, "not in my drawing room."

Lord Peakes subsided, his face red, while his wife continued to look shocked. "But Lady Dawson raised Miss Carrington, who is her niece. Is it not entirely possible that she transmitted her own peculiar ideas to the girl?"

Her mother thought for a moment. "Did Miss Carrington curtsy to her betters?" she asked.

"Now that I recall it, she did not. She gave me her hand in parting, quite as if we were two tradesmen concluding a bargain over fish or coal."

Lady Blagdon sniffed. "Flora Dawson did not believe in rank or titles. She claimed a scullery maid was, in many cases, just as good as, if not better than, anyone in the *ton*. We all wondered what she would do if she were ever presented to the king, but that never happened, for which I am sure all society was grateful."

She closed her eyes for a moment and then added, "It is, of course, unfortunate that the girl was in your drawing room last evening, but everyone, knowing the nicety of our standards, will put it down to an unfortunate mistake, brought about by the stupidity of Lady Wilson. From now on we will have nothing to do with her. I myself will cut her if she dares to approach me."

"But, Mama, if Drew is showing a partiality for her, we must acknowledge her."

The dowager sat up even straighter, if that were possible. "It has often been my opinion, Marion, as you know, that Andrew delights in being difficult, but in this case it will be unnecessary for us to take steps. He has only to spend a little time with the young woman and all will be made plain. You cannot be suggesting, daughter, that my son is so lost to all reason and sensitivity that he would overlook ill-bred oddity, or wish to consort with peculiar females?"

Lady Peakes was quick to say that she was sure Drew would do just as he ought, but remembering the mischief in her brother's dark blue eyes, she could not be comfortable. Mama might think Drew's inherent good taste and the fact that he was her son would make him conform, but I have no such reliance on his good sense, she thought as she gathered her stole and reticule and went to give her mother a chaste kiss of farewell on her high, narrow forehead. After all, men have been caught before by the unusual, especially men as bored as Drew appears to be. She was very quiet on the drive back to St. James's Square.

Lord Blagdon was prompt to arrive at Belgrave Square at three that afternoon, and if he was surprised to see Miss Carrington waiting for him at curbside, instead of seated in the general's drawing room beside her hostess, he managed to hide his astonishment. As his groom ran to the horses' heads, he prepared to get down and help her into the phaeton, only to find her springing up with a light step to take the seat beside him before he could play the *galant*.

This afternoon she was wearing a severe gray gown and matching cloak which privately he thought made her look somewhat nunlike, but he was quick to compliment her on her appearance, for he knew all girls expected it.

Miss Carrington seemed surprised and she glanced down at herself as if she had forgotten what she was wearing. "This, sir? Well, it does have the advantage of not showing the dirt, and London, as you know, is a filthy city."

Lord Blagdon stared at her and promptly forgot the gray gown. Her cheeks were rosy as if she had been out-of-doors for some time, and under the brim of her bonnet a few short curls peeked out, black and shiny. Her large gray eyes were sparkling, and he noticed they were fringed with ridiculously long thick lashes. Miss Carrington was better-looking than he had first supposed.

"I hope I did not keep you waiting, ma'am?" he asked next.

"No, you were very prompt, a trait I admire. It was I who ran the risk of delay, for I was just coming home as your carriage entered the square, and I had to run the last hundred yards so I would be before you."

"You ran? Through Belgrave Square?" Lord Blagdon asked, somewhat stunned.

"Of course! Running is very good exercise, and exercise makes a healthy body. Don't you agree with me?"

Lord Blagdon was glad the gates of Hyde Park had to be maneuvered just then, so he did not have to answer. He wondered what Michaels, his groom, was making of his companion and her conversation. He himself had never heard a young lady even acknowledge she had a body, much less call it by name.

As the team settled into a steady trot, another thought occurred to him. "But where was your maid, or your footman?"

Miss Carrington chuckled. "I never have a servant in attendance, sir. I dislike being trailed by them, and I consider it an unnecessary waste of their time."

The marquess stole a glance at her profile, somewhat at a loss for words. That anyone would consider it important whether a servant was wasting his time or not was an alien thought to him. "But they serve as protection, Miss Carrington," he said. "They are not there merely to lend you consequence."

She turned toward him and smiled. "At my age, sir, I am well able to take care of myself. Of course, when I venture into a rough part of town, I take a hackney or Lady Banks's carriage. I have traveled extensively with my aunt, and there is nothing in London to compare with many Italian districts for *banditti*, or the Paris streets for pickpockets. If I can protect myself there, I am sure London holds no greater evils."

Lord Blagdon nodded to his friend Mr. Venables, who was escorting his mother on a stroll. It was clear that Mrs. Venables had noticed him and his companion, for she could be seen to begin questioning her son at some length, a fact the marquess was quick to point out to the lady by his side. He was not averse to changing the subject in any case, although he wondered what rough parts of town Miss Carrington felt it necessary to frequent, and for what reason.

"Mrs. Venables will be a great ally of ours, Miss Carrington, for she is one of London's most accomplished quizzes. She will spread the news of our drive throughout the *ton*, and I would wager anything you like that by tomorrow morning we will be the latest *on-dit*."

"Do call me Claire," she invited. "Miss Carrington this and Miss Carrington that can hardly suit our purpose. And I shall call you Andrew."

"You don't feel that once around the park and a half-hour spent at a musicale together might not be considered enough of an acquaintance for such informality, Miss . . . er, Claire?" the marquess asked.

Miss . . . er, Claire tilted her head a little in the way he was beginning to recognize meant she was considering his words. Instead of answering, she asked, "Tell me, Andrew, are you very conventional and straitlaced? I only ask because I can see that if you are, we will have a hazardous road to travel. There are a great many things you do not know about me, and I would hate to shock or delude you. Perhaps it would be best if I tell you more about myself while there is still time for you to withdraw from our agreement.''

"I should be delighted to hear everything at a time when we can be private,'' Lord Blagdon announced, motioning with his head to where the groom clung to the back of the phaeton. Miss Carrington's eyes widened and gleamed with some inner mirth, but to his relief, she did not persist, and followed his lead when he began to discuss the guests they had met at the musicale.

"Tell me, ma'am, do you attend the Willoughby ball this evening? I would beg a dance or two,'' he said next.

"No, I will not be there. I received an invitation, but I refused it.''

"What a shame! Lady Willoughby is noted for her balls, and it would be the perfect occasion to further our friendship.''

Miss Carrington laughed, the same silvery scale he had heard last evening. "It would certainly be that, for we would have the entire evening to converse. You see, Andrew, I do not dance.''

The marquess dropped his hands inadvertently, and the team picked up the pace. "You don't dance? But . . . but everyone dances.''

"What a ridiculous thing to say when I have just told you I do not. My aunt did not consider dancing a proper activity for me.''

Lord Blagdon smiled in some relief. "It is unfortunate that she was so prim and strict, for you will miss some wonderful parties.''

"Oh, Aunt Flora was not at all prim or strict.'' Miss Carrington gurgled, as if she were vastly amused by his comment. "You see, she considered dancing, and most especially the waltz, a form of stylized, substitute mating between the sexes that it was better not to indulge in.''

The team began to canter before the marquess brought them back to a more decorous pace, while faintly behind him he heard his groom stifling a cough.

"My aunt said the birds did it better than any humans she had ever observed,'' the irrepressible Miss Carrington explained.

Lord Blagdon, who had been about to suggest she have private lessons, bit his tongue and pulled his team to the side of the road. "Michaels, walk the horses if we should be delayed," he ordered as the groom ran to their heads. "Miss Car . . . Claire, I suggest we walk for a bit."

His voice was so stern that Claire looked at him in surprise, to find his mouth set in a firm line and his blue eyes cold.

"Wait until I come around before you try to get down," he ordered when he saw her begin to rise obediently. Miss Carrington allowed the marquess his chivalry, although she was perfectly capable of descending from even a high-perch phaeton without any help, and she took the arm he held out to her, not noticing the openmouthed stare of his groom as they walked away.

The marquess did not attempt a conversation until a narrow side path was reached, but as soon as he had taken her that way, he said, "Do you delight in shocking people, Miss Carrington, or is it merely bad manners?"

"Bad manners?" she asked, her voice incredulous. "How can you possibly say that, Andrew? Surely my aunt's opinion of ballroom dancing cannot have occasioned this stern disapproval of yours. After all, you did ask, and if you have ever observed a peacock courting a hen, you would have to agree with her."

"I think you had better tell me about Lady Flora Dawson right now," he said.

"Of course. We are certainly private here." They had reached the Serpentine, and as she looked around, she spotted a bench. "Shall we be seated, or do you prefer to continue our walk?"

The marquess led her to the bench and seated her, but he did not take his place by her side, preferring to stand before her, one booted foot on the bench and his arms folded across his thigh as he leaned forward slightly in order to better see her face.

Her aunt's eccentric life-style was not soon told, although Claire was as brief as possible. She looked straight into his eyes as she spoke, and so she was able to see a myriad of expressions cross his face in only a few minutes: shock, surprise, disapproval, horror, and, yes, she was relieved to see, even amusement.

"So you see, when my parents died when I was just three, Aunt Flora was the only relative I had left to bring me up,"

29

she concluded. "She died a year ago, and I miss her still. But I will always be grateful to her, for taking over a baby's care meant she had to curtail her traveling for some years. I know she was planning a trip to Brazil and she was not able to go for the first time until I was twelve and could accompany her. She was most anxious to see the Amazon, and she had always been fascinated by tales of headhunters and snakes."

"Headhunters? Snakes?"

"Yes, she made a study of them and kept several at Dawson Hall. Snakes, I mean, not headhunters," she added at his uplifted brows. "It was not an area where I echoed her enthusiasm," she admitted when she saw his grimace.

"You have certainly had a singular education, Claire," he muttered. "But did she teach you nothing that would be of benefit to a young lady in society?"

"Not a thing," Claire admitted cheerfully. "And thank heaven she did not! I could not have stood fancy sewing and simpering and dancing and dalliance, not when there are so many other things in the world to learn that are of such great importance."

"What things?" the marquess asked suspiciously.

"Why, literature and art and music . . . science and mathematics and languages. The world is full of wonders, Andrew, as I am sure you, a man, must know. Aunt Flora brought me up as if I were her son, and I must always thank her for that. She told me the waste of a mind is a terrible thing, and women have minds too, as well as bodies."

"This constant reference to 'bodies' must cease," Lord Blagdon said, running a hand through his blond hair in some agitation. "Could you not delete the word from your conversation, Claire?"

"I suppose so," she said, a slight smile coming and going in an instant. "But I never suspected you would be so starched up. Most men, I believe, think nothing of discussing any number of topics relating to the human physique."

"But not when they are with women—ladies, I mean," he was quick to add. "What men discuss at other times would not be at all suitable."

"What a humbug!" Claire sighed and smoothed her gray skirt. "I see I was right. Well, Andrew, you are excused. It is clear that any liaison with me would not be suitable for you at all, and I shall release you from our agreement."

"I did not say I wanted to be released," he said, his deep voice rising in volume a little.

"Surely you cannot want to spend the next two months in my company, being constantly shocked and in a dither worrying about what I am going to say next?"

"No, of course I do not. But couldn't you moderate your conversation? Couldn't you at least give the social amenities a try? You might even find you get along better. It cannot be comfortable always to be offending people. I shall be glad to instruct you and help you."

She tilted her head to one side to consider his words. "I suppose so." She sighed. "Very well, if you are still determined to continue, I will try to conform, at least when we are in company. My hand on it."

She held out her hand, and as he took it and looked down into her glowing gray eyes and rosy cheeks, and saw the little curls stirring on her forehead in the early-May breeze, he could not resist lifting it and kissing it. At once she snatched her hand away.

"There, now, that is what I so much dislike! There was no need for you to do that."

"I wanted to," the marquess said simply as she rose, her glance reproachful. "Besides, it is merely a courtesy that you might expect from anyone. It does not mean that I, or any other men who so honor you, have nefarious designs on you," he assured her as they began to retrace their steps.

"Well, I do not like it," she muttered. "And if I am to moderate my outspoken opinions, you must forgo such gallantries."

"Then how are we to convince the *ton* that we are *épris*? No one who knows me will believe it if they do not see some sign of fondness, some small secret smiles and hand kissings. Perhaps it is you who wish to draw back, Miss . . . er, Claire?" he suggested.

"No, I do not," she said. "Do you realize that today was the first day since I have arrived in London that Lord Wilson was not on the doorstep with a bouquet, an invitation, or a silly poem about my black curls or the deep, stormy pools of my eyes? Such fustian! For that benefit alone I agree to gestures of intimacy between us, but only in company. In private, we can relax and be ourselves."

The marquess refrained from pointing out that gestures of intimacy were almost always better when indulged in in private, asking instead, "And perhaps you might control yourself before my groom as well? I cannot tell you how you have shocked Michaels. He is a very conventional old man."

"Isn't the whole thing ridiculous, Andrew?" she asked, trying for his sympathy. "How much simpler life would be if people could say what they think instead of having to wear masks all the time."

In thinking this remark over, the marquess could not agree, but he did not argue the point. "You may rely on me to assist you in your new education as a lady of quality, Claire. Before long, I am sure you will be as accomplished and easy as any debutante. I wish you would reconsider dancing, though, even if I am not a peacock," he added as they regained the main walk and he spotted his phaeton waiting a short distance away. "It is such an exhilarating pastime, and almost as good exercise as running."

Claire looked up at him, suspecting he was teasing her, to see him smiling down at her, a devil dancing in his dark blue eyes. "I did not come to London to dance," she said, wondering at the sudden constriction in her throat.

"Sometime you must tell me why you did come," he said as he helped her to her seat and nodded to Michaels. "Unless, of course, one of the snakes got loose at Dawson Hall, and unable to locate it, you beat a hasty retreat."

Claire laughed, that silvery scale of complete enjoyment that he remembered as he took his seat beside her and picked up the reins. "The snakes have all been given away to other herpetologists, and the spiders, the monkeys, and the jaguar are gone too. Poor Adonis! I did hate to see him go, he was so beautiful, although not of a very pleasant disposition, of course."

The marquess laughed out loud. "Claire, you have to be funning me. A jaguar?"

"Aunt Flora could not resist him when she saw how badly he was being treated by the natives who had captured him. She meant to release him in the jungle, but somehow he came back on the ship with us. She named him Adonis and he was handsome, although he was never tamed. The Royal Enclosure was delighted to have him when I inquired after her death, for I could not keep him. You see, my aunt was the only one who could even halfway gentle him."

Lord Blagdon was beginning to enjoy himself, especially

when he pictured his groom's face behind him. "I am delighted you do not have similar zoological enthusiasms," he remarked.

"No. It was a disappointment to my aunt, of course, but when she saw my interests lay in quite another direction, she insisted I concentrate my studies in my own field."

"I do not think I will ask what that might be at the moment, devout coward that I am," the marquess said. "Shall we pull up so I can introduce you to Mrs. Venables and you can begin to practice your new resolution?"

Claire nodded and promised to be good. And so she was, Andrew noted as he exchanged a few quiet words with Paul Venables and watched Claire answer his mother's probing questions with an ease of manner that could not be faulted, before she changed the subject to the clear May day, such a rarity in spring, and to the current London scene. He was quite in charity with her as he drove her back to Belgrave Square. "I shall miss you at the ball tonight, Claire, but perhaps you would care to go to the theater tomorrow? I shall be happy to assemble a party."

Miss Carrington denied him. "I have already accepted an invitation for tomorrow evening, sir. General and Lady Banks are taking me to the opera."

"In that case I shall call on you in Belgrave Square tomorrow afternoon at three," Andrew said firmly.

"Do make it four, if you please, Andrew. Generally I do not return home until then."

Before he could question her further, he had to pull up at the Banks's door, and unfortunately for their new rapport, Claire insisted on getting down from the phaeton before Michaels could assist her.

She waved cheerfully. "Thank you for the drive, sir. I enjoyed it very much," she told him, her oval face uplifted to his and her warm smile brightening her face. "Until tomorrow."

And then she turned to the groom and said, "And thank you for accompanying us, Mr. Michaels."

By the time the elderly groom rose from an astonished bow, she had run up the steps and the front door was closing behind her. Michaels, who had known the marquess since before he was breeched, climbed up beside him, shaking his head, although his wrinkled old face was wooden.

"Yes, yes, I know, it is too bad of me, is it not, Michaels? But you must admit the lady is quite out of the common way, and I find that intriguing. One never knows what she will say next.''

"Only that it won't be at all suitable, m'lord," the groom mumbled, but at the marquess's haughty frown he subsided for the remainder of the journey to Upper Brooks Street, where Lord Blagdon kept rooms.

Andrew was unaware of the disapproving, silent presence beside him, for he was busy remembering the unusual Miss Carrington's conversation and the story of her childhood and upbringing. If anyone else had told him such a tale, he would have said they were bamming him, and refused to believe such a fairy story, but somehow Claire's huge eyes were so honest that it was impossible to doubt her, no matter what absurdities she mentioned. Headhunters . . . snakes . . . a boy's education . . . trips up the Amazon and across the Mediterranean in a native *felucca* . . . a jaguar named Adonis . . . reading Plato in the original Greek . . . even dressing most of the time in breeches for comfort—and all of this related in such a matter-of-fact voice that it was impossible to think she was lying.

He raised his whip to two friends who were strolling along Park Lane, feeling a little uneasy. What had he gotten himself into? Perhaps it would have been more politic if he had taken Miss Carrington's suggestion and extricated himself from their pact as gracefully as possible, for he could foresee a Season that would not only be the most unusual one he had ever spent but also one in which he would have no idea of or control over what was going to happen next, except that as Michaels had said, it was sure to be something entirely unsuitable. And then he grinned to himself. To escape Pamela Greeley would be worth any number of contretempts, even to the point of having to teach the girl the social niceties that most young ladies began learning in their nurseries.

Besides, Miss Carrington was interesting; no, *Claire* was fascinating. "Interesting" was much too tame a description of that young lady. The time he had spent with her had passed as quickly as if he had been amusing himself with his cronies in some enjoyable masculine pursuit. She did not simper or blush or dissolve into girlish giggles, nor did she succumb to bashful reticence, and it was refreshing not to have to edit his conversation for expressions and ideas that might be upsetting to the little dear. Claire did not flirt—lord, how tired he was of flirting! She did not demand or even seem to want his compliments—and how tired he was of praising his companion of the moment, extolling her eyes, her hair, her grace. Altogether, Claire was the most singular, distinctive girl he had ever met, and with her by his side, he would never be bored. The word for Claire was "stimulating," he decided, and in some perverse way, "restful" as well.

He pulled up at the front steps of his house, tossed the reins to Michaels, and got down from the phaeton, a little smile still playing over his lips.

The groom watched him enter the house, two steps at a time, and he shook his old grizzled head. "Aye," he muttered as he drove around to the mews, "you're mighty pleased with yourself, m'lord, but if I'm not mistaken, this time you've bitten off a deal more than you can chew. There's trouble ahead, you mark my words."

Chapter Three

Lord Bladgon called round in Belgrave Square shortly after four the following afternoon, to find that Miss Carrington was already entertaining callers. When the butler led him to the drawing room, he discovered that as well as Lord Wilson and his mama, Sir Reginald Randolph was there, and it was obvious from their glares at each other that both men were determined to wait each other out, although only one of them was under direct orders to do so. Noticing the militant look on Lady Wilson's pudgy face, the marquess decided that Sir Reginald didn't stand a chance. Claire managed to hide both her annoyance and a reluctant amusement tolerably well as she sat amongst them.

And well she might be amused, Lord Bladgon thought as he gave her his elegant bow and a nosegay of flowers. While she introduced him to her guests, he had time to take their measure. Lord Wilson was dark and thin and betrayed his youth by his stammering replies to the marquess's polished greeting. His mother was another kettle of fish. Gray-haired and dumpy, she was attired in an afternoon gown of dark purple with a matching feathered turban, but it was obvious to anyone of the meanest intelligence who wore the breeches in that family.

The marquess was somewhat acquainted with Sir Reggie and knew him to be a few years older than his reluctant rival, perhaps twenty-six or -seven. He was a handsome man even with his startling red hair and pale hazel eyes and the sneer he had adopted as his normal expression. The marquess was not at all surprised to see him in Lady Banks's drawing room, for he knew, as all London did, that Reggie had to marry a rich wife. As he bowed to the others, he decided Claire's fortune must be more than just respectable to attract the almost penniless peer.

"Thank you, Andrew," Claire said, giving him her warm

smile as she admired her posy. "I shall ask the butler to put these in water if you will all excuse me for a moment."

The gentlemen rose as she left the room, and the marquess turned back to see three pairs of eyes fixed on him in disbelief and chagrin.

"Posies, m'lord?" Sir Reginald asked. "From you?"

His attempt at scorn came out sounding more like petulance at the advent of yet another suitor. Besides, although he could disregard Lord Wilson, the Marquess of Blagdon was another matter.

"She calls you 'Andrew,' sir, so soon?" Lord Wilson wondered aloud, as his mother sniffed and glared in disapproval.

"As you can see," the marquess agreed, his deep voice cordial as he took a comfortable chair, crossed his elegantly clad long legs, and prepared to enjoy himself. "You have been here some time, m'lady? M'lords?"

"Not long at all. Not nearly as long as Sir Reginald," Lady Wilson said firmly while her son squirmed.

"I am of course desolated to have to correct you, m'lady, but I was before you by only a moment," Sir Reginald said in his sneering light baritone.

Lord Wilson flushed and his mother's mouth dropped open, but what she was about to say in rebuttal was lost as Claire returned.

"Do say you will give me the honor of your company, my dear Miss Carrington," Sir Reginald demanded, returning to the conversation the marquess had interrupted. "On my honor, 'tis the only thing that will make the expedition bearable at all."

"Claire is as good as promised to me," Lord Wilson interrupted. "I told you that before." Beside him, his mother patted his hand.

"I do not recall promising either one of you, and since I have accepted the invitation of the marquess, I am sure I did not do so. Isn't that right, Andrew?" she asked, her gray eyes twinkling as she turned toward him.

"Of a certainty you did, my dear Claire," he replied, his smile intimate even as he wondered where they were going.

"But . . . but I did not know that *you* were to be one of the party," Lady Wilson remarked with a frown and a massive pout as her son darted a nervous glance in her direction.

"I am generally included in most of society's amusements, ma'am, and have been for years. I am so sorry."

"Not at all your type of thing, m'lord, I assure you," Sir Reginald pointed out, sounding a little surprised to find himself allied with his rivals.

"Oh, I am sure I will be able to amuse myself tolerably well, especially with Miss Carrington by my side," the marquess remarked, even as he wondered what he was getting himself in for, and wished Claire would give him a hint.

"Well, in that case, there is nothing more to be said." Sir Reginald's stiff tones softened as he added, "But perhaps you would honor me some other day, Miss Carrington? I particularly want you to see my new team, so if I am not to be allowed the felicity of driving you to the picnic at Richmond, you must permit me to take you to Hyde Park instead."

Lord Blagdon felt a chill of foreboding, even as he noticed the way Lady Wilson was poking her son in the ribs to prod him into checkmating this plan. The only picnic to Richmond that the marquess knew of was being given by Lady Greeley, and he had already refused her suggestion that he escort her daughter there. How he was to appear now, and with another young lady on his arm, he did not know, for to do so would be an intolerable snub. He dragged his thoughts back to present company as Claire said, "I find I cannot tell you when that would be possible, sir, for my time in town is much bespoke."

Lady Wilson positively beamed, and Sir Reginald tried a teasing note. "Come, come, dear lady! Even someone as lovely and sought-after as yourself must have some free afternoons. I am prepared to await your pleasure, and I will not take no for an answer. I am quite a determined chap, y'know," he added, his green eye glinting with *double entendre*.

The marquess saw Claire's pointed glance at the clock, as he was sure everyone present did, and knew she was wishing Sir Reginald would take himself off.

"I shall have to let you know, sir. I can make no promises at this time," was all she replied, and then she turned to Lady Wilson to chat.

Andrew was content to sit and watch the maneuvering that ensued until Lady Banks came in. Her greeting to the marquess was especially fervent in its welcome, and he had to hide a grin. In a few moments, she had drawn Lady Wilson aside for some private conversation, but when Sir Reginald would have reopened his campaign, Lord Wilson was before him, and he began to talk of Berkshire and recall some childhood memories that he and Miss Carrington shared. Claire allowed him the diversion for a few minutes, but at last she rose and held out her hand.

"It has been pleasant to see you, Wilfred, and you too, Sir Reginald, but I would not dream of detaining you further."

Both gentlemen were forced to rise, but while Sir Reginald seemed dumbstruck at this unusual method of clearing a drawing room, Lord Wilson bit his lip and looked resigned.

"Lady Wilson, so good of you to call," Claire added, going to lead the fat little lady to the door. "You are spoiling me with your constant attentions. You are much too good, but I cannot permit it."

"Dearest Claire," Lady Wilson purred, although her little eyes gleamed with barely concealed anger, "I have told you time out of mind that it is our pleasure."

She glared back over her shoulder at the marquess, who had risen but showed no sign of joining the exodus. "May we drop you somewhere, m'lord?" she asked, honey-sweet.

"I thank you, but no. I must discuss the picnic arrangements with Claire, among other things." As her face settled into lines of profound dissatisfaction, he could not resist adding, "Besides, I have only just arrived."

When Claire offered her hand to Sir Reginald, he pressed it between both of his before he lifted it to his lips to kiss, and at such a liberty, Claire stiffened and pulled away.

"Good day, sir," she said coldly, and somehow Sir Reginald found himself in the hall without further ado. Lady Banks bustled after him, a look of distress for Claire's rudeness on her face. Claire closed the door behind them all.

"Should you do that, Claire?" Andrew asked as she came back and sat down across from him. At her questioning look, he explained, "Shut the door like that? After all, you are here alone with me. It does not do to flout convention that way, you know, and an unmarried girl is never allowed to be private with a gentleman unless he is a member of her immediate family."

"How silly! I never regard such conventions, and Lady Banks will pay it no mind either, for she knows me too well."

"Somehow I feel I have been insulted," the marquess murmured, and then, as he recalled the picnic party, all else fled from his mind. "I find I have a quarrel with you, Claire.

How could you say I had invited you to the Greeley expedition? Are you always so precipitate? Lady Greeley has already asked me to be her daughter's escort, and so I was forced to refuse the party. What on earth am I to do now?''

Claire smiled at his expression. ''Forgive me, Andrew, I had no idea. But perhaps if you said you had changed your mind and asked Miss Greeley to join us . . . ? I would like to make her acquaintance, and you see how it solves the problem.''

The marquess pictured the outraged pout Pamela would be sure to sport if she found she was not to be his exclusive companion, and he shook his head, explaining in succinct terms why this was not at all feasible.

''How ridiculous she is,'' Miss Carrington remarked, and then she added, ''Well, then, we have only to ask Wilfred or Sir Reginald to come. Then Miss Greeley cannot remark it or be uncomfortable.''

''But we will be uncomfortable in that case. What a pleasant afternoon of rare enjoyment would be in store for us! No, you must allow me to select the other gentleman, for I confess I do not find either of your admirers agreeable for any length of time.''

Claire nodded. ''It is unfortunate, is it not? But just as I told you—for you see, they have no idea that they are bores.''

''How came Sir Reginald into your net, ma'am?''

''I have no net! He attached himself to me at one of the first parties I attended. Alas, it was more for the yellow of my gold than the gray of my eyes, I am afraid.''

''But even if that is so, Claire, you were very impolite to him,'' the marquess insisted, determined on his critique. As her eyebrows rose, he added, ''Allow me to instruct you. When he asked you to drive, you should have returned a more gentle answer, and tempered your refusal with a smile. As for your old friend Lord Wilson, your manner was almost disdainful.''

''Of course. I can feel nothing else for Wilfred lately. He is no more in love with me than Sir Reginald is, and yet there they both sat awooing. Bah! I do so hate hypocrites. Besides, I do not want to encourage either one of them.''

The marquess privately thought that that was one thing she did not have to worry about, but he could see she was becoming upset, and so he turned the subject. ''Tell me, why do you not curtsy as custom demands? It looks so odd, I am sure everyone must remark it."

Claire studied the hands that were clasped in her lap. He noticed that today she was wearing a very plain dark blue gown and wondered if she had anything in her wardrobe that was more attractive. None of the outfits that he had seen her in could be called anything but serviceable. They did not flatter her slender, graceful figure, for they were cut much too large, and they did not sport so much as a lace collar or a knot of ribbon to relieve their starkness.

He recalled himself as she answered, "I was taught that to curtsy was to acknowledge someone's superiority to myself. I consider all men and women equal; therefore, I do not give obeisance."

Lord Blagdon frowned, and his dark blue eyes grew stern. "Now, this is the outside of enough, Claire! It is only a matter of courtesy to observe someone else's rank or his more considerable years. Was this another of your aunt's beliefs?"

"Yes, it was, but I completely agree with her. If I were to curtsy to Sir Reginald, for example, I would hate myself. He is not my superior, in fact I find him deficient in every way. He has no education, and no interests beyond his horses, his clothes, and his consequence. If I were to curtsy to anyone, it would be to someone I admire, a great artist or philanthropist, or a learned scholar."

The marquess was at a loss for words, and he rose and paced the room, running a hand over his face as he thought. He wondered, if she were to learn of his own special charity, if she would consider curtsying to him. At least he was not the worthless fribble Sir Reginald was. Putting this wayward thought from his mind to concentrate on the problem at hand, he said, "Claire, come here."

His handsome face was so stern she was surprised, although she rose at once and went to him. He took her hands and stared down into her face. "It will not do. Your bad manners in refusing to curtsy will be remarked, and you will be talked about and scorned. Then how are we to manage?"

Claire shrugged. "May I suggest we ignore the gossip? I have been doing so for years, for what people say matters little to me."

"I can see that. But how can you embarrass and distress your hostess and General Banks? Surely their contentment is important to you. And then, there are my feelings as well."

Claire's gray eyes opened wide. "Your feelings, sir? How can my beliefs reflect on you? It is only a game we play, after all."

The marquess dropped her hands. "Let my feelings go. I will explain them some other time. But what we are to do if you continue adamant, I do not know. You don't dance, you won't curtsy—what other social customs do you scorn?"

Claire tilted her head to one side as she thought, her eyes alight with mischief. "Perhaps I will explain them 'some other time' too, Andrew. But come, is it so important that I dance? If you do indeed say so, O my mentor, perhaps I will agree to learn."

"Splendid," the marquess said with enthusiasm. "I missed you at the Willoughby ball, by the way, for I was forced to stand up with Pamela Greeley twice, and take her in to supper as well."

"Now, how did that happen? Did she ask you to dance?"

"No, but my mother deserted the card table that evening," the marquess said glumly, and then, as if he were afraid she would change her mind, he moved a few chairs, remarking as he did so, "No time like the present, and you shall have your first lesson now. One of my talents, as yet undiscovered by you, is that not only am I considered an accomplished dancer, I can hum in tune and to the correct tempo. Miss Carrington, may I have this dance?"

He bowed, and since she still refused to curtsy, lifted her hand as he bowed. A strange look came over his face, and Claire saw him sniff.

"Is there something wrong, Andrew?" she asked.

"What is that peculiar odor that I smell? It is very sharp, like vinegar, but it is not vinegar precisely." He sniffed again, and then he raised her hand to his nose. The look on his face made her burst into laughter, that silvery trill that meant she was completely amused.

"It is I, I'm afraid," she said when she was able to speak. "Or perhaps it would be more truthful to say it is the turpentine."

The marquess looked perplexed as he studied her hand. He noticed that although it was well kept and of a beautiful shape, the nails were trimmed to a no-nonsense length, and the cuticle of one of her nails was stained a brilliant green, while another fingertip was blue.

"Turpentine? And why do you sport those colors?"

"You have discovered my dark secret, Andrew, and my particular field of work. I left the studio late this afternoon and so I did not have time to clean the paint from my hands as I should."

"Studio? Paint?"

She smiled at him. "I am an artist. I came to London expressly to study with Joseph Turner, but in spite of all my entreaties, he would not take me as a student."

Her expression darkened and she shook her head. "It is because I am a woman, of course. Even though he knew I was serious and complimented me on my work, he would not consider me. He does not admire, or indeed, admit the existence of artists of my sex. It is so unfair!"

She pulled her hands from his and took a deep breath to calm herself. "But never mind that. Perhaps one day he will change his mind. He is doing such fantastic things with light now, and his paintings are so vivid and glowing and free. But one of his students, Emil Duprés, has taken me on. He has four students in his *atélier* on Dilke Street, and he is a competent artist in his own right and an excellent teacher."

The marquess found his voice as she paused for breath. "Er . . . are all his students female?" he asked, somehow knowing the answer before she spoke. My Lord! Dilke Street, he thought.

"No, I am the only one. Why?"

"What matter of subject do you paint in this man's studio?" he asked instead of answering her question.

Claire considered him, her huge gray eyes serious. "Why, still lifes, portraits, and of course, the human figure."

There was a sudden silence while the marquess leaned against the mantel and began to swing his quizzing glass, his eyes never leaving her face. Somewhat to her surprise, he did not question her further, although she saw that his expression was serious, and there was no laughter in his blue eyes. Unaccountably, she missed it. After a pause he said, "I should like to see your sketchbook sometime. I am sure your drawings are charming."

Claire could have told him that her sketchbook had nothing in common with those that most young ladies produced and that she resented the word "charming" when it was applied to her work, but she felt she was treading on dangerous ground here, and so she only said, "Thank you. I should welcome your opinion of my skill, but today, I believe, I was about to learn to dance.''

The marquess returned to her side and took up her hand again, his face still solemn and stern. To distract him, Claire smiled up at him and said, "Do you suppose it was the odor of turpentine that made Sir Reginald so overcome when he kissed my hand, sir? How lowering if it should be so.''

The marquess was not proof against her demure smile, and his dark blue eyes crinkled shut in an answering grin. "I wish I did not foresee that you will set society all about on its ears, Miss Carrington, but at least you will dance while doing so. Come, watch my feet, if you please. We will begin with one of the simpler country dances. The basic steps go thus . . .''

When Lady Banks came back half an hour later, she was stunned and pleased to see her young cousin whirling about the floor, and no one could take exception to the behavior of the marquess, for far from behaving amorously now that he had her in his arms, he was busy scolding and instructing.

"No! One *and* two *and* turn *and* pause! Not one *and* two *and* pause *and* turn. And you must learn not to tread on your partner's feet, Claire: that is the unforgivable sin.''

Claire stopped, and he noticed she was not even breathing hard. "How ungallant, sir! You should be extolling my grace and the quickness with which I learn, should he not, dear ma'am?''

"Not until you can perform more creditably than that, Claire,'' Lady Banks had to reply in all honesty, and both Claire and the marquess laughed.

"I must be off. I have trespassed too long on your hospitality, ma'am,'' the latter said as he bowed. "It would be a great kindness if you would see that the young lady applies herself to this new form of study before our next meeting.''

Lady Banks promised to do so, even offering to play the pianoforte so Claire could learn her steps to music, and a date was set in two days' time for another lesson.

On his walk back to Upper Brooks Street the marquess was deep in contemplation of Miss Carrington's new and startling revelations, and so he completely missed his sister's wave as her carriage turned into Hyde Park, where she was taking her mother for a drive. The dowager marchioness, although she saw her son, did not wave or even smile, for to do so would be unbelievably vulgar, in her opinion.

Her daughter sank back in her seat, a frown in her hard

blue eyes. "There, you see how it is, Mama," she said. "Drew did not even see us, and he was coming from the direction of Belgrave Square as well. I would wager anything you like that he has been calling on that hubble-bubble girl."

Lady Blagdon inclined her head an inch in acknowledgment of the Duchess of Trent's smile. "Be so good as to moderate your conversation, Marion. It ill becomes you, as my daughter, to use cant expressions," she scolded in her cold voice. "I fail to see why you are so agitated in any case. Andrew knows very well that I do not approve of public waving and excessive expressions of familiarity, even among the family. I am pleased to see that at last he is adopting a more sober, formal mien, as befits his station. He must always bear the burden of knowing that it was his fault that he attained the title at such a young age. Since that is the case, he also knows how important it is for him to take his father's place with dignity and restraint."

Marion opened her mouth to protest, but only a moment's reflection told her it would be useless to disagree. Mama was even more stubborn than Drew; there was nothing she could say that would get her to change her mind once she had voiced an opinion. Marion sighed. She saw that she would have to handle this matter herself. Perhaps a visit to Lady Banks was in order. She would be sure to discover more about Miss Carrington, and about Drew's inexplicable attraction to her. Yes, she would call tomorrow, for it had been some time since she had done so, and the general and his wife were such old dears.

That evening, at Lady Gardner's reception, she saw her brother and Miss Carrington again, in company with a dark, thin young man she had no trouble identifying as Lord Wilson. He seemed to cling to Miss Carrington's side with grim determination, although Marion was quick to note that neither that young lady nor her own brother paid him much mind, as they were too busy conversing and laughing together. She was not the only one who noticed that the Marquess of Blagdon seemed to be fixing his interest with this new face in town, and several ladies nodded to themselves, remembering Mrs. Venables' report of their drive in the park.

Lady Peakes studied the girl through narrowed eyes. She was not at all in the style of Drew's usual flirts, for up to now he had been attracted only to shapely blonds or fiery redheads of the first stare. This lady was altogether too slim and boyish, too dark, and too unfashionable. Her gown this evening was a pale gold muslin, completely unadorned. Lady Peakes thought it positively provincial, and wondered that anyone could ever have admired it long enough to purchase it. As for the lady's short black curls, they looked as if she had dragged a comb through them at the last moment without even consulting her looking glass. Whatever did Drew see in her?

She saw Lady Greeley beckoning to her and went to her side, glad that Pamela was talking with some young friends and flirting with the gentlemen as if she had not a care in the world.

"I see your brother is busy attending Miss Carrington, my dear Marion," Lady Greeley began, her eyes disapproving. "However, you will be happy to learn that I had a lovely note from him today, begging to be allowed to come to the picnic party at Richmond after all, and asking if he might bring some friends and take Pamela up with him, so I do not despair."

Marion wondered if the friends included Miss Carrington, and was afraid they did, although she did not think it necessary to apprise Lady Greeley of her suspicion.

"What on earth does he find so fascinating about her?" Lady Greeley asked next, echoing her own thoughts. "Look at her, dowdy and plain and skinny. Why, next to Pamela, she is almost an antidote, and I daresay the marquess has as much hair on his head as she does."

"I have no idea. Perhaps she is a wit, or perhaps he is doing it just to be annoying. So like Drew to bring a nobody into vogue, just to tease us, and then, when all society takes her up, to drop her in an instant, completely unconcerned," his loving sister said, her voice tart.

"Men can be so difficult, can they not?" Lady Greeley asked. "We must hope that is the case here, although I do find it in my heart to be sorry for any young lady so deceived. Someone should warn her before she makes a fool of herself. I see Lord Wilson continues attentive, however. His mother has told me of her hopes there, so perhaps any sympathy of ours is misplaced. The girl will have a husband waiting when the marquess has had his fling."

Marion agreed, but in a few moments she excused herself and went to find her husband. She was feeling restless tonight, and wished her mother had come so she could see Miss

Carrington and her son with her own eyes. She noticed that Mr. Venables had joined Miss Carrington's group, as well as Lord Allenton. It was altogether too bad of Drew!

The following morning she ordered her carriage and drove to Belgrave Square. Lady Banks was delighted to see her, and she herself was not at all disappointed to find that Miss Carrington had gone out, as she took a chair in Lady Banks's sunny morning room.

"Dear Claire will be so sorry she missed you, my dear," Lady Banks said, her little round face wreathed in smiles as she told this bald white lie. "She is out most mornings, however, and three afternoons a week as well."

"Yes, she told me she finds London full of fascination," Marion agreed. "No doubt she is shopping or seeing the sights?"

"Not exactly," Lady Banks replied, a little frown replacing the smile of a moment ago. "If only I could interest her in fashion! I am sure those gowns she wears are enough to give anyone the mopes, but when I pointed out to her how dowdy they were, Claire only laughed. She is not interested in such fripperies as new gowns, you see, nor laces or reticules or stoles."

"Indeed? How very unusual. But what is she interested in, my dear Lady Banks?" Marion asked, adding silently: Besides my brother.

The old lady wrung her hands and looked self-conscious, almost, Marion thought, as if she did not care to say. There was quite a long pause before she whispered, "Well, you see, she is interested in art. And books and learning and . . . and anthropogomy or some such thing."

"Art and books and . . . ?" Marion asked. "Never tell me that she is blue!"

Her voice was horrified, but Lady Banks did not notice, for once past the dreadful hurdle of admitting that Claire was an artist, she was quick to come to her defense. "I do not know if you are familiar with her background, and her aunt, Lady Flora Dawson. She raised Claire as if she were a boy, introducing her to all manner of studies that I for one thought ridiculous, although Claire would stare to hear me say so. Thank heaven she is to have one Season in town, at Flora's express command."

"But if what I have heard of the lady is correct, she had no time for Seasons or society herself. Why would she insist her niece come to town?'' Marion asked, somewhat perplexed.

On firmer ground now, Lady Banks opened her budget and confided, ''She wanted to be sure that Claire knew what she was giving up if she did not marry and have a family. She told me once that although she herself needed no other way of life, she would not let Claire embrace it without giving her a chance to discover if she would prefer a more conventional existence. Claire tried hard to dissuade her, but Flora was adamant and made her promise that she would try London for one Season at least, and that is why she is here now. Not that she has any intention of changing her mind about it,'' she added somewhat obscurely.

''I see.'' Lady Peakes nodded, her heart lightened by this informative conversation. ''So it is merely a respect for her aunt's wishes that brings her to town?''

Lady Banks opened her mouth to reply and then shut it firmly, only nodding, although she looked as if she wished she could say more.

Marion changed the subject then by asking after the general's health, and the remainder of the visit was more pleasurable, for Lady Banks at least, for she was able to dwell at great lengths on sciatica and gout, failing hearing and an uncertain temper, without any return to the dangerous subject of her young relative.

Marion went away much heartened. If there was anything that would repel Drew, it was the knowledge that the lady he was honoring with his attentions was a bluestocking, she told herself. True, Drew was no illiterate himself, for she remembered how well he had enjoyed his books and tutors, and the honors he had won at Oxford when he was there, but she was sure he was not at all the type to look with approval on a lady scholar. It was only a matter of time before he discovered the girl's failing, along with her peculiarities, dowdy clothes, and insignificant beauty, and cut the connection. Mama had been right after all.

She would not have been so complacent and relieved if she could have seen her brother that same afternoon with Miss Carrington in his arms, teaching her the intricacies of the waltz while Lady Banks played a rousing piece in three-quarter time on the pianoforte.

After one badly misplaced step, when Claire tried to turn to the left while the marquess was determined to go in the opposite direction, he shook her a little and scolded her, while she laughed at herself.

"How clumsy I am," she said, her voice mocking.

"You are not clumsy at all, Claire, you were simply not attending. See here, you must follow my lead, you know. You cannot strike out on your own that way. I am the one to decide in which direction we turn, and when, and you have only to follow me. The pressure of my hands will tell you what I plan to do."

Claire quirked an eyebrow at him, her gray eyes, so close to his, sparkling with fun. "So the man has the say, as always, and we mere females must bow to his dictates without question. How typical! I am sure this dance was invented by a man, aren't you, Cousin Martha?"

Lady Banks replied without thinking. "Oh, no, my dear. I have always thought it must have been a woman, for it is such a delicious feeling, waltzing in someone's arms."

Her face turned bright red as both dancers laughed, and she hastened to add, "Not that I have ever waltzed myself. In my day, to dance so intimately would have put anyone beyond the pale." She sighed as if she regretted that she had been born too early for such enjoyment.

"Shall we try again, Claire?" the marquess asked, holding out his arms, and Claire came to him and took his hand while he put his other arm around her slim waist, nodding as he did so to Lady Banks. He knew it was only a matter of time before Claire would be an accomplished dancer, for she was quick to learn, and so lithe and graceful that even missing her steps now and then could not detract from the pleasure he got in clasping that yielding waist and looking into her big gray eyes with their abundant thick black lashes.

He put such wayward thoughts from his mind as he began to count out loud. "One and two and three and turn . . . Good! One and two . . ."

Chapter Four

The morning of the picnic party to Richmond dawned warm and sunny, more like a day in midsummer than early May. The marquess, cocking a knowing eye at the sky as he sat in his landau being driven through the London streets to pick up Paul Venables and the two young ladies, thought it would very likely turn sultry and come on to shower before the conclusion of the expedition, but as he had seldom attended any *al fresco* entertainment where the weather at some point did not become inclement, this prospect failed to dampen his spirits.

Paul Venables voiced the same opinion as he climbed into the carriage after greeting Michaels, in his place on the driver's perch, with a warm smile. He was the same age as the marquess, for they had become friends when they were both up at Oxford, a friendship that had grown and deepened over the intervening years. Mr. Venables was of medium height, with smooth black hair and brown eyes, and he always looked as neat as a pin. He was not in the forefront of fashion, nor considered a top-of-the-trees Corinthian, but he was well liked for his easy manner and his integrity. If Paul Venables promised to do something, you could be sure it would be accomplished without delay.

"Don't care for this heat, Drew," he said now. "Bound to pour before nightfall, and we shall be lucky to escape thunder and lightning as well."

"But of course. This is a picnic, and that automatically ensures some natural disaster, whether it be storms, twisted ankles, high winds, ants, or bee stings. Be easy, old friend. By nightfall we shall be restored to civilization once more."

As they reached the general's house, he climbed down and said to his groom, "I shall not be long; there is no need to walk them."

Paul laughed. "You mean the lady comes on time? I do

50

not believe it. You must marry such a prodigy at once, or allow me the privilege.''

''You shall see,'' Drew threw back over his shoulder as he climbed the steps and sounded the knocker.

It seemed only a moment before he reappeared escorting Miss Carrington. Mr. Venables greeted her with his usual aplomb and grace, but as he insisted on taking the seat facing back, he thought it was no wonder she was on time, for she had not spent much of it on her toilette. Although he knew of his friend's pursuit of the lady, he could not help but wonder at the usually demanding Andrew Tyson's choice. Miss Carrington was wearing a light muslin gown of a peculiar shade of gray-green, and her plain bonnet was adorned only by a matching grosgrain ribbon. He noticed she carried a shawl, but disdained sunshades and lacy handkerchiefs, trimmings and fans. A very ordinary girl, he thought, and not at all in Drew's customary style.

Miss Greeley more than made up for any deficiency of hers. When she finally appeared, Michaels had walked the team twice around the block and Mr. Venables and Miss Carrington were well on the way to becoming old friends by that time. The pretty blond was attired in a pale blue muslin sprigged all over with tiny white flowers and caught tight under her breasts with a ribbon of royal-blue velvet. Her wide-brimmed straw hat was bound with a matching ribbon that fell in long streamers down her back, and decorated as well with an abundance of blue cornflowers and white roses. On her feet she wore a dainty pair of white satin sandals over matching silk stockings, and she carried a little blue sunshade trimmed with lace.

If only she would smile, she would be breathtaking, Paul thought as he helped her to her seat, but her distaste at seeing the other members of the party was written clear in her stormy blue eyes and on her pouting rosebud mouth.

As the marquess performed the introductions, she seemed to control her chagrin, as if she were determined to be pleasant. Andrew noticed how she stared at Claire's gown and hat, and the self-satisfied little smirk that she gave her before she adjusted her own bouffant skirts and settled back.

''How delightful to meet you, Miss Greeley,'' Claire remarked in her deep warm voice, a pleasant smile on her face. ''I have been admiring you from afar at several parties, and although I would not put you to the blush, I must tell you that you invariably outshine every other girl present.''

Unable to ignore such a compliment, Pamela gave her a brief smile, but then her eyes returned at once to the marquess and his friend as they sat facing them, their backs to the horses, to see if they agreed with the lady's assessment. She smiled more enticingly now, her glance lingering on the lean planes of the marquess's face, sure he could not fail to notice how much she was outshining one particular lady today as well. Thank heaven she is a dowd, she thought, opening her reticule for a lavender-scented handkerchief that she pressed to her nose. The landau was passing through the poorer sections of London now, on the way to the post road, and she made a little *moue* of distaste for the smells of rotting vegetation and slops that lay about the cobblestones and curbsides. Miss Carrington did not appear to notice, for she was chatting with Mr. Venables with some animation.

The marquess was content to lounge back in his seat and watch the expressions that came and went on her face as she did so. She was asking Paul his opinion of the exhibition of Elgin Marbles, and since Mr. Venables was able to chat knowledgeably on almost any subject, the conversation flourished.

"You are comfortable, Miss Greeley?" the marquess inquired, afraid she might feel neglected. "I know there is no need to offer you a rug on such a day as this, but I can see that you are distressed by these mean streets. We will be out of town soon and then we can spring the horses."

Pamela lowered her eyes and dimpled. "Your carriage is prodigious comfortable, m'lord. Indeed, you are too kind, although it is true that I have such a sensitive nature that the sights and smells to be found in neighborhoods such as these can be upsetting."

She paused to look around with distaste, and then she exclaimed, her voice surprised, "M'lord! Who are those children waving to you? Dirty little beggars! How dare they presume?"

The marquess glanced over to where a line of small children, attended by two women in navy stuff gowns, were smiling and waving. His face lit up, and he waved in return before he said, "You are mistaken. I am sure they were waving only to the pretty horses."

His voice was cold and Miss Greeley said hastily, "Pray

lo not regard my distaste for them. My mother says I am a leal too nice in my requirements. Why, I had to send this gown back to the modiste's three times before I was satisfied.''

She paused expectantly for his compliment, and Lord Tyson noticed the laughter in Claire's gray eyes for his predicament and was hard put not to grin at her in return. "You ladies are all alike, I know,'' he said in such a careless manner that Paul Venables made haste to add, "But when the results are so breathtaking, Miss Greeley, we men can only applaud your taste and discernment.''

Miffed that the marquess had been so offhand, Miss Greeley sniffed a little as she nodded her head in thanks, and then he turned to Claire.

"Of course that does not hold true for all ladies,'' she remarked, her eyes sliding over Claire's plain muslin gown. To her surprise, this blighting remark drew a gurgle of laughter from the lady, who did not seem to realize she had been snubbed and insulted.

"How perceptive you are, Miss Greeley, and of course you are right. Although I know I am in the minority of my sex in this regard, I do not consider clothes and personal adornment to be at all important. Besides, fussing over outfits and accessories takes too much valuable time.''

Miss Greeley's little mouth opened in astonishment and her blue eyes grew wide. "How strange,'' she remarked in a disbelieving tone, and then she added, "I, however, must admit I adore new clothes and fripperies. I have never found that it required too much time to shop, for of course it must be an object with ladies to appear at their best. What in the world could be more important?''

Claire opened her mouth to tell her, and then she caught Andrew's warning eye. "Tell me, Miss Greeley,'' she asked instead, "how do you spend your days? You must not mind my curiosity, for I am so interested.''

Pamela replaced her handkerchief in her reticule before she answered. They had reached the open road and Michaels had increased the pace, which caused her to put a hand to her elaborate bonnet to ensure it was not blown away in the speed of their passage.

"Why, like anyone else. How can you ask? I wake around ten unless there has been a late party the evening before, I eat breakfast and dress. Then there is shopping, parties, afternoon calls, teas—why, the days just fly by! And of course I am out most evenings, as I am sure you are yourself.''

"Hardly," Miss Carrington replied, her tone wry. "But do you do nothing else all day? By that I mean, nothing to better yourself or to benefit mankind?''

The marquess interrupted, although Miss Greeley was speechless. "But she has just told you, Claire. She benefits mankind by being better dressed than anyone else, for man's edification and enjoyment. I say, Paul, isn't that Sir Reginald's phaeton coming up behind us? I am sure those showy chestnuts are the breakdowns he had from Jones-Smythe. Rackety, don't you think?''

Mr. Venables took the hint, and since he was just as tired as the marquess of this boring conversation, was quick to agree. "He's tooling them right along, too. At the pace he's traveling, he'll have to change teams before Richmond is reached.''

Both men laughed, and everyone waved as Sir Reginald swept by with a flourish of his whip, his red hair gleaming in the sunlight, and his light hazel eyes on Miss Carrington to see if she admired the dashing picture he made. He was gone in a cloud of dust, and then Pamela recalled the company to herself by uttering a piercing scream. She had let go of her bonnet in order to wave, and the wind had swirled under the wide brim and plucked it off her head to send it sailing away behind.

"Pull up, Michaels, Miss Greeley has lost her bonnet," the marquess ordered, and Claire wondered if she was the only one who heard the impatience in his voice.

"Oh, dear, my hair," the young lady wailed, trying in vain to control her blowing curls. "Now I shall look a perfect fright when we arrive. It is too bad!''

By this time Michaels had pulled the team up at the side of the road, and the marquess jumped down in one fluid motion and set off to fetch the lady's bonnet. Claire soothed the girl as best she could. "No, no, Miss Greeley, there is only the slightest disarrangement. You look charming.''

She turned her head to see the marquess climbing up an embankment and pushing through some tall grass to where the bonnet had come to rest on the branch of a hedgebush. "See there, Andrew has caught your hat and will soon restore it to you.''

Indeed, it was not long before he returned and handed Miss

Greeley her bonnet, but this restoring of her property only called forth further wails.

"It is ruined, ruined," she sobbed, touching a dirt stain with a fastidious finger and eyeing the limp cornflowers and rumpled ribbons with distaste.

"Nonsense!" the marquess said as he took his seat again and gave Michaels the office to start. "You must expect such things to happen on a picnic expedition, Miss Greeley, especially if you wear such a large hat."

The girl sensed the barely veiled boredom in his voice and made an effort to smile. "Of course you are right, sir. I shall look the perfect ragamuffin, but I shall not regard it."

She replaced the slightly damaged bonnet on her blond curls as the marquess added, "Be sure you hang on to it, then, for it cannot be improved by any more bouncing along the road. What a shame those decorative streamers do not tie under your chin."

Claire could see Miss Greeley's blue eyes begin to fill with tears at his tone, and although she was just as impatient as the men that the conversation had centered for so long on nothing of more interest than a hat, she made haste to say, "It is not much farther now. I am sure your mama will be able to set it straight in a trice."

Andrew eyed the limp flowers and the peculiar droop of the straw brim as if he doubted it, but he was too wise to refer to the bonnet again.

Richmond was reached without further mishap, and Sir Reginald was there to greet them as the marquess helped the ladies down.

"I shall escort Miss Greeley to her mother, Drew," Paul Venables volunteered, wondering at Sir Reginald's eager smile and the marquess's annoyed frown.

Claire looked around and took a deep breath. "How very warm it is, and yet it is pleasant to be in the country. I may not have the sensitivity of Miss Greeley, Andrew, but even I admit the air is much fresher here than in town. Shall we walk?"

Sir Reginald hastened to extend his arm, declaring that a walk with Miss Carrington was just what he liked best.

"You must excuse us, sir," the marquess said firmly as he took possession of Claire's hand and tucked it in his arm. "There is something of a private nature we have to discuss."

The redheaded peer bowed, his face disappointed. The

servants were busy preparing the picnic feast and setting out some lawn chairs and tables, and it was obvious that it would be some time before all would be ready. Under the shade of a large elm, Lady Wilson could be seen poking her son and speaking to him with every sign of displeasure even as she waved to Claire.

Claire did not appear to notice either Wilfred or his mother's beckoning hand as they strolled away, and the marquess saw that she matched him stride for stride. Not for Miss Carrington little satin sandals or a dainty step, even though they were climbing a steep rise that led to a beech wood.

As they entered one of the winding paths, she said, "How much cooler it is here," and then she removed her bonnet and ran a hand through her cropped curls. Andrew watched, fascinated. The curls, black and shiny, sprang back into place to frame her face, and although he still considered them very strange, he could see why she preferred them to a more elaborate coiffure that would take so much "valuable time."

"I am sorry about Pamela Greeley," he said to break the silence that continued between them. "But allow me to compliment you. You behaved very well in spite of her sniping remarks."

"Why, thank you, sir. Coming from you that is praise indeed. But there is no need to apologize. You cannot help it if she is a widgeon. All that fuss over her clothes and her hat—so silly!"

"Claire, tell me something," the marquess demanded as he helped her over a fallen log.

"Of course, anything," she said cheerfully, even as she wondered at his sober expression.

"Why do you wear such unattractive gowns? Is it truly because you cannot be bothered to fuss? Since you must purchase clothing, why don't you choose pretty ones?"

Claire looked down at her gray-green muslin for a moment and her lips tightened. "I only want my clothes to be serviceable and long-wearing, and since I am not interested in entrapping a husband, why should I not be practical?"

"But why are they cut so loosely?" he persisted. "You look as if you had had them made and then lost a great deal of weight. Such ill-fitting gowns make you look very odd."

"They are cut for comfort," she replied, ignoring his last remark. "As I told you, at home I am more used to breeches

56

and riding boots and I hate petticoats and corsets and lacing and tight binding bodices.''

"Good heavens, girl, you should not mention such things to me,'' the marquess protested, and then he returned to his original complaint. "Your appearance does reflect on me, you know, much the same way your behavior does.''

Claire stopped short, and took his hand, one finger to her lips. "Shh! Look there, Andrew, through the trees.''

The marquess looked in the direction she indicated to see a small herd of the deer for which Richmond Park was famous, grazing in a small clearing. There were several does and fawns just losing their spots, and it was such a peaceful, bucolic scene that he had to smile down at his eager companion. Claire was leaning forward, almost not breathing, her eyes intent. "How I wish I had brought my sketchbook,'' she whispered, and soft though the murmur was, one of the does lifted her head and stared in their direction before she whirled and leapt into the woods, her white tail flagging, and the rest of the herd followed.

Claire sighed. "How graceful they are, how lovely.''

"And how destructive,'' the marquess pointed out. "The crops they consume, the trees they girdle and kill.'' He saw her little frown and asked, "You are not against the hunt, are you, Claire?''

"No, indeed, I am not so foolish, although it makes me sad that they must be controlled. But I know there is only so much graze, and it is better to kill them cleanly than let them starve through a hard winter. If only the venison could be given to the poor, who need it so badly! But we stray from the point, sir. You were saying that my attire is detrimental to you?''

Her tone was a little stiff, and the marquess drew her hand in his arm again and pressed it. "Only insofar as it might cause others to wonder what I find to admire in you.''

Claire laughed now. "As if my appearance was of any great matter! It is what is in my mind and heart that is important, not an outward show. Yes, yes, I know all about the world and its opinions, but not even for your sake, Andrew, will I imprison myself in the tight ridiculous garments that men have decreed women wear to entice them. Such fustian—bah!''

The marquess shook his head in despair and suggested they return to the party. As if she did not notice the coolness in his

57

voice, Claire went on, "Has it ever occurred to you that you are demanding a great deal from me, Andrew? First I must moderate my conversation, next learn to dance. I am treated to a lecture about curtsies and then instructed in how I should dress. And yet I have asked nothing of you in return. That does not seem fair, now, does it?"

The marquess stopped and turned to face her. The sunlight sifting through the spring leaves lit her face and he saw her soft mouth curve in a smile, and the provocative sparkle in her gray eyes. For a moment he did not speak, and then he reached out with his free hand and tilted up her chin, caressing it as he leaned closer and said in his deep, intimate voice, "Ask any boon you want, my dear. I will be delighted to comply with your wishes."

Claire twisted her head away from his strong hand, a slight color tingeing her cheeks as she backed away from him. "Then I would ask you to stop this . . . this lovemaking at once. I told you I do not care for it, and yet you still persist. If you want to play the *galant*, do so where the Wilsons and Sir Reginald can see you, not when we are alone."

For a moment she thought she was in for a thundering setdown, but then the marquess bowed, the expression in his dark blue eyes ironic. "Very well, that boon I grant you. Passion in public, prudity in private. However, Claire, what you called 'lovemaking' was no such thing. If ever I treat you to any in earnest, you will discover the difference."

Claire thanked him, her voice calm as she said she would really rather not find out and so must forgo such a treat, and he tousled her black curls with one big hand.

"Perhaps you will change your mind, minx! But come, is there nothing more you would ask of me?"

"Not at the moment, but perhaps something will occur to me as time goes by, so beware. Oh, what a lovely vista!" she exclaimed as they came out of the woods to see the park stretched before them, while in the distance the Thames wound between its banks on its tranquil way to the sea. The marquess was not looking at the view, for his narrowed eyes were scanning the sky and the clouds massing over the western horizon.

As they came down the slope and rejoined the other guests, he saw that if Lady Greeley looked most displeased, Lady Wilson sported an even more dissatisfied expression. Of Miss Greeley and Paul Venables there was no sign, so he knew his friend had gathered that his role today was to amuse Pamela while the marquess remained by Miss Carrington's side. His mouth twisted wryly. He was sure Paul would exact payment for such an act of generosity, young ladies in their first Season with no conversation being as little to his taste as to Lord Blagdon's.

The picnic that was spread before the thirty guests was lavish and delicious. There were little birds in aspic and slices of smoked ham, as well as tiny biscuits filled with chicken, and asparagus vinaigrette, and several wines to accompany each course. The meal concluded with pastries and jellies and baskets of peaches and grapes. The marquess led Claire to some seats beneath an ancient elm when he saw Miss Greeley and Paul taking their places there, and no further private conversation was possible.

After luncheon, Mr. Venables suggested a walk along a small brook that ran through the grounds, eyeing Lord Wilson and Sir Reginald, who had somehow attached themselves to their party as he did so. For a while they all strolled along in a large group, but then the marquess found himself alone with Miss Greeley when Claire stopped to admire some wildflowers that grew along the bank, and the others remained beside her. He was forced to slow his pace and offer the young lady his arm when she pretended to stumble in the grass.

Hugging his arm, she began chatting in her breathless way of the picnic and the delightful day, and then suddenly she stopped in mid-sentence, uttered a little scream, and threw herself into his arms. The marquess caught her up neatly as she fainted, and Claire and the others hurried to join them.

"What on earth is it now?" Claire asked, pushing her curls off her damp forehead, for the afternoon was growing steadily more sultry.

"Whatever did you say to her, you rogue?" Mr. Venables teased, as he saw the young lady's eyelashes quiver and knew she had only suffered a momentary weakness. Lord Wilson's eyes were full of concern, and even Sir Reginald had lost some of his sneer.

"On my honor, nothing. Come, now, Miss Greeley, it is all right. Whatever caused you such distress?"

"Oh, a snake, a huge snake," she sobbed, her arms clinging tighter around his neck as she stared at the ground in horror.

Claire walked past them, her gray-green skirts swinging,

and suddenly a thin rust-and-black snake less than a foot long slithered through the grass and out of sight.

"Oh, it will bite and poison me," Pamela wailed, burrowing her head against the marquess's chest, to the detriment of his cravat. "Kill it for me at once, m'lord!"

"Nonsense," Claire said firmly. "It is only a common garter snake of the Colubrinae subfamily. I daresay it is more frightened of us than we are of it. Snakes are very shy and do their best to avoid mankind. Do not kill it, m'lord, it is doing no harm."

"So, already you have found another boon to ask of me, Claire," the marquess teased as he set a reluctant Miss Greeley back on her feet.

"Oh, let us return to the carriage," the girl continued to implore as she hung on his arm. "I do not feel at all safe here."

"As you wish, and perhaps it might be as well to take our leave. I dislike the look of those clouds."

Paul Venables looked to the west and nodded. "Yes, it will come on to storm before long. See, others are preparing to depart as well."

Obediently Claire started back to the picnic site, but after a few dawdling steps, Pamela Greeley found herself swung up into Lord Blagdon's arms again, and after one startled look, she settled down there, completely happy.

At Claire's raised eyebrow, he explained, "Miss Greeley is walking as if the path was strewn with reptiles all hanging about just waiting for a chance to pounce on her. It will be quicker this way, so lead on."

Claire was surprised at the little pang she felt to see a blushing Pamela dimpling and smiling her pleasure as she nestled in Andrew's arms, her blond curls so close to his handsome face, but she soon forgot it as she began to ponder what paints she could use to capture the color of his hair, especially those golden highlights that gleamed so brightly in the sunlight. Not chrome or aureolin or Windsor lemon, she thought, but perhaps a combination, mixed with a touch of zinc white? Beside her, Sir Reginald continued to chatter, and on her other side Lord Wilson interjected a comment whenever his rival paused for breath, but she heard not a word. She decided she would like to pose him in an outdoor setting, and in more casual clothes than he wore today, perhaps an open-necked shirt and breeches, sitting on a log in the woods and leaning forward, his arms on his knee, with one long leg outstretched as he took his ease.

She was recalled to the others when they reached Lady Greeley and the marquess restored her daughter to her arms, and reassured her she had taken no hurt.

"Of course not, if she was in your care, m'lord," the lady simpered, her tone coy. The marquess waved away the compliment.

"Delightful as the picnic has been, m'lady, I do feel we should make haste and return to town. Those clouds may break long before the outskirt villages are reached. I see you came in your barouche; perhaps it would be wise for Miss Greeley and Miss Carrington to travel with you? I would not run the risk of their getting wet and chilled."

He ignored the flash of indignation for such a plan on Claire's face, but Lady Greeley was quick to pooh-pooh his caution. "I am sure you refine on it too much, m'lord, for I daresay it will not rain before sunset. No, no, do run along, all of you. I am sure Pamela would prefer to travel in your dashing equipage rather than a stuffy barouche, now, wouldn't you, my love?"

Pamela hesitated and looked doubtful, but her fond mama only gave her a little push. "Be off with you now, my dear. I shall see you in town."

Shrugging, Claire allowed Mr. Venables to lead her to where Michaels was waiting beside the landau, the team harnessed and ready to travel.

"Cutting it a bit fine, m'lord," she heard him murmur as she climbed up to take her seat. "Shall I put up the top?"

"No, just spring 'em, Michaels, and if it begins to rain, we'll stop and raise it," the marquess instructed, and the groom touched his forelock.

They had covered perhaps half the distance of ten miles when the first distant thunder was heard. Each noisy rumble was followed almost at once by Miss Greeley's startled scream, so only the marquess, who was sitting across from her, saw how pale and strained Claire became, and how tightly she clasped her hands in her lap. It appeared that she was frightened, but surely a girl who could travel the jungles of Brazil would not succumb to terror in an ordinary English thunderstorm.

But as the storm came steadily closer, and the claps grew in intensity and duration, he could see how she winced, her huge gray eyes growing wide with fear, even though she made not a sound. Miss Greeley more then made up for her silence, however, by her incessant wails, and Mr. Venables was kept busy calming and soothing her.

The marquess wished he might sit beside Claire and put his arms around her to comfort her, but then the wind rose, and before he could suggest changing places, a heavy downpour began and he was forced to shout to the groom, ordering him to pull up so they could raise the hood.

Miss Greeley began to cry in earnest as her gown became soaked and her golden curls drooped in limp tangles under her sodden hat. Claire put her shawl around the girl, but by the time the two men had the top secured in place, they were all wet through. The air had grown much cooler, and Miss Greeley shivered as she clutched Claire's shawl and complained bitterly that she was cold and wet and miserable, and m'lord must do something about it, and at once!

The marquess took his seat again and ignored her as he noticed that Claire had a better figure that he had thought, for now her too-big gown clung to her body, from her gently curving breasts to her slim waist and hips. He took off his coat, and leaning forward, put it around her shoulders, grasping them as he did so and whispering, "It will be over soon, Claire. Do not be afraid."

She tried to smile, but her lips were quivering, and when a particularly loud clap sounded right over their heads, and the lightning lit up the dark sky, she reached up and grasped his arms. Vaguely he was aware that Michaels was calming the frightened team, for he could hear his soothing voice over the sound of their neighs and stamping hooves, but the strength of Claire's hands as they held on to his arms through his thin shirt surprised him.

The thunder and lightning were almost continuous now, and he called up to the groom that they would not try to continue until the storm passed. As the rain drummed on the leather hood so loudly that it seemed impossible that it could rain any harder, he spared a glance toward Pamela Greeley and saw that Paul, bless his heart, had taken both her hands in his and was patting them while he told her what a famous story this escapade would make, and how very brave she was. The marquess was relieved to see that these blandishments were working, for the girl had quieted now and a little smile played over her lips.

Claire, however, was another story. Her lips were as white

as her face, and her hands still gripped his arms so hard he was sure she was leaving marks.

"Gently, my dear, gently," he said, and his deep, easy voice seemed to calm her fear. He saw her make a visible effort to regain her control as she took a deep breath and released him.

"I beg your pardon, Andrew," she whispered, and then she winced as the thunder sounded again.

"Do not worry, Claire. You will notice that that one was not so close, for the storm is already moving away from us. We will be able to continue in only a short while."

She smiled, but it was a tremulous thing, as if she did not believe him, although his prediction proved correct. In only a few minutes more the rain had lessened to a gentle shower and the thunder and lightning were far away to the east.

The marquess leaned from the landau to call to his groom. "Good man, Michaels! Set 'em along now, but at an easy pace, for they are probably still skittish."

"Aye, m'lord," the groom replied, and then he clucked to the team and the landau jerked into motion.

Paul Venables leaned back in his seat, smiling at both girls. "A bit of excitement, what? I have never heard thunder so close. Your man is to be congratulated, Drew, for holding the team. I was sure they would bolt."

Andrew settled back as well, still watching Claire's face. "Oh, the team doesn't live that Michaels cannot control. Do not worry, ladies, you will be home and dry in no time, my promise on it."

A bedraggled Pamela tried an arch smile of relief, looking more than a little ridiculous as she did so, and he was glad to see that Claire looked more at ease as well.

She insisted that they take Miss Greeley home first, and neither man was at all reluctant to do so, after having had to listen to the girl bemoan the ruin of her gown and hat and coiffure all the rest of the way back to London. After she was safely delivered at her mama's town house, the marquess instructed Michaels to drop Mr. Venables off next, for he wanted a moment alone with Claire so he could be sure she was fully recovered from her fright.

When they were alone in the landau, he sat beside her and took both her hands in his. "You are all right now, Claire?" he asked, his deep voice concerned.

Her short black curls were already dry, and the color had

returned to her face, and since she still wore his coat, he knew she was not cold or uncomfortable. She smiled at him and nodded, and then she took a deep breath and said, "I suppose I should have warned you how stupid I am about thunder. It has always been so, and even though I am ashamed of my weakness and try very hard to overcome it, the terror never seems to lessen."

"Was it because your aunt was afraid of storms?" he asked gently.

"Heavens, no! Aunt Flora wasn't afraid of anything. But she did tell me that it was during a thunderstorm that my parents were killed. We were all together in an open carriage, much like today, but that time the horses did bolt with fright. Of course I was barely three and do not remember it at all, but the truth is that when the carriage was overturned, I was thrown clear, while my mother and father were trapped underneath."

She paused, biting her lip a little, and then she said softly, "So you see, being such a baby, I never really knew them. I cannot tell you how much I have always regretted it."

At her rueful confession, Andrew realized how lucky he had been to have known his father, even for the short space of eight years. Then, as he recalled the manner of his death, his lips tightened and his blue eyes grew remote. He forced himself to shake off his sad memories and concentrate only on Claire's phobia.

"No wonder you have this awful fear! And to think you endured it without making a single sound, while all the time Miss Greeley screamed and cowered."

His voice was admiring and he held her hands tightly. She tried to laugh his admiration away, and her sad thoughts as well. "You will be happy to know, Andrew, that after spending the day in Miss Greeley's company, I am more determined than ever to continue our charade. Your marriage to her does not bear thinking about, for a sillier peagoose I have never seen. At all costs, we must make sure you are protected from a life spent with her, and I promise you that I shall spare no effort to ensure your safety."

He grinned at her, his dark blue eyes crinkling with amusement. "Even to purchasing some new gowns, Claire, as well as speaking only social platitudes, learning to dance, and perhaps, if she appears to be gaining on me, condescending to curtsy?"

"Yes, even that, but such sacrifices on my part will not be at all necessary," she said severely, although an answering smile lit up her face. "No one, having spent ten minutes in the young lady's company, would ever expect you to offer for her. Why, you would be sure to murder her in a month."

The marquess laughed. "Thank you for your compliment on the strength of my character, but in honesty I must correct you. I rather think another day like this one would be the limit of my endurance."

Chapter Five

The marquess was back in Belgrave Square late the following morning, for he wanted to be sure that Claire had recovered from her terror and the outing. Lady Banks received him in the morning room, her round face wreathed in smiles, but when he inquired for her guest, she had to admit that Claire had gone out.

"Well, I can see she came to no harm from her wetting, if that is the case, m'lady," he remarked. "Dare I hope that she has gone shopping?"

He grinned, secretly amused, and Lady Banks thought his conversation quite as difficult to follow as Claire's.

"No," she said slowly, lowering her eyes, "she has not gone shopping."

"I knew it was too much to expect, but may I ask where she is and when you expect her to return? We must make arrangements for another dancing lesson, for the St. Marlowe's ball is to be held next week."

"I do not know if Claire has told you, m'lord . . . Well, that is, I do not like to betray . . . Surely it is not my place, when she knows how much it distresses me . . ." Lady Banks said, starting several sentences and abandoning them all in turn.

"Aha! I deduce she has gone to her painting lesson, ma'am," the marquess said, putting an end to her confusion.

"So she has told you! Yes, she goes three mornings a week, as well as some afternoons. I do not understand it, and as for the paintings she brings home, I do not understand them either. Why she does not paint a nice bouquet of flowers, or do portraits of children, or fields of gentle sheep, all quite unexceptional, you know, and no one would think that at all peculiar, at least, not much, but no. She says she is not interested in such subjects. I don't know what she plans to do with a painting of dead rabbits, or women without so much as . . ."

Suddenly the elderly lady blushed bright red and buried her face in her handkerchief to give herself time to recover. The marquess was quick to rise and bid her farewell.

"I shall return later, ma'am. No, do not bother to ring. I can find my own way out," he said, and Lady Banks was so glad to see him leave before she blurted out Claire's unforgivable secret that she did not try to detain him.

Maybe Claire will never show him her paintings, and then he will not cut the connection, she thought to herself. It would be so wonderful if he offered for the dear girl and she was able to lead a normal life at last. She sighed and sat dreaming of the bridal while her coffee grew cold.

Lord Blagdon stood on the general's doorstep for a few moments, lost in thought. He remembered clearly that the studio was located on Dilke Street, for that location had so horrified him he was hardly likely to forget it, but the name of her teacher took longer to recall. He was just about to give up searching his memory, when the name Emil Duprés came to mind, and he strode down the steps and hailed a passing hackney.

When he asked to be driven to Dilke Street, the elderly cabdriver looked surprised. "Sure you got the address right, m'lord? Not at all the place for the likes o' you, Dilke Street ain't," he added in a fatherly way.

"I do not agree with you, since it is necessary that I go there, and at once. If you cannot bring yourself to drive me, let me know so I can hire another, not so fastidious cabbie."

The driver clucked to his horse, who was as elderly as himself. "No need to get mifty, guv, and if it's Dilke Street you wants, Dilke Street you shall 'ave."

The hackney rumbled on its slow way, soon leaving the broad squares and tree-lined thoroughfares of the rich, and winding through ever meaner and narrower streets. When the driver drew up in Dilke Street, the marquess asked an elderly crone for the lodging of a Monsieur Duprés, but since he used the French pronunciation, she was not able to help him until he mentioned that the man was an artist.

"Oh, 'im! You means the Frenchy wot 'as the loft. Aye, your lordship, 'alfway down the block, number forty-seven, top floor."

The marquess gave her a coin for her trouble and motioned the cabbie to continue. When he alighted and looked around, he tried to keep the horror he felt that Claire frequented such a location from showing on his face. A crowd of dirty urchins stopped playing in the crowded street, their eyes wide to see such a toff in their neighborhood, and the women who were abroad whispered to each other behind their hands. He himself, in the course of administrating his favorite philanthropy, was often in the poorest sections of London, but what was suitable for a man would not do for a girl, especially one who went about unattended by servants. He shook his head at such folly as he went up the steps of number forty-seven, missing the speculative look a young, brawny man who hadn't shaved for some time gave him from across the street.

Five flights up brought the marquess to a landing and a single door which still showed a few flakes of its original paint. He saw the name "Duprés" on a card tacked to the door, and tapped it with his cane. Although he could hear sounds of movement and voices within, no one came to answer his knock, and finally he opened the door and peered around it.

Before him was a huge, open room lit by a bank of skylights in the peaked roof. It was cluttered with tables and easels and stools, and at one end, directly under the windows, was a model's stand containing an ancient divan covered with a burgundy throw on which reposed a voluptuous woman. She was reclining with her eyes closed, one arm resting on the back of the divan and the other holding the discreetly placed scarf that was her only covering.

For a moment the marquess stood frozen, so stunned at the sight before him that he forgot to breathe. There were four artists, in various positions before the model, who had their backs turned to him, but he had no trouble spotting Claire at once, in spite of her odd attire, for she was the only other woman present.

He drew in his breath sharply. To think she stood there in the company of men, while only a few feet away an almost nude woman displayed herself on a divan. How dare she be so bold, so unconcerned, so immodest? The marquess stared at her, his eyes narrowing with his anger.

She wore an old brown gown, and over it a voluminous smock, much spattered with paint, while on her head she sported a mobcap, the likes of which he had not seen since childhood. As he watched, she stepped back several paces from her easel and tilted her head as she studied her painting, and then she began to mix a new color on the palette by her side.

From what the marquess could see from his position by the door, her painting was an excellent study of the model, the whiteness of her skin thrown into bold relief by the dark red of the throw, and in spite of his fury he was impressed by her competence and talent.

To her right, a small gray-haired man with a flowing beard, dressed in a velvet jacket, was staring at another student's work, and suddenly he waved his arms and burst into a torrent of French. For the artist's sake, the marquess hoped he did not speak the language, and that must have been the case, for in a moment the teacher changed to English.

"No, no, Tompkins, eet weel not do! Not burnt umber there! And see 'ere, where you have muddied the color and smeared the line? That will not gain you patrons or fame, my boy. You must paint it true . . . 'ow can I say eet? You must paint from the *inside* out. There are bones there, and tendons and muscles under the flesh. But your painting, bah! There is nothing but blobs of fat."

" 'Ere now, watch it, ducky, or you'll 'ave to get another model," the voluptuous lady on the divan remarked in a coarse, husky voice.

The artist ignored her, and the marquess eased the door closed and leaned his shoulders against it, intrigued in spite of his anger at Claire.

"And you do not 'ave the proportions right yet. See there, from shoulder to waist, too long, and from waist to thigh, too short. Draw and study before you paint, draw and study!"

He held up a long brush and squinted past it to demonstrate, and the young man beside him leaned forward as if to capture the correct perspective through his master's eyes. Monsieur Duprés patted him on the shoulder and returned his brush, and then he moved to Claire's easel.

"That is better," he said as she added another stroke to a rounded knee. "But watch the 'ighlight there, Carrington. Is eet really of such a boldness?"

Claire stepped back again, frowning as her eyes went from her canvas to the subject and back again, and then the model yawned and opened her eyes. Spotting the marquess at the back of the room, she uttered a little shriek as she jumped to her feet to draw on an old brocade robe.

The others turned as one, and Lord Blagdon was stunned to see Claire's frown when she saw him standing there.

"Andrew, why are you here?" she asked, her tone belligerent, and Monsieur Duprés bustled forward, rubbing his hands together.

"Sair?" he asked, bowing very low from the waist. "How may I serve you?"

It was obvious that Claire's teacher thought him a wealthy collector, come to admire and hopefully buy his work.

"Your pardon, sir," he said through stiff lips. "I have come to escort Miss Carrington home—when she has finished the morning's work, that is. I did not mean to interrupt . . ."

In spite of his conciliatory words, his voice was haughty and cold, and everyone seemed uneasy as Claire came up to him and said, "But you have interrupted. Furthermore, I do not need you to take me home."

Aware that her truculent words sounded as ungracious as his, she paused, but her gray eyes still flashed, and furious himself, the marquess wondered why she had any right to be angry.

"Now, now, Carrington, eet does not matter," Duprés interposed. "The gentleman is welcome to stay and observe my methods. And perhaps, sair, you might care to see some of my work? I am a student of Turner's."

"Thank you. If you are sure I will not be in the way?"

"Of a certainty! Here, sit here, sair. The class continues only another half-hour in any case."

He bowed the marquess to a chair, and then bustled away, clapping his hands as he did so, and the students turned back to their easels.

"Mimi, the pose, if you please. To work!"

The model resumed her position, sans robe, eyeing the marquess as she did so, until she was reminded that the pose required her to close her eyes. The marquess watched Claire pick up her brush again and turn her back on him without another word, but he thought her shoulders looked stiff under her paint-smeared smock, as if she were feeling self-conscious. I shall have more than a few words to say to you, my girl, he thought grimly, and then he turned to inspect the studio more carefully, his curiosity piqued.

It was very plain, almost stark in its appointments in spite of the clutter of easels and painting equipment. Over against one of the walls was a stack of canvases of various subjects and different sizes, and every wall was covered with more of them, some framed, and some still in different stages of completion. Where canvases were absent, drawings were pinned up, the newest efforts overlapping older, more yellowed papers. In one corner was a spacious cupboard, and such disparate items as a broken marble column, a bowl of rotting fruit, a large urn, and a stuffed partridge stood about the room or rested on various tables amid broken sticks of charcoal, discarded sketchbooks, old tubes of paint, and a mismatched set of teacups. The smell of turpentine, linseed oil, and paint was very strong, but not unpleasant. He studied the other students, now completely engrossed in their work once again. The man Duprés had called Tompkins was short and dark-haired, with a pale face that did not look as if it saw much sun or good food. Next to him, a tall older man, who was almost bald, was carefully painting the velvet that draped the sofa, with tiny, precise strokes. The other student was a handsome young blond man, and although the marquess could not see his canvas, he was painting with quick, feverish stabs of his brush, holding another brush in his teeth as he did so. Monsieur Duprés moved from easel to easel, scolding and instructing, and very occasionally praising.

The time passed quickly, for the marquess had never been in a professional studio before, and he had not realized with what intensity and concentration artists approached their work. His only experience had been accompanying ladies on a sketching expedition, or admiring the occasional watercolor they executed, and he knew they did not bring such singlemindedness to their work. Why, everyone here had forgotten he existed.

When at last Duprés called "Time!" and the model rose and put on her robe again, he felt he had learned a great deal, and had more respect for the creative process, even though he had every intention of taking Claire to task for being here at all, as soon as they were alone. She was a woman; it was not at all seemly.

While Claire and the other students cleaned their palettes and brushes and inspected each other's work, he allowed Monsieur Duprés to show him some of his own canvases. He thought them more than competent, although somewhat lifeless and stiff, but he was willing to admit he knew very little about art and was not a qualified judge. He was careful not to look at Claire's painting after one brief glance, for in the face of her earlier anger he did not want to seem to be spying on her, although he saw the others clustered around it. He could not restrain a spurt of anger when the young blond man put a hand on her shoulder as he pointed out some detail of her work, talking volubly all the while.

At last she came toward him, and he was glad to see that she had regained her composure and had removed the smock and mobcap as well.

"*Merci, maître*," she said to her teacher. "I shall be here tomorrow if Mimi will be available to pose."

"Of a certainty, Carrington, 'ave I not said so? And you must bring m'lard sometime again. A pleasure, sair."

The marquess nodded and then followed Claire to the door as she called her farewells to the others. Somehow it fanned his anger to see how completely at ease she was in this most unsuitable environment. Mimi sent him a seductive smile from the stand where she was lounging eating an apple, and her robe fell open in a casual way to disclose her full breasts and one gently swinging leg. He felt his anger increasing; this situation was intolerable!

The five flights down to the street were not traversed quickly. No sooner had he closed the door of the studio behind them with a decisive snap than Claire rounded on him and began to berate him before he could speak, not that he had any intention of taking her to task then and there.

"How dare you come here, Andrew?" she demanded, her gray eyes flashing fire again. "How dare you interrupt my work, make me uncomfortable by singling me out before the others, when it has taken me so long to gain acceptance as one of them? I have never been so angry!"

At that insolence, the marquess forgot his good intentions and grasped her arms and shook her. "You are angry? Let me tell you, my girl, your anger is as nothing compared to mine! How do you think I felt when I entered to find you, in the company of men, staring at a . . . a naked jade? Have you no sense of decency at all?"

He shook her even harder, and Claire gasped and tore herself away from him to clatter down the first flight. He followed close on her heels, and when she reached the landing, he caught her arm again.

"Let me go at once, sir! May I remind you that what I do is no business of yours? Furthermore, your description of what I—what we were *all* doing—is far from the mark. We were staring, yes, but not in the way you think, for we were painting her."

She sniffed her scorn, but before he could reply with a suitable setdown, she added, "Not being an artist yourself, you compare our concentration to the way you go to admire the scantily clad opera dancers or the *ingénue* at the theater dressed in a tight gown with her breasts only half-concealed to tantalize the men. You should be ashamed of yourself! What we were doing was nothing like that. We look at a peach or a stone wall or a horse in exactly the same manner, but you, sir, with your genteel moralizing, are disgusting."

The marquess felt he was getting much the worse of this encounter, and he shook his fist at her. "Be quiet!" he thundered. "And I suppose you expect me to believe that such immodest activity on your part does not lead to familiarity from the others? What about that blond man? I saw him touch you myself, and I am sure it was not the first time, for what can he think of a young lady who would lend herself to such a scene?"

To his surprise, she laughed, albeit a little bitterly. "You refer to Frederick Peckham. He would be astounded to hear you accuse him, and his wife and children would be sure to take offense. He considers me only a fellow artist and I am grateful for the compliment. Besides, how can you think anyone would make advances to the wretch I appear in my working clothes? You are naive! They don't even make advances to Mimi, and that is not only because she is Madame Duprés, but it is impossible to make you understand, you tiresome, ignorant man!"

Stunned by this uncomplimentary assessment of his intelligence, and the disclosure that the artist allowed his wife—his wife!—to pose unclothed, the marquess dropped her arm, and she preceded him down another flight.

"Is it to keep them in their place that you appear so odd?" he could not help asking. "That mobcap, for example . . ."

Claire turned to face him again. "You have a very poor opinion of your sex, m'lord. You seem to think all men are nothing but lascivious beasts. Is it because of your own inclinations that you come to that conclusion?"

At the sudden blaze of fury in his dark blue eyes, she faltered, and then she continued down to the next landing, saying more quietly over her shoulder, "Forgive me, that was not kind. To answer your question, I wear the cap to protect my hair. I have a bad habit of running my fingers through it without thinking when I work, and I have had to clean out too much cerulean blue and sienna to leave it unprotected anymore. Painting is messy work."

"But why do you persist in it, Claire? It is such an unwomanly thing to do, and what in the world do you hope to accomplish? Do you hope to show . . . to sell? I doubt anyone would take your work seriously, for after all, you are a woman.''

She paused and stood still, one hand clutching the scarred banister, for his tone of voice was quieter, and he seemed genuinely puzzled, as if he really did not understand, yet wished he did.

"I do it because I must," she said at last. "It is my work, and the most important part of my life. Oh, I know that women of my quality are not expected to work, but if I could not draw and paint, I would feel I was nothing, a truly worthless human being. Painting is all I know, and all I want to do, and since I have been given this talent through no effort on my part, it behooves me to make the most of it. I must work as hard as I can to perfect it, otherwise I would be ashamed of myself. As to what I hope to accomplish, why, Andrew, I hope to become a better artist, perhaps even a great one who gives pleasure to the world. Do you really think it matters if a woman, rather than a man, holds the brush? And even if my ambition is unwomanly, so be it, for I do not care.''

They continued down the stairs, each deep in his own thoughts. "But why did you feel you had to come and escort me home?" she asked, suddenly recalling what had fanned her anger in the first place. "I have been studying here for two months. Believe me when I tell you that I am capable of coming and going on my own.''

"In this neighborhood?" he asked, his voice incredulous. "You need a man, perhaps two, to ensure your safety. It will require all my ingenuity to get you away from here unmolested.''

To his surprise, she laughed again, this time in genuine amusement. "And you think your presence will guarantee my safety? We have spent some time discussing my appearance, m'lord, but now I beg you to look at yourself.''

Puzzled, the marquess inspected his person, from the pale blue morning coat and pristine whiteness of his high shirt points and his cravat, secured with a diamond-and-onyx stickpin, down his tight-fitting breeches of delicate biscuit hue to his shining boots. He knew his beaver was tilted at the correct angle, his hair combed to a nicety, and his rings and clouded cane the height of elegance, but he was suddenly all too aware of what was amiss with his attire.

"Yes, you are the complete town beau, a top-of-the-trees Corinthian, I agree. As such you will be sure to attract the attention of every thug and pickpocket of either sex to be found in Dilke Street. I assure you there are a great many of them here. I, on the other hand, blend right into the locale in my old painting gown and gray shawl. I have never been accosted. Why, no one has even spoken to me. Of course, I do take a cab here, and it returns to fetch me when the day's work is over. I beg you to allow me, Andrew, to see *you* safely home."

By this time they had reached the final flight, and Lord Blagdon was impressed in spite of himself by her wisdom and foresight. Never before had he thought of women as being capable of logic, and he was ashamed of himself, for here was Claire not only pursuing her painting in such a single-minded way but also seeing to her safety in a slum district. As he was not unacquainted with such districts himself, her competence was doubly impressive.

As they reached the dark hall that led to the front door of the tenement, he heard Claire gasp from her position below him, and looking into the shadows under the stairs, he saw a heavyset man sidling toward them brandishing a long knife. Without a moment's hesitation, he picked Claire up and put her behind him before he went into a defensive crouch, his cane upheld. The thug laughed even as he came closer.

" 'Ere now, guv'nor, 'and over the baubles, and your purse and that there fine toge too, and I gives you me word you'll not get cut, no, nor the little lady neither," he growled.

Andrew was well aware that without any weapon other than a flimsy cane, and even with his competent fists, he was helpless to defend himself or Claire against that shining steel, and although if he had been alone he would certainly have attempted it, now he reached into his pocket for his purse. He could not run the risk of her being hurt, he knew, and then he heard her say from behind him, "I think not."

He had not taken his eyes off the thief, and now he was surprised to see the terror in the man's eyes as he backed slowly away, crying, "Gawd, missus, don't do it!"

The marquess turned his head then to see Claire holding a very businesslike pistol in her small but steady hands. "Be off with you at once," she ordered, her voice cold. "I am a very good shot, and at this range I can put a bullet in you any place I choose."

It seemed they all stood frozen in place for several heart-stopping moments, and then the thief dropped his knife and scampered away toward the back of the hall. A moment later they heard the door slam behind him.

"What on earth?" the marquess demanded, turning to inspect her pistol more carefully. "Where did you get that weapon?"

"I told you I could take care of myself, Andrew. Of course I would not dare to come here unarmed."

"Is it . . . is it loaded?"

"Of course! If it were not, of what use would it be?" she asked, and then put the pistol back in her reticule and moved toward the door. She opened it a crack and peered through, and then she threw it wide and beckoned to him. "Come, Jeremy is here now. It is quite safe."

He followed her almost meekly to where a hackney cab waited, the burly driver scowling as he held the door open for them. The marquess thought there was very little to choose from between him and the robber who had just confronted them as regards to looks, but Claire gave him a sunny smile.

"In good time, Jeremy. Do not look so black! This gentleman is Lord Blagdon, a friend of mine. Belgrave Square, if you please."

The marquess climbed into the ancient cab behind her and took his seat, a million questions spinning in his mind. His previous anger had been replaced now by a sense of mortification, for never since he had been a child had a woman had to come to his defense and save him from harm.

"Forgive me for asking such a personal question, Claire, but have you ever shot anyone?" he inquired as the cab began to make its slow way through the crowded streets. "Of course, you need not answer, if you prefer not to," he added quickly.

"Not in London," she said promptly as she settled back on the dirty squabs.

The marquess eyed her patrician profile, but even his brief acquaintance with the lady had taught him not to doubt her words.

After a short pause she turned toward him and said with a frown, "Once I had to shoot some natives in the Brazilian jungle. Aunt Flora said they were headhunters—you see my predicament?"

The marquess stared at her, and then he nodded as if he had this kind of conversation every day in the week, and she

76

continued, "It was awful, Andrew. I was so frightened and I hated to think I was killing other human beings, but . . . well, headhunters, you know."

"The alternative does not bear thinking about," he remarked, and she smiled a little at his wry tone.

"Wherever did you find this singular cab and driver, Claire?" he asked next, as he inspected the cracked leather of the squabs, and the dirty floorboards and grimy windows as well.

"I chose it deliberately because Jeremy was the driver, not for the hackney itself. You see, I wanted someone I could rely on if the need arose, and of course a cab from the vicinity of Hyde Park would never come into Dilke Street."

The marquess took a deep breath and braced himself by the leather strap as the cab lurched into a hole. "You must accept my profound apologies, ma'am, and my sincere congratulations as well," he said, his voice a little stiff. "I see that you are well able to take care of yourself, and it was presumptuous of me to think you needed my aid. Indeed, I see my attendance on you has subjected you to even greater danger than normal."

Claire reached over to clasp his free hand. "You refine on it too much, Andrew, and your motive was only to help me. I daresay ninety-nine out of a hundred other girls would not only have welcomed your assistance, but been in great need of it as well."

"You are wrong. All one hundred of them would have needed it, but I forgot how unusual your qualities are, Claire."

She laughed and thanked him, and then she said, "I must apologize to you as well, for becoming so angry. I do not like to be watched when I work, but that was no excuse for my sharp words. Shall we forgive each other and cry friends again, sir?"

For answer, he looked deep into her eyes and made as if to kiss her hand in agreement, but then he only shook it and placed it back in her lap with such an air of virtuous restraint that she had to laugh at him.

"May I ask a few more questions, Claire?"

"Of course, as many as you like, and in honor of our new truce, I promise not to rip up at you, no matter what they are."

"Why does Monsieur Duprés call you 'Carrington,' then? It is so rude!"

"It is a small conceit of his to call all his students by their last names, and when I began to study with him and he called me 'Mademoiselle,' I insisted I be treated like all the rest. Since we study together, we must all be equals. I do not mind it, truly."

"But why don't you paint from a clothed model?" he asked next, and the unease in his voice told her that this part of her studies continued to bother him out of all reason.

"We do at times, but for now it is important that we learn the human body. You cannot paint the clothing that covers it until you understand how it works and how the skeletal structure fits together, as well as what the muscles do and why, and what those muscles look like."

She paused for a moment and then confessed. "I admit there was some little shyness when I began, but that soon passed. After all, you are not embarrassed when examined by a doctor, are you? Well, an artist is just like that, Andrew. When we look at a model so intently, we do not see just the obvious flesh, we see pectora majors, tensor fascia lata, and biceps, femurs, and patellas."

"Do not tell me what those are, if you please! I see, but still I am surprised that Monsieur Duprés allows his wife to pose almost nude."

"Oh, Mimi was an artist's model even before they met, and she is a good one. She rarely feels fatigue, so she can hold a pose longer than anyone I have ever seen and can assume it after a break exactly as she held it before. Then too, she does not cost anything, and that is of prime consideration to Monsieur Duprés. Poor man, he does not have much money, for his art does not take."

"So that is why he was so eager to sell me some of his paintings," Andrew remarked.

"Of course. His students do not bring him much income, and he has never been lionized or achieved fame. He has been struggling for some years now, but he has yet to attract a patron."

"Although I am no judge of art, for I have no knowledge of it beyond the ordinary, I thought his work very competent, and yet there was something stiff and stilted about it."

Claire turned toward him, admiration in her eyes. "But you are a good judge if you can see that. Poor Emil! He is a technician of the first rank, but the spirit, the originality he should have, is missing. Perhaps that is why he is such a

78

good teacher, for there is nothing he does not know about technique and he has studied with some of the finest masters. He cannot do it, but he can tell us how to, you see. It is too bad. I am afraid poor Roger Tompkins is another such one."

Andrew thought to ask her of the other students then, and for the remainder of the drive he leaned back in his seat and watched her eager face and the animation of her expression as she described her work and her own particular problems with light and shade, and he felt a warmth for her enthusiasm. What would it be like, he wondered, to be so involved, so intent on something that it consumed you, and constantly fired your spirits and revived your heart? And what would she think of his own particular hobbyhorse that he kept so secret from the *ton*? Perhaps someday he would have the courage to admit it to her as honestly as she had spoken to him.

When he helped her down at the general's house and she dismissed the cab with a reminder that she would need it on the morrow at nine, he took her hand and held it for a moment in farewell, and she pressed it back.

"I am glad now that you came to the studio, Andrew, for I feel as if some barrier between us has been removed. I have not liked deceiving you, but you do see how I could not explain, even to you, and certainly not to society, what I was doing?"

A picture of his mother's and sister's horrified faces came into his mind, and he was fervent in his agreement that she must on no account mention it to another soul, and then he reminded her of the St. Marlowe ball and the need for further dancing lessons, and a time was set for the following afternoon.

As they climbed the steps together so he could summon the butler for her, she said, her tone a little diffident, "I have not had a friend who entered into all my concerns since my aunt died, and I cannot tell you how I have missed her companionship. How wonderful it is to know that you will stand my friend, Andrew—someone I can confide in honestly that I know will listen and understand, even if you do disagree and argue with me on occasion. You may be sure I will be your good friend too."

She smiled up at him and the marquess bowed and thanked her, feeling a little distracted as he made his graceful farewells.

Now, why did I feel disappointment when she said that? he wondered as he strolled away.

Chapter Six

The marquess did not make the mistake of going to Dilke Street again, but contented himself with seeing Claire at those few evening parties he could coax her to attend, in driving or walking with her in the park, and of course by attending to her further education as a young lady of quality, all the while making sure she perfected her dancing.

But even with his constant tutoring and occasional scoldings, the lady often forgot herself and made provocative remarks that at best could only be considered extreme, and at worse, downright rude.

One evening, after being twitted by Lady Greeley about her plain muslin gown, worn so many evenings already, she had so far forgotten herself as to make the mistake of informing the older lady that women who did nothing more than think of their clothes and appearance were no better than parasites on the men they had married, and that any such woman who brought up her daughters to emulate her example was a disgrace to her sex. The marquess took her away from the sputtering Lady Greeley before she could enumerate the areas in which she believed girls in 1817 required an education, but he was not always near enough either to still her unruly tongue with a frown or a shake of that gleaming blond head, or, as had been necessary with Lady Greeley, to remove her from the scene.

Although Paul Venables himself never repeated the story of his setdown, he was one of a group of men that Miss Carrington took to task for remaining in town involved in worthless activities of indulgence, when they should have been employed on their own acres overseeing their land, or engaged in some study that would further the progress of mankind. Unfortunately, Mr. Venables was the only reticent gentleman present, and this stunning and unexpected criticism was soon the talk of the *beau monde*.

Claire also announced one evening, in Lord Liverpool's hearing, that people, not property, should be represented in Parliament. In addition, she was quick to inform anyone who asked—and a great many who did not—that she was against enclosure, the Corn Laws, any remnant of the feudal system, and child labor, and she wholeheartedly subscribed to free schools, a university education for women, and the philosophical radicalism of Jeremy Bentham. This man was teaching that legislation should promote the greatest happiness for the greatest number of people.

None of these beliefs endeared her for a moment to the wealthy lords and landowners whose major desire was to preserve the status quo that had brought them all their wealth and permitted them to retain it.

From these gentlemen to their wives' ears was a very short step, and presently all the *ton* began to buzz and whisper about this outspoken young lady, recalling her aunt and all her escapades, and shaking their heads at such folly.

In view of the gossip, there was no question of obtaining vouchers at Almack's for Claire, and wisely, Lady Banks did not even try, for even if there had been no gossip at all, Claire's continued refusal to curtsy to the nobility made her entering those sacred portals unthinkable.

In spite of this, Lord Wilson and Sir Reginald Randolph remained attentive, a fact that the dowager marchioness was quick to point out to her daughter, Lady Peakes, when Marion bemoaned Drew's infatuation with such an unworthy girl. Lady Blagdon refused to share her sentiments, for she had convinced herself that Andrew, being her son, would soon come to his senses as regards the unusual Miss Carrington, and that her daughter's despair was only a tempest in a teapot. No Tyson had ever behaved so, she said, and therefore of course it followed that Andrew would not either. He was the Marquess of Blagdon and he knew his worth.

It was on the afternoon following her setdown of Lady Greeley when Andrew came for Claire's dancing lesson that he proceeded to chastise her for her unseemly words and quick temper.

"Well, I don't care. I meant it when I told her that it was pure folly for her to bring her daughter up to consider her appearance of primary importance," an unrepentant Miss Carrington told the marquess, darting a little glance at his stern face as she did so. "After all, Andrew, of what use has it

81

been? She has become a simpering bore. Why, even her beauty could not hold you.''

"But I am not the only man in London, and believe me, Claire, many of my fellows do not require anything in a wife *but* a beautiful bore. They would choose Pamela over a woman who insults her elders, scorns society's rules, and speaks her mind on each and every occasion. And why you felt a discussion of the Corn Laws at all appropriate at Lady Danver's ridotto, I shall never know. You are impossible!''

The marquess paused, afraid he had been much too severe, but when he looked at Claire, it was to see her smiling.

"That takes the trick, m'lord. How unkind of you to leave me without a word to say in my defense. Very well. I agree I was rude, but so was Lady Greeley when she made fun of my gown.''

Andrew swallowed another quick retort. He had seen Lady Banks before Claire came down, and asked her point blank if her young cousin owned a ball gown. Poor Lady Banks had wrung her hands and stammered, but although it was unheard of for a gentleman to inquire after a lady's wardrobe, with Claire his concern was perfectly understandable.

"Oh, m'lord, if only she did not,'' the elderly lady mourned. At the marquess's raised eyebrow, she explained. "Then, you see, she would have to purchase a new one, and you may be sure I would be beside her to guide her choice. But unfortunately she has a gown that is adequate for the occasion and that she has not worn before.''

"May one hope it is not a serviceable gray or navy, and that it fits her, ma'am?'' Lord Blagdon inquired next.

Lady Banks shook her head. "It is white, as befits a debutante, but it is so plain that it does not become her overmuch.''

This revelation did not improve Lord Blagdon's temper, and now, as he recalled the conversation, he said, "If Lady Greeley did twit you, it is your own fault. I quite agree that appearance should not be the be-all and end-all of anybody's rational thought, but to care nothing about it at all is equally arrogant.''

He said no more, for Lady Banks came in then to play the pianoforte, but Claire seemed lost in thought for some time during the lesson, and it was only when the general put his head inside the door to see his young guest and the marquess twirling around the floor that she lost her abstracted air and laughed out loud.

Lady Banks stopped playing at her husband's frown, so they all heard his disgusted snort and saw him shake his head before he withdrew, growling, "Demned caper merchant, and in my drawing room too! What is the world coming to when a man cannot come home at four of the afternoon without finding his house full of noisy music and town beaux. Martha, I must see you!"

As Lady Banks rose obediently, he added, his white mustache bristling with his indignation, "At your convenience, ma'am. There is no need to interrupt your dancing academy."

The marquess was quick to join in Claire's laughter after the door shut behind the irate old man, and Lady Banks made haste to explain that his sciatica and gout had made him testy, and then she wondered out loud what there was about the army that it could turn a perfectly nice man into a tyrant.

When the marquess finally took his leave, Claire asked her cousin for a few minutes of her time. Lady Banks was not at all loath to delay her visit to her husband's library, and sank down next to Claire on the sofa.

"It has become necessary for me to buy some new clothes, dear cousin," she began, "and a ball gown is of primary importance."

Lady Banks threw her arms around her guest, exclaiming that she was so pleased, she was sure Claire would outshine everyone, she would be delighted to help, and ended with the guileless statement that now the marquess could be easy. At this, Claire frowned.

"Andrew can be easy? Is it possible, ma'am, that you have been discussing my clothes with him?"

Lady Banks was forced to confess, and Claire made her promise that she would not say a word to him. "It is the outside of enough that he feels his influence extends even to what I wear. Let him remain in ignorance until the ball. It will serve him right!" she exclaimed, and then she added, "The problem is that I will need the gown in just a few days. I am determined to be the most elegant, entrancing lady at the St. Marlowe ball. But how to go about it, I do not know. Where does one find a gown like that?"

Lady Banks straightened up and said, "Do not worry about it, my dear, only be ready to accompany me at nine in the morning. I will send a note round to Mrs. Fetherington. She is not a modiste of the first stare as yet, but her reputation is growing. She will be sure to help us after I explain the problem.''

Claire hid a sigh. She knew she must forgo her painting lesson, and she could be almost positive that it would take most of the rest of the day before she was through with fittings and shopping for stoles and fans and slippers and other finery.

Lady Banks did not notice Claire's tiny frown at this loss of her freedom. She stared straight ahead of her, and then she nodded her head, setting all her gray curls to bobbing.

''I shall send a message to your man of business as well, asking him to bring Flora's jewels here tomorrow afternoon. Or, I should say, your jewels, my dear. I know you have not cared to wear them, but they will be the perfect finishing touch for your ball gown.''

Claire was glad to agree. She had forgotten the casket of jewelry her aunt had left her, and her interest was stirred. She remembered that there were some unusual pieces. That four-strand *parure*, for example, composed of the rubies and diamonds that an African chieftain had given her aunt, and the emeralds set in heavy gold that Aunt Flora had brought back from Brazil.

As she went up to her room to finish a sketch she was doing of Andrew from memory, leaving a happy Lady Banks at her writing table, she tilted her chin. She would say nothing of her shopping or her finery to Andrew or to anyone of the *ton* who talked about her and thought her a dowd. They would be all the more surprised to see that she could appear the elegant lady whenever she chose. And then, of course, they would be forced to realize that her plain appearance was of her own choice, and not from ignorance or lack of taste, or genteel poverty.

The next day she was surprised to find that she was more interested in her shopping than she had supposed she would be. Mrs. Fetherington, a tall imposing matron with a keen eye, had not been able to restrain a little shudder of distaste when she saw Claire's gray morning gown and shawl and her sturdy bonnet, but as if challenged by such unattractive garments, she was quick to produce a number of patterns for fashionable walking outfits and evening gowns, driving ensembles and morning muslins in various colors and styles.

Lady Banks explained about the St. Marlowe ball, and Mrs. Fetherington snapped her fingers to a hovering assistant.

"The scarlet silk, Miss Fordham, if you would be so good," she ordered.

As the assistant scurried away, she turned back to her clients and said, "I made this gown for another lady this season. Unfortunately, her husband took exception to the amount of her quarterly bills, and the gown was returned."

She sniffed, looking offended at such parsimony, and then Miss Fordham returned, a drift of silk and gauze over her arm.

When she held it up, Claire gasped. It was cut with the fashionable low round neckline, and tiny pleats made up the short puffed sleeves and bodice. Under the breasts it was confined with a twisted braid, and from there it fell in narrow folds of silk and gauze to the floor.

"It is not quite as ornate as it should be for a *grande toilette*," Mrs. Fetherington conceded, "but that can be remedied by the addition of some pearl rosettes here, and here, and more pearls sewn into the braid."

"Oh, no!" both Claire and Lady Banks exclaimed together. Mrs. Fetherington raised haughty brows.

"No?" she asked, as if she could not believe her ears.

Lady Banks hurried into speech. "Claire cannot wear that gown. It is not at all the thing for a young lady in her first Season. Why, every feeling must be offended! It is much too revealing and much too strong a color for a debutante."

The modiste stared. "But the young lady is hardly a miss just out of the schoolroom, ma'am. If she were a blushing eighteen, I would agree with you, but it is obvious that she labors under no such handicap. She appears to have more than her share of confidence and sophistication."

Now it was Lady Banks's turn to stare, for to her Claire was very green, in spite of her years and world travel and education.

Mrs. Fetherington turned to the lady in question. "What is there about the gown that you cannot like, miss?"

"Nothing at all! It is beautiful, but I would not have it further adorned. You see, I intend to wear a most elaborate set of rubies. The gown is perfect for them, but pearls would be too much."

Mrs. Fetherington inclined her head and suggested Miss Carrington try on the gown so she could have her first fitting.

"The lady for whom it was made was much stouter than you are. It will be necessary to make extensive alterations before it becomes you."

Claire sighed and steeled herself, and for an hour she was pushed and turned, pinned and tucked and draped, as well as advised on everything from accessories to undergarments to coiffures.

After promising to return in two days' time for another fitting, the ladies left the shop carrying a small piece of the silk with them so they could exactly match the color. Two afternoon gowns and another evening gown of soft green, the color of new leaves, were bespoke as well. In the Burlington Arcade, where they repaired next, a pair of satin sandals was purchased, and in another shop two doors away, new chemises and petticoats.

Lady Banks was all smiles, for when she had seen Claire actually wearing the scarlet silk, she had had to admit it was the perfect color to set off her white skin and gleaming black hair, and when she and Claire inspected the casket of jewelry that Mr. Lawton had brought to the house, she was ecstatic at the ruby-and-diamond set.

The *parure* had four diamond strands of ever-increasing length, each connected to the others by ruby clusters, the longest strand ending in a giant stone that glowed a rich bloodred. There were bracelets as well, and a pair of matching combs to set in her hair, and Claire was satisfied that her appearance would be as stunning as she had hoped.

In the following days, she was not often at home when Lord Wilson or Sir Reginald called, and even the marquess was denied twice by Lady Banks's butler. He went away with a frown, sure that Claire was spending more and more time in Monsieur Duprés's studio. True, the dancing lessons were a mere formality now. Except for the most formal court dances, Claire had conquered all the rest, but he found he missed their afternoons together.

The day of the St. Marlowe ball, one of London's premier hairdressers appeared, and although he was stunned to see the length of his newest client's hair, he rose to the occasion when presented with the ruby-and-diamond combs. Wisely, he did not try to concoct anything elaborate, but brushed her hair up into a topknot that ended in a mass of curls that was secured by the glittering combs. He coaxed a few of those curls to fall over her high forehead. With Claire's elegant profile and long slim neck, it was superb.

The maid carefully lowered the scarlet silk over this masterpiece and hooked it up before she fastened on the *parure* and bracelets and stepped back, clasping her hands and assuring Miss she looked beautiful.

Claire stared at her reflection in the pier glass, her large gray eyes widening as she contemplated the stranger staring back at her. Was this really Claire Carrington, this slim, sophisticated lady in the low-cut gown of scarlet silk, with magnificent jewels sparkling on her white bosom and crowning her high-dressed hair?

She was amazed at how comfortable she was in her disguise. Mrs. Fetherington had scoffed at any suggestion of corsets and lacing for a lady with such a slim waist and high bosom, and so Claire was able to go down the stairs to join Lady Banks and the general, who in honor of the occasion had been persuaded to lend his presence, with almost the same ease she had when wearing one of her old gowns.

While Lady Banks clapped her hands and exclaimed, the general inspected his young cousin from head to toe through his monocle. He pronounced her as fine as ninepence and admonished his wife for making such a cake of herself, telling her to come along at once. The ball was scheduled to begin at ten, and the old army man intended to be on the doorstep at a minute before the hour.

As it turned out, there was an accident near the Stanhope Gate of Hyde Park that delayed them, and such a crush of carriages and sedan chairs in the street where the St. Marlowes had their town house, that it was well after the half-hour before their carriage was beckoned forward to the red-carpeted front steps to discharge its passengers.

General Banks was red with impatience, but his wife whispered to Claire that it could not be better, for now she could be sure that others would be there when she made her entrance.

Lady St. Marlowe was a good-natured woman who had a fondness for the Bankses. She was all graciousness as she greeted their young relative. Never having seen the girl before, since she had only recently come up from the country, she did not know how controversial a guest she welcomed.

Passing on into the ballroom with her elderly escort, Claire looked around. It was her first ball, and she was impressed in spite of herself by the beauty of the huge room with its hundreds of lighted tapers and masses of hothouse flowers, as well as with the crowd of richly dressed members of the *ton* who had already assembled. She felt no qualms, however, as one slim hand came up and touched her necklace. No, this evening she was sure she was more than the equal of anyone, even royalty.

She saw Wilfred Wilson staring at her, his mouth falling open in shock before he hurried toward her, and then Sir Reginald was there, bowing and complimenting her, with every sign of a sneer gone from his fervent words. When he would have signed her dance card for the first waltz, she denied him, but she remembered to smile as she did so.

"The first is bespoke, sir, I am so sorry," she said.

"Then you must grant me the second, dear lady," he persisted, and she nodded, wondering where Andrew was.

Lord Wilson managed to engage her for a set of country dances, before Paul Venables came up to chat, his glance approving. He was followed by several other members of the Corinthian set, who seemed identically stunned by her metamorphosis. Claire wished she might ask Mr. Venables where the marquess was, but she did not dare.

And then she saw him. He was escorting his sister into the room and making sure she had a comfortable seat, but when he straightened up and looked around, his glance fell on the slender figure in scarlet silk, and his eyebrows rose as his dark blue eyes grew intent in a thorough inspection.

Claire smiled at him even as she unfurled her fan and waved it gently to and fro before her face, and then she turned away to answer a question of the Duke of Severn.

When she turned back, Andrew was beside her.

"Miss Carrington," he said, taking up her hand and raising it to his lips, his dark blue eyes dancing with his approval. "My compliments, ma'am. You are looking very beautiful this evening."

"Thank you, m'lord. I am so glad you think so," she said demurely.

"Dare I hope you have been able to save me a dance?" he asked next, calmly taking the little card that dangled from her wrist and inspecting it.

"But of course, O my mentor. How would I dare the first waltz with anyone else?" she teased as he signed her card for the supper dance she had kept free as well.

The orchestra began to play then, and he drew her onto the

floor, holding out his arms in that now familiar gesture. Claire went into them without another word, wondering at the strange lump in her throat as she did so.

For a moment they danced in silence, and then the marquess said, "What a revelation you are, Claire! And to think that all these weeks you have been hiding your light under a bushel. But perhaps you are offended that I compare your former attire to a bushel? You must forgive me, and put my gaucheness down to my delight and surprise."

"I am very fine, am I not?" Claire asked.

"Breathtaking," he agreed, pressing that pliant waist and sweeping her into a turn. "Well done, Claire," he whispered.

Her large gray eyes under the long black lashes laughed up at him. "Of course. I have had an excellent teacher, you see. However, I seem to keep hearing you count 'one and two and three,' but perhaps that will fade in time."

He laughed, his eyes crinkling in amusement as he bent his blond head closer to her midnight-black one.

"And may I also say how fine you are, sir?" she asked, her voice complimentary. "I have not seen you in full formal attire before, but now I know why Pamela Greeley is so determined in her pursuit. Perhaps you should dress more carelessly if you are serious in your refusal to marry."

The marquess smiled at this sally, wondering why his reluctance to enter that holy estate was fast being undermined, as her eyes admired his black evening coat of superfine with its long tails, and his satin knee breeches worn with white silk stockings and black pumps.

"And do you feel yourself as confined and breathless in your new gown as you feared, Claire?" he could not help asking next.

He felt her move a little in his arms. "As you are very well aware from the tight way you are holding me, Andrew, I do not. The modiste assured me there was no need for any such . . . ah, restraints. But this is a very improper conversation, even between old friends."

"Oh, surely not, Miss Carrington," he insisted, a devil dancing in those dark blue eyes now, and his mouth twitching in amusement. "Not for someone who daily spends hours before unclothed models, painting their likenesses on canvas."

"Andrew, do be careful," she whispered. "Sir Reginald is nearby, and your sister as well. Why ever is she glaring at me?" she wondered aloud, giving Lady Peakes a warm smile.

"She is sure you have seduced me, but having chosen Pamela, she will permit no substitute for my hand," Andrew answered, his voice calm. "But come! Let us enjoy the music. I do not desire to talk about Marion right now, or think about Pamela Greeley either." He paused and then added, "What a shame I am allowed only two dances."

"Why is that?" Claire asked, bewildered. "You know you may have as many as you like."

The marquess shook his head in contradiction. "To dance attendance on you all evening, Claire, especially after all my attentions these past few weeks, would lead to gossip, and you have already discovered the *ton*'s penchant for gossip. We must be discreet; otherwise everyone will be searching the columns of the journals for an interesting announcement," he instructed her.

"I see," she said, her deep contralto colorless.

He thought this reply most unlike her, but then any questions he might have asked her fled from his mind as he looked down into her oval face. Her black lashes rested on her cheeks now, but as if she knew he was staring at her, she raised her eyes. At the look in his dark blue ones, serious now with some unknown speculation, her color rose a little, but she did not look away.

How honest her eyes are, he thought, how true. He admired the way she held her head so proudly, the slim column of her throat, and the expanse of smooth white skin exposed by the low décolletage of her gown, and only slightly masked by her magnificent necklace.

Suddenly he realized they had been silent too long. "Where had you those beautiful jewels, Claire?" he asked, his voice a little strained.

Claire wondered at the way her breath seemed to catch in her throat, and she had to swallow before she could reply. The African chieftain provided an interesting—and safe—topic of conversation, and from his beneficence she went on to speak of the other jewels Lady Dawson had acquired over the years.

"I shall look forward to admiring them too," the marquess said, and then the music ended. All around them, ladies were sinking into deep curtsies, but not even this evening, bejeweled and clad in scarlet silk, would Claire compromise her principles. Lord Blagdon bowed a little and kissed her hand, well aware that as the only erect couple on the ballroom floor, he and Claire stood out as oddities, and he drew her hand in his arm to lead her to where Lady Banks was sitting with some friends. Of the general there was no sign, of course, for he had sounded the retreat at the first musical note and retired to the card room.

But Claire was not allowed to take her place beside her elderly relative, for the Duke of Severn came up to claim his dance. Andrew bowed and gave him her hand, but felt unaccountably reluctant to do so.

William Fairhaven, the Duke of Severn, was a tall man in his late thirties, with hair as dark as Claire's, and soaring black eyebrows above a strong, aristocratic face. He had married when he was very young, but his wife had died in childbirth some years ago. Since she had presented the duke with three sons and a pair of twin daughters before her death, there was no need for him to remarry if he did not care to, and up to this time he had seemed content with the single state and his return to bachelorhood.

Now Andrew watched the way he was admiring Miss Carrington, and even the grace with which she was performing the intricate country dance could not still his unease. The duke was nothing like Lord Wilson or Sir Reginald. He was a handsome, sophisticated man, and a knowledgeable one, as well-traveled as he was well-read. From the way Claire was smiling and conversing with him, Andrew could tell she was enjoying their conversation. He saw the duke throw back his head and laugh at something she said, and then reply, and he saw Claire's answering smile as well.

Somehow the marquess was delighted when the music ended, and he felt a stab of elation when Claire refused to curtsy yet again, only holding out her hand to her noble and very surprised partner.

As they came off the floor, he could see the duke questioning her, and listening intently to her reply, but then he lost any feeling of complaisance when he saw him smile and nod and raise her hand to kiss it in tribute. Who would have thought the duke would take this slight to his title so calmly?

He was glad when Wilfred Wilson joined them and seemed determined to remain by their side, and then he realized that by standing on the sidelines staring at Claire throughout the dance, he had made a spectacle of himself. Blindly he asked Miss Beck, who was standing beside him, for the next dance, and he was careful from then on not to look Claire's way too obviously.

Lady Peakes was not reassured, not even when he asked Pamela Greeley for a dance, and when she went to speak to her mother, she found that the dowager's massive calm had also been a little dented by Miss Carrington's stunning appearance and her son's admiration.

"We shall speak of this later, Marion," Lady Blagdon said, her cold voice stern. "I shall summon Andrew for an interview tomorrow. This has gone on quite long enough; he shall be brought to see the error of his ways."

Lord Peakes, standing to attention behind his mother-in-law's chair, spared Andrew a brief pang of sympathy, only glad it was not he who had to face this reprimand.

When the supper dance was announced at last, the marquess was quick to separate Claire from the group who surrounded her. She thought his face looked stern and set as he took her in his arms, even as she regretted the dance was not another waltz.

"Are you enjoying the ball, Andrew?" she asked, concern in her voice.

"Not as much as you are, I can see," he replied. Claire ignored the pique in his voice as she tilted her head to one side to consider his words.

"Do you know, I am, and I never thought to do so," she admitted. "I have met some interesting people tonight. Not all the *ton* are silly and worthless, I see, and it was arrogant of me to think so without any more knowledge than I had of them. Why, the Duke of Severn is a fascinating man; he has been in South America too."

"Yes, you are quite the belle of the ball," Andrew agreed, and she leaned back in his arms for a moment to search his face.

"And that does not please you?" she asked, her voice wondering. "But it was at your instigation that I bought this new gown and had Aunt Flora's jewels brought to me. Lady Banks let slip that you were concerned about my ballgown, and I'm afraid I made up my mind to show you that if I wanted to, I could be as grand as anyone. You did say once that my appearance reflected on you, after all, and yet it seems I have displeased you."

She looked so upset that Andrew felt ashamed of himself, and since he had no idea why he was taking her to task, he

92

changed the subject. "No, no, Claire, you have not displeased me. But tell me, why did you agree to a Season at all? I know that you wanted to come to London to study in a real artist's *atélier*, but it was not necessary for you to enter society as well. I do not understand."

Claire explained how she had promised her aunt that she would have one Season. "You see, she wanted me to be sure that I knew what I was giving up when I decided to remain single," she said, her gray eyes steady on his. "And although I had made up my mind and wished only to paint, I had to agree."

"But by entering this pact with me to trick society, you are not fulfilling your promise to your aunt," Andrew reminded her.

Claire's brows contracted in a little frown. "Well, perhaps not quite to the letter of the law, but I am here, and I do go to *ton* parties."

The marquess was struck by a sudden unwelcome thought. "Claire! If you change your mind and do find someone you want to marry, you must tell me at once. I would not hold you to our agreement, you know."

She smiled up at him and pressed his hand. "Silly! I shall never find anyone I like better than you, and if I don't want to marry you, it follows that I shall not want to marry anybody."

Her huge eyes were so honest and her words so matter-of-fact that the marquess caught his breath, but then the dance ended and he was not able to ask her to explain her last remark. As he took her into the supper room, he wondered why he felt relief as well as chagrin at her guileless words.

Their table was very popular. When he returned from the buffet with a plate of delicacies for Claire, he found that the Duke of Severn had taken the seat on her other side, and Paul Venables was there as well, escorting Miss Greeley, who did not look as if she were enjoying the ball at all, even though she was an angelic vision of white satin and golden curls.

The duke insisted on pouring Miss Carrington a glass of champagne himself, and Andrew noticed that although he was polite and included the others in his conversation, his eyes went most often to Claire's face.

Miss Greeley was not used to playing second fiddle. Toying with her breast of partridge and new peas, she said, "I have not had the chance to tell you, Miss Carrington, how much I admire your gown and those jewels you wear." Her hand went up to the single strand of debutante pearls she wore as she stared at Claire's necklace. "Such an unusual set, are they not? Almost barbaric in their size and splendor, in fact."

In her voice was also the unspoken thought that they were most unsuitable as well, but Claire only smiled.

"They belonged originally to my aunt, the Lady Flora Dawson, and were given to her by the head of an African tribe."

"Really?" Miss Greeley asked, her voice sweet. "I wonder what the circumstances were that he was obliged to show his gratitude in such an extravagant way?"

Her words were insulting, and Andrew saw the duke's frown, and the way Paul Venables' face stiffened a little, but Claire continued to smile.

"She did not tell me, Miss Greeley, but knowing my aunt as I did, I doubt if there would have been anything to stare at. She was always scornful of the way ladies in society expect to be rewarded with jewels in return for their favors."

Miss Greeley gasped and raised her napkin to her suddenly flushed face, and Claire turned to the marquess. Ignoring the censure in his eyes for her boldness, she changed the subject. Pamela Greeley became very interested in her supper.

As they all rose from the table at last, after a final course of ices and *petits fours* and more champagne, the marquess saw the intent way the duke was studying Claire, and he could not help but overhear his quiet remark that he would do himself the honor of calling on Miss Carrington on the morrow, before he bowed and went away.

As he escorted Claire back to the ballroom, Andrew hoped for the very first time that she was planning an early trip to Dilke Street and a long session at her easel.

Chapter Seven

True to her word, the dowager marchioness sent a note around to her son's rooms the first thing the following morning. Her footman was instructed to wait for m'lord's reply, and so he was forced to cool his heels for some time. Andrew had gone out for an early canter in the park, and after returning to change his clothes, had just left Upper Brooks Street to visit White's when her message arrived.

Lady Blagdon found herself growing more and more angry as the morning wore on, and when James returned at last and she learned that Andrew would not be able to call on her until the following morning, having engagements that afternoon that he could not cancel, such respect for the social niceties did nothing to endear him to his mother on this occasion.

She pursed her thin lips and wrote a note to Lady Peakes, asking her attendance at that time as well, and then she ordered her carriage and was driven to the shops in Bond Street, a location she had had no intention of visiting that day.

Lord Wilson was not so fortunate in avoiding his mother's censure, for since they had taken rooms together, Lady Wilson was able to scold and threaten and instruct until he had the sudden inspiration that he would be remiss if he did not order flowers to be sent to Claire at once. Lady Wilson allowed him to escape, but she sat on at the breakfast table for some time, her fat face settling into lines of profound disappointment. The suit of Sir Reginald Randolph she could ignore, but the attentions of the Marquess of Blagdon, and now the Duke of Severn as well, were impossible for her to contemplate without serious feelings of unease. Fond of her son as she was, she was not blind, and it was obvious that Wilfred didn't stand a chance in the face of their competition. For the first time, she cast about in her mind for other wealthy debutantes of her acquaintance who might be suitable for her purposes.

Lady Greeley also spent an unpleasant morning. Her daughter was quick to tell her of Miss Carrington's shocking conversation at the supper table, and in doing so revealed her part in it as well. Lady Greeley had lost her temper at her daughter's inability to see that she had appeared jealous of the older girl, and no better than a backbiting shrew.

Shaking an astonished Pamela, who had been sure of her mama's sympathy, Lady Greeley told her daughter in no uncertain terms that she was fast losing any chance of attaching the marquess with her tempers and pouting and ridiculous starts, and then instructed her, until her voice grew a little hoarse, in the ways it was best to go about forcing a reluctant gentleman to propose marriage.

Pamela went away much chastened, and Lady Greeley shook her head. She knew she herself had never been so silly and stupid, and she did not understand how she could ever have brought up such a beautiful widgeon. Why, Lord Greeley had asked for her hand after only three meetings; surely the marquess had had more than enough time to fix his interest if he were ever going to do so at all. She sat on in her morning room, making and discarding plans to bring him to his knees, and like Lady Wilson, reviewing other candidates as replacements if he failed to come up to scratch.

Claire had gone early to Dilke Street, as Andrew had hoped she would, for she was beginning a large canvas on a classical theme. Monsieur Duprés had encouraged her to attempt a painting of *The Judgment of Paris* as an exercise to see how she would handle several figures on a large scale. It was not a subject she would have chosen herself, but she had become more and more interested as she made sketches of the placement and poses and background of the various figures in a formal yet pleasing design. She had prepared her canvas a week before, stretching it and applying the gesso, and blocking out the figures in charcoal, and was now engaged in beginning the actual painting, from the sky and clouds that formed most of the background, to delineating the figures in their classical robes.

She was not at home when Wilfred's bouquet was delivered, and she had still not returned when the butler accepted several more floral tributes—a sheaf of gladioli from Sir Reginald, a bouquet of spring flowers from the Duke of Severn, and an elegant posy of scarlet rosebuds from the Marquess of Blagdon that was accompanied by a note of congratulation for her triumph and a reminder that he was escorting her and Lady Banks to the theater that evening.

That elderly lady was in raptures over the floral tributes, and she was admiring them in the hall, where they had been placed on a table awaiting Claire's attention, when the general came down and took instant exception to his house being turned into a florist's shop. After delivering several pithy comments in a loud voice, he stamped out the door, and was not seen again until after teatime, for which his long-suffering wife could only be grateful.

Claire herself did not come back to Belgrave Square until midafternoon. She admired all her flowers, but Lady Banks noticed that only the marquess's posy was honored by a place in her bedroom, the others being relegated to the drawing room.

The Duke of Severn came to call while she was changing from her painting clothes, and Lady Banks immediately sent an urgent message to Claire to be sure to wear the smart new dark gray afternoon ensemble with the braid trim. Then she ordered some Madeira for her noble guest, and proceeded to engage him in conversation until her cousin should come down.

Claire had put on the new gown, she saw with relief when she came in to join them some minutes later, but she had brushed her curls in quite the old way. Instead of a sophisticated coiffure, they tumbled over her head and framed her face with what Lady Banks considered a milkmaid's attempt at elegance.

The duke did not appear to be disgusted, however, and he remained with the ladies for half an hour. Lady Banks sat quietly with her embroidery, content to play the silent *dueña* as he and her cousin discussed South America, and especially Brazil, with great animation. When he rose to take his leave, Claire walked with him to the drawing-room door. He had asked if he might not drive her in the park the following afternoon, and they were arranging the time.

"Not before four, if you please, Your Grace," she said in her rich contralto, and the duke was happy to agree. When he would have bowed, she put out her hand, and he took it and held it for a moment, his dark eyes twinkling with amusement as he said, "I had forgotten. Very well, Miss Carrington, no curtsies and no bows. I wonder if the day will ever come when you will be glad to curtsy to some one particular gentleman? I will be most interested to learn that gentleman's identity."

He inclined his head then and went away, and Claire asked her cousin what he could have meant by that remark.

Lady Banks had to admit she had not been attending, but before she could begin to question Claire about it, her butler announced Sir Reginald Randolph, and she was forced to take Claire to task instead for the expression of distaste that appeared on her face.

The marquess arrived in his carriage at the time he had appointed to escort both ladies to the theater. He had engaged a box, and not even the sight of Claire in one of her old gowns, without jewels and wearing her hair in the old, careless way, upset him.

At the first interval, while Lady Banks was busy waving to all her acquaintance, Claire leaned toward him and whispered, "Are you enjoying the *ingénue*, sir?"

Her voice contained a barely controlled amusement, for the actress had an abundant figure and was in constant danger of falling out of her low-cut gown.

"Claire!" he warned, his tones admonishing, although he could not help responding to the sparkle in her eyes.

"But we are alone now, my friend, so I can say what I want," she pointed out. "And that reminds me, I feel I must apologize for wearing my old muslin tonight. My new gowns will be ready soon, and I cannot tell you how delighted I will be when they arrive. All these fittings, and the endless shopping for sandals and bonnets and trim. Bah! Besides, they are so expensive, I cannot be easy."

The marquess, who knew Claire's fortune was not at all contemptible, raised a brow. "You are worried about the expense?" he asked, his voice disbelieving.

Claire waved her hand. "I can afford them, of course, but it seems such a waste of money, all those guineas for one ball gown. Why, it would feed a family of four for a month, and think of all the canvases and paints and lessons it would buy."

Lord Blagdon laughed, and then in a casual voice he asked if the Duke of Severn had called on her that afternoon.

Claire admitted the visit, and mentioned their coming drive in the park.

"I like him, for he is an interesting man, but I really

cannot continue all this gadding about," she told him, and for some reason his heart lightened. "I have begun a major work," she explained, "and it will require all my attention from now on."

The marquess was unable to ask her any more about it, for the house lights were being extinguished and the curtain was rising on the second act, which for some unknown reason he enjoyed much more than the first.

The Duke of Severn would have been amazed at the jealousy he was causing in so many masculine breasts, and the hatred with which Lady Wilson now regarded him. Having been on the town forever, he had no intention of enjoying more than a friendship with Miss Carrington, for although she was a well-enough-looking girl, she was not at all in his style. There was that of singularity about her that intrigued him of course, for to discover a young lady who was not only intelligent but also well read, who had traveled almost as extensively as he had himself, and who was able to conduct a sensible yet sparkling conversation without pregnant pauses, titters, or innuendos was too much for him to ignore. He was determined to spend as much time with Miss Carrington as she would allow him, but when the Season was over, he would make his elegant farewells and retreat, still unwed, to his estates in the country.

During their drive in the park, he discovered by devious questioning that this program had Miss Carrington's heartfelt approval, and although he looked sideways at her, one black eyebrow quirked in disbelief when she announced she had no plans for matrimony either now or at any time in the future, there was something in her voice that made him believe her.

"But surely, in that case, Miss Carrington, it is most remiss of you to be so constantly in Lord Blagdon's company?" he asked, his voice calm. "One might almost say you are raising false hopes there."

Claire opened her mouth to explain her pact with Andrew, and just as quickly closed it. "The marquess knows my mind, Your Grace," she said, and then she changed the subject, asking him to tell her more about his journey to Russia the previous year, for it was a place she had never visited.

The marquess arrived at his mother's town house only a few minutes late the following morning. Marion and her husband, Lord Peakes, were already installed in the drawing room, and Lady Blagdon was once again sitting bolt upright on her throne.

As Andrew came in on the heels of her butler's announcement, he took in the situation in a glance, and for a moment his dark blue eyes gleamed.

Not a sign of his amusement showed, however, as he strolled into the room. He was dressed with great propriety in the correct attire of a gentleman making a morning call, so there was nothing in his appearance to give his mother a disgust of him, although from the stony expression on her thin face this was not immediately apparent. Rather she looked as if he had called on her in his dressing gown.

"My word, Percy, you here too? For shame!" Andrew said as he went to kiss the cool cheek his mother offered for his salutation, and then he waved a careless hand to his sister, who was sitting opposite her mother in an identical upright position.

Lord Peakes was heard to try to voice his apologies to Andrew, saying he had really rather not come, until a glare from his wife and a sniff from his mama-in-law caused his disjointed mumbling to die away.

"That's all right, old man, perfectly understandable," Andrew reassured him. "I shall not regard it or hold it against you."

Unbidden, he took the most comfortable chair in the room, for he had no intention of standing before his mother like a small boy waiting to be chastised, and then, looking at Lady Blagdon, he asked, "I am sure there is some grave reason for your summons, Mother? Not, of course, that I am not always delighted to attend you, but I gathered from the tone of your oh-so-loving note that there was something of great import you wished to discuss with me?"

Lady Blagdon inclined her head a fraction of an inch. "That is correct. I have asked you to call so that I might apprise you of my feelings concerning your present conduct."

The marquess's blond eyebrows rose as he settled back in his chair, throwing one arm over the back and crossing his legs before him, completely at his ease. "My conduct, Mother?" he prompted.

Lady Blagdon eyed his handsome, lounging figure with distaste. The times she had ordered him to sit up straight! The board she had insisted be strapped to his back for hours at a time when he had been a boy, so he would learn the correct posture for the future marquess! Now she decided to be magnanimous and ignore it as she said, "It has come to my attention, Andrew, that far from fixing your interest with Miss Greeley, a young lady who you are well aware has earned my approbation, you have been in constant attendance on a most unsuitable young female; to wit, a *Miss Claire Carrington.*"

She paused and sniffed. Her scornful tones as she uttered Claire's name would have wilted the hardiest plant at twenty paces, and Lord Peakes moved uneasily in his chair, his nervous eyes darting from one to the other of the adversaries.

"Well?" she asked when her son made no comment, "I am waiting for your explanation. You will not attempt to deny it, I hope."

"Certainly not," Andrew agreed, completely cordial.

"Perhaps you were not aware of my distaste for this *Miss Carrington?*" she asked next.

"It is unnecessary to enumerate your reasons, ma'am," the marquess said, holding up a deterring hand. "The tone of your voice when you speak her name makes it very clear in what light you regard her. In fact, one may say that all its usual gentle cordiality is most definitely *in absentia.* Someday you must explain how it is possible to dislike someone that you are not even acquainted with, for I find that impossible to fathom."

"Since I do dislike her, you should as well. You are well aware that Pamela Greeley is the young lady I have approved for the position of the next Marchioness of Blagdon. I cannot tell you, Andrew, how disappointed I am that you have not asked for her hand as yet. I am sure Lady Greeley also is mortified by your continued reluctance."

"How can this be? I have never given any sign that I wished for a warmer relationship with her daughter. You will not accuse me of leading the young lady on, I trust?" Andrew asked, and Marion saw the way his blue eyes darkened before he lowered his eyelids.

"It would be unnecessary and unbecoming for you to engage in such an undignified occupation, my son," the dowager said, folding her thin hands in her lap as she kept her cold eyes on the marquess. "Not after I have told you the match has my sanction."

"And therefore is as good as accomplished?" Andrew

asked, his voice still quiet, although with a hint of steel in it that had not been there earlier. "You are too good, ma'am, but I must beg you not to trouble yourself over my affairs."

The dowager stiffened. "Are you daring to defy me, Andrew?" she asked, as if she could not believe her ears, even as she thought with regret of the thick leather strap she had had the governess use on him so often when he was a boy. Lord Peakes rolled his eyes at his brother-in-law in warning, and then looked longingly at the decanter of wine that sat on a side table.

The marquess rose to his feet and stretched his arms wide.

Lady Blagdon closed her eyes in disgust for a moment, making a prim mouth at such physical carelessness, and in her drawing room, too.

"You may consider it defiance, but I beg you to reconsider your position, ma'am. I owe you filial respect and courtesy; I do not owe you the ordering of my future. I have told you time out of mind, and Marion as well, that I will never be coerced into matrimony. I intend to choose my bride myself, and all these plans and approvals of yours will not force me to a match that can bring me nothing but misery and boredom."

"And I suppose a marriage to that woman's niece will not?" the dowager asked, her voice outraged.

Andrew grinned. "No, with Claire I would never be bored. Miserable, perhaps, on occasion, but never bored. But come! The occasion is not likely to arise, for I have not proposed to that lady either, as yet."

Seeing that her mother was speechless, Marion spoke up for the first time. "It is too bad of you, Drew! How can you cause Mama this pain and upset all her plans by insisting on having your own way?"

"Probably because it is I, not Mama, who will have to spend so many years as Miss Greeley's husband," Andrew was quick to reply.

"But, Drew, Miss Carrington is so . . . so unsuitable! Her background and upbringing, the tone of her mind . . . But I cannot bring myself to speak more plainly. Perhaps you have not heard some of the things she has said?—in company, mind!—but let that go. The very fact that she refused to curtsy to her betters should be enough to give any gentleman a disgust of her. I do not understand you at all."

"You never have, nor has our mother either," her fond brother told her. "Both of you have always maintained that I was difficult and hard to manage. Well, I dislike being managed as much as the next man, perhaps even more so, since after my father died I spent my childhood under an iron hand.''

His bow to his mother was ironic, but she did not seem to notice, only inclining her head a trifle as if to thank him for a compliment he had never intended.

"I would remind you both, with all due respect, that I am no green young man, to be easily led and manipulated. No, I cut my eyeteeth years ago, and attained my majority quite thirteen years past. I shall decide my future. I, alone.''

He bowed again to both indignant ladies in turn and added softly, ''Of course, if I ever find myself in need of advice, be certain I shall know where to come, since you both seem so preoccupied with my private affairs.''

Lady Peakes gasped at her brother's sarcastic words, her blue eyes going in horror to the rigid figure of her mother.

"That will be quite enough,'' that lady said through stiff lips. "If you continue to carry on in this nonsensical way and dare to disobey my clearly expressed wishes, Andrew, I shall be forced to take steps.''

She paused after this awful statement, and the marquess, who had been adjusting the lace at his cuffs, looked surprised.

Nodding her head, she continued in her cold, colorless voice, "I shall cease to acknowledge you, and your name shall never be mentioned in my presence again.''

She might have been discussing a boring book she was reading, or the inclement spring weather, and, taken aback, the marquess stared at her.

"Indeed? You would cast off your only son forever, simply because he would not do your bidding? How . . . how very unmaternal, ma'am, even for you.''

Lady Blagdon rose and faced her unrepentant son. "You have been warned, Andrew, and I believe your hearing is excellent. You will cease dancing attendance on that woman's niece at once, or you will suffer the consequences of my banishment, and be dead to me from this time on. Since it is entirely your fault that your father is not still the Marquess of Blagdon, I expect you to honor my wishes.''

She did not notice how her son had stiffened, nor the dangerous light that came into his dark blue eyes, nor Marion's little gasp of horror as she continued, "It is unfortunate that you cannot like Pamela Greeley, but I will not insist on your obedience in this instance. Some degree of liking and respect there must be, although of course it is not at all seemly to love. Indeed, that emotion is beneath the notice of those who have noble blood.''

She paused, and then with the air of one granting a tremendous concession, she said, ''I shall allow you to choose your own wife, with the stipulation, of course, that she meet with my approval, and I shall expect to be accepting the congratulations of my friends before the year is out.''

''You are too good, ma'am,'' the marquess murmured.

''Indeed I think so. I have been more than patient with you, Andrew, but now that patience is exhausted. That is all I have to say. You are excused.''

She inclined her head in dismissal, and for a moment there was a stunned silence in the drawing room that was broken at last by Lord Peakes's nervous cough.

''I shall take my leave, then, ma'am. You have given me a great deal to ponder, and I shall, of course, apprise you of my decision as regards your ultimatum in due course,'' the marquess said, but as he bowed to them all, Marion noticed that he did not offer to kiss his mother good-bye, and there was a light in his dark blue eyes that startled her in its intensity and regret.

She could not help feeling that this time Mama had gone too far in referring to Andrew's unintentional part in his father's demise, and she herself would never have tried to handle him by threatening him and giving him orders. She knew that if her brother was as stubborn as a pig, and always had been, her mother was twice as likely to insist on getting her own way. She sighed. In that respect, they were really so much alike.

She considered this impossible impasse as she began to draw on her gloves and the drawing-room door closed softly behind the marquess. It was not at all like Andrew to go without further argument, and this new, quiet man who spoke up for himself in such a firm way was a new come-out indeed. She wished she did not feel so uneasy, even as Lady Blagdon took her seat in the high-backed wing chair again and said in a satisfied voice, ''And now I think we have seen almost the end of Andrew's inappropriate alliance with that terrible woman's niece. I shall allow him two weeks to come to his senses, but that is all.''

Marion was not so sure that two weeks or even two years

would suffice, but she did not voice any contrary opinion. She had been stunned on the night of the St. Marlowe ball to see Claire dressed in such a stunning gown, and although she could not approve the vulgarity of the display, had had to admit that her jewelry was most impressive. And then when she had seen her waltzing with Andrew, she had been struck by the ease and grace with which they performed, almost as if the two of them had been intimate for years. Her brother's brooding stare when Miss Carrington had danced the next set with the Duke of Severn had not escaped her notice either, nor the way his eyes had sought out the slender figure in scarlet so often throughout the evening.

Marion wished her mother had not issued such an ultimatum, for she knew that, having spoken it, she would never retreat, and she did not like to contemplate a future in which she and her only brother must live estranged.

Marion was cold and proud, but as much as she was capable of loving anyone, she loved Andrew. Since he was six years younger, she had often felt protective and compassionate toward him when they were growing up. Sometimes she had had the thought that she was more his mother than the dowager was, especially after their father died and her mother had turned all her efforts into making eight-year-old Andrew a worthy successor to the title, with no regards for his feelings or his needs. She herself had succumbed without question to the rigorous training her mother insisted she have as the sister of the future marquess, even as she tried to shield her brother from his mother's cold severity. Lady Peakes had adored her father, with his hearty laugh and the blue eyes and golden hair that were so much like his son's, and in Andrew she could imagine that he lived again.

As they drove away from the dowager's town house, Lord Peakes noticed how sad and distracted his wife was, and patting her hand, said he was sure everything would be all right, but this comforting platitude only drew a heavy sigh from the lady. And then he startled her by adding, "She shouldn't have done it, Marion!"

At her questioning look, he explained further, "Demn all, Drew's a man, ain't he? And he's thirty-four to boot. If a man can't order his own life at that age, when can he? Not to put too fine a point on it, m'dear, your mama is a fool. He'll not stand still for this arrogance and she'll lose him, you mark my words."

Stunned by this flow of critical words from her generally tongue-tied husband, Lady Peakes could only nod and agree with him. He patted her hand again.

"Aye, she'll lose him, but you won't, m'dear. After all *we* didn't say he would be dead to us, now, did we? And we don't have to abide by *her* decision!"

Marion felt so much better at these comforting sentiments that she was able to smile a little.

In the meantime, Andrew had dismissed his carriage and walked directly to Hyde Park. It was not a time of the day when he expected to meet any of his acquaintance there, and he felt the need for solitude. As he strolled the almost deserted paths, he reviewed the morning's meeting.

How could Mama? he wondered. How could any woman be so proud and cold, so completely unconcerned with her son's happiness that she insisted he do exactly what she wished or be exiled forever from her presence?

A little boy rolling a hoop was skipping toward him, while behind him his parents strolled arm in arm, keeping a watchful eye on him. When he tripped on a stone in the path and fell to his hands and knees, Andrew noticed how the lady hurried forward at once to draw him up and hug him, before she dusted him off and set him on his feet again with a kiss. Had his mother ever cared about him that way? Had she ever kissed and hugged him?

His blue eyes darkened and he frowned. He could not recall any contact between them except for the filial salute he was allowed to press on her cheek at certain formal, specified times. She had always been reluctant to participate in physical closeness, but after his father's sudden death she had seemed to harden into even greater frigidity.

Andrew reached the bench where he and Claire had talked the first afternoon he took her driving, and he sat down and stared at the calm waters of the Serpentine.

He did not want to give his mother or sister pain, but he knew without questioning his decision that there was no way he would stop seeing Claire.

Then he wondered why he was so firmly committed to this course, when after the Season was over he had every intention of parting from her, as she did from him. After all, wasn't that their agreement?

Surely this adamant attitude of his was only because he

resented being treated as if he were still in the nursery. Or was it?

He sighed and removed his high-crowned beaver to run a hand over his smooth blond hair. Was it possible that he was developing a *tendre* for Claire? No, no, he told himself. It was just that his friendship with her was much too important to be discarded lightly, even though he viewed the severing of all ties with his mother with extreme reluctance. It was such a final step—why, almost it would seem as if one of them had died.

He sat there on the bench for over an hour, and when he rose at last he felt a sudden ache in his heart, for after all his introspection he had come to realize that he would not care all that much if his mother did refuse to speak to him or see him again. He had been pretending all these years that she loved him, as he had been pretending he loved her too. His eyes were bleak with the pain of his discovery as he made his way back to the carriageway.

When the day comes that I do marry, I shall marry only where I can love, he promised himself, and I shall be careful to choose a lady who is warm and caring, so that the next Marquess of Blagdon will grow up in a happy, close-knit family.

Suddenly it seemed the most important thing in the world to him, and he made a vow that his sons—and his daughters, too—would be able to depend always on his support, a support he would make as loving and encompassing as he possibly could. And Blagdon Hall would be filled with laughter and love and the enjoyment of its inmates once again, as it should have been all these years. Why, he could hardly wait to change it!

As he walked with firmer purpose toward the Brook Gate, he knew now, with a clarity he had never experienced, why he had kept his secret philanthropy hidden from his mother all these years. She would never have approved the houses he maintained, or the moneys he so willingly gave, to shelter and feed and educate the children of unwed mothers who had deserted them at birth.

He had begun this work while still in his early twenties, and it was the business of overseeing their care that kept him in London the greater part of the year. Not a one of his friends, with the exception of Paul Venables, knew of his charity, nor had he ever wanted anyone to know, but now he wondered what Claire would think of it. Why, one of his homes was located not far from Dilke Street, he recalled, a ghost of his old grin lighting his lean face for a moment.

He walked along more quickly now, for he remembered he had a meeting with his agent about the possible acquisition of another building, and then he stopped suddenly and stared straight ahead.

It is no wonder that I took deserted children as my special charge, he told himself sadly, for after all, I have been as much an orphan as any of them all these years.

Chapter Eight

Lady Banks was delighted to welcome her cousin Lizzie to her morning room when that lady called a few days later, for she was big with the news of Claire's success, her stunning new gowns, and her abundance of suitors. The two old ladies sat over their teacups for an hour, discussing this gratifying situation in endless detail.

Miss Elizabeth Boothby, after years of diligent application to a study of the art, was fast becoming London's most accomplished gossip. As such, she stored each new item that was related to her away in her head, and brought it out again during her afternoon calls for all her acquaintance to admire.

No matter that Lady Banks almost always preceded her stories with the admonition that what she was about to say was for her cousin's ears only, and begged her not to tell a soul. Miss Boothby could never resist being first with the latest *on-dit*, although of course she assured Lady Banks that her lips were sealed.

By the time she rose to take her leave, she had several new stories, and she was moved to reward her cousin with a tidbit of her own.

"It has come to my ears, dear Martha, that the Dowager Marchioness of Blagdon is not at all pleased with her son's attendance on a certain lady," she confided, her faded eyes glistening in her excitement. "Lady Warner told me, in strictest confidence, of course, that she positively glared at dear Miss Carrington only two evenings ago at the concert where she was being escorted by Lord Blagdon."

"How could Lady Warner be sure she was glaring?" Lady Banks inquired, her tone disbelieving. "What I mean is, Lady Blagdon always looks disapproving. I am sure it was only her habitual expression, for we both know how much she wants the marquess to wed. Of course Claire's birth is so excellent, she is such an heiress, and . . . and there is so much to say to her praise, I am sure any mama would be delighted to welcome her into the family."

Lady Banks's voice was a little militant, for she was well aware that there were those in society who did not approve of Claire Carrington at all, those who thought her odd and bold and impolite, but she would never admit these things to Lizzie. Lizzie was not a relation of Claire's, she told herself, and it was none of her business. Little did she realize that Miss Boothby knew more about it than she did.

Now that lady was quick to smooth her ruffled feathers. "I am sure it is as you say, dear Martha. I have often remarked on Lady Blagdon's disagreeable air myself. And do you favor the marquess as Miss Carrington's future husband? Is he, perhaps, in the forefront of her suitors? I am sure if anyone knows, it must be you," she added coyly, bending forward in her eagerness.

Lady Banks did not appear to notice, for she was busy thinking. "I would certainly have said so a week or so ago. He was forever on the doorstep. Why, even the general remarked it. But now there is the Duke of Severn as well." She sighed and smiled. How wonderful it was that Claire could choose between a duke and a marquess!

"I am so sorry to have missed seeing Miss Carrington," Miss Boothby said as she gathered up her shawl, her reticule, and her umbrella. "I do not believe she was home the last time I called either, was she?"

Lady Banks shook her head and said in an airy tone, "I do not recall, but no doubt you are right. Claire is seldom home these days."

"Is she shopping, or perhaps walking with one of her beaux?" Miss Boothby asked, and Lady Banks tried not to look self-conscious as she said, "I am sure I cannot say, for I have no idea of Claire's engagements today."

"I shall not be at all surprised to hear some happy news from you at any moment, Martha, and I shall hope it is a duchess or at least a marchioness you will be welcoming to the family. I am sure we can cross Lord Wilson and Sir Reginald Randolph from the list, can we not?"

Lady Banks tittered as she escorted her cousin to the front hall. "Oh, my, yes! As the general would say, they are outflanked, outgunned, and outmaneuvered."

"I quite long to see dear Miss Carrington in one of her new gowns," Miss Boothby said after she had laughed politely at this sally. "I shall make it a point to be driven through the park at five, and perhaps I shall be lucky enough to be able to admire her with my own eyes. Such a stunning young woman," she enthused as she kissed her elderly cousin good-bye.

The stunning young woman was at that very moment in her large paint-stained smock, her hair concealed under the old-fashioned mobcap, and with a smear of yellow ocher on her cheek.

"No, no, Carrington," Monsieur Duprés was exclaiming, his hands on his hips as he studied her painting. "You cannot 'ave zee light coming from two directions at once. *Incroyable!* See 'ere, thees figure is lit from the left, yet over 'ere the shadows fall on that side. It will not do. Scrape it off and begin again!"

Claire sighed, but she could see her error as soon as he pointed it out, and without a word she took up her palette knife and scraped away the paint she had just spent an hour applying. On the model's stand, Frederick Peckham, who had been pressed into service to pose as Paris, twitched at his classical robe and grinned at her.

"While you are scraping, may I rest, Claire?" he asked. "I cannot tell you how difficult it is to maintain this position with my arm raised to such a height."

"That's 'cause you're not a trained model, Mr. Peckham," Mimi volunteered from the side of the room where she was busy making tea for them all.

The young artist climbed down from the stand and massaged his sore arm. He was dressed in a white sheet that was draped over one shoulder, leaving the other arm and most of his chest bare, and he was barefoot.

"Put some coal on that fire, if you please, madame. It is cold in here, wearing nothing more than this so-called robe."

Duprés nodded a reluctant approval to his wife as he inspected the other students' work, and Mr. Peckham came over to look at Claire's painting.

"Yes, it's really coming along now," he complimented her. "Those clouds are especially good—don't touch them!"

Claire promised she would not as she wiped her knife on an old rag, and then he leaned closer to peer at the golden-haired figure of Paris that occupied the center of the crowded canvas.

"I say, Claire, you haven't made the face at all like mine."

He sounded almost disappointed, and Claire smiled. "This is not a portrait. I am painting an ideal, a god, not a man. Besides, I should think you would be glad of it, Frederick. If I keep making stupid errors about the light direction, you would not want to be associated with the work, now, would you?"

Her fellow artist stepped back and with narrowed eyes studied the canvas as a whole for many minutes, and Claire found she was holding her breath.

"I have no desire to be a professional model, no matter how Madame extols the profession," he said at last, "but I must say I am delighted to be associated with this work. It is good—no, much more than good. It is excellent!"

Claire's huge gray eyes lit up with pleasure. "Do you really think so? I must admit I am pleased. It has come so easily, so quickly."

"How much longer will you need 'Paris' to pose? I am anxious to get back to my own painting of Madame Duprés before the oils begin to set."

"Not much longer, perhaps another half-hour or so. There is that troublesome piece of drapery here, and the left foot is not quite right. Can you hold the pose that long?"

Mr. Peckham assured her he would do his best, and went back to the stand. Since Claire had insisted on paying him generously for his time, he was not at all loath to pose for as long as she wished, no matter what he said. He was not a well-to-do young man, for he had come into only a small inheritance, and the extra money made it possible for him to buy some small treats instead of just the necessities for his growing family. He had great hopes as well that he might sell his entry in the show at the Royal Academy that was to open shortly. He had been accepted as an exhibitor for the first time, and he could not help but dream of a success that would establish him as a painter of the first rank, bringing wealth and fame at last.

As he took up his position, Claire rubbed her aching neck and right shoulder. She had been working for hours at a time, almost every day, and she too grew weary of standing before her easel, constantly raising her right arm and extending it as she painted. In her concentration, she was able to forget, but when at last the light faded, or Monsieur Duprés reminded her of the time, she was glad to sink down on her stool, her shoulders bowed in fatigue and her legs throbbing. By the time she cleaned up her palette and brushes and her own hands, and took her hackney to Belgrave Square, it was all she could do to change her clothes to join her cousin in the drawing room. Two days this week she had even denied the marquess and the duke when they came to call, to fall on her bed in an exhausted sleep.

Well, she told herself as she rode home sometime later, staring out at the dirty streets with unseeing eyes, at least I am almost finished. She felt a quiver of excitement as she recalled Frederick Peckham's words. Yes, she knew the painting was good, the best she had ever done. It had flowed from her brush as if her hand were being guided by some force outside herself. Although she had had this feeling before, this time it had been stronger and more persistent than ever.

She was so glad she had come to London to study, for the hours she spent in the *atélier* had made all the difference. Now she could approach that big white rectangle of canvas, which used to intimidate her so with its emptiness, with assurance and competence. And she was gaining knowledge every day in technique, augmenting her strengths and correcting her weaknesses. No longer did she have to hide a model's hands behind a scarf or a book because she could not draw them accurately, and now she knew, without thinking of it consciously, what paints she should mix, and in what proportion to get the exact shade of a violet shadow or a golden highlight.

I must tell Andrew that, she thought. For some reason, she had not again mentioned to him the large classical painting she was doing. In the back of her mind was the thought that she would like to surprise him with it when it was finished, and then she smiled at herself. I am like an eager child, she thought, waiting until I can show my teacher a perfect alphabet on my slate. And then I do want to ask his opinion about the subject of my next painting, and see if he approves. She planned to do a modern work of the *beau monde* gathered in Hyde Park at the fashionable hour of the promenade. In her mind's eye she could see the bright colors of the ladies' dresses, the handsome, gleaming horses and smart carriages, and the well-dressed gentlemen, all illuminated by the golden afternoon sunlight as they mingled and talked and exchanged greetings.

She had left the studio early this particular day, for she was engaged to drive out with the marquess, and she had left behind her a pensive Monsieur Duprés.

He stood before her almost finished canvas for a long time, one hand caressing his beard as he studied it, and then, coming to a sudden decision, he nodded his head. Mademoiselle Carrington invariably signed her canvases with two capital C's. He could enter this painting in the exhibition at the Royal Academy and no one would suspect it had been done by a woman. It was so good, he knew it would be accepted, and for a moment he felt a pang of envy. He had worked hard all his life, but he knew he would never be the artist Mademoiselle was, for she brought such talent, such freshness to her work. Life was not at all fair, he decided as he wandered over to stare at his own paintings, but at least I can let it be known that this artist is a student of Emil Duprés. Surely such excellence will attract others to my *atélier*. He felt a rising excitement at this coming good fortune and called to his wife. He gave her enough money to buy them a lavish meal, and for once, a good bottle of wine.

At that moment the marquess was just escorting Claire to his phaeton in Belgrave Square, his handsome face unsmiling. If Claire had not been so preoccupied with her painting these past several days, she would have noticed Andrew's growing air of abstraction, and seen the tiny frown that so often of late furrowed his forehead. He seldom corrected her social manners these days, but she assumed that was because it was becoming unnecessary for she had learned all her lessons. She did notice how gentle he was when he spoke to her, but she failed to see how often he stared at her profile before he shook his head and turned away, nor did she see the little despondency that had come into his dark blue eyes, and remained, a permanent feature.

This afternoon she was wearing a new gown of primrose muslin, with a dashing hat of chipped straw that dipped over one eye and was crowned with yellow and white wildflowers and a mass of pale green veiling. Her gloves and sandals matched the veiling, and over her shoulder she had tilted a tiny parasol of pleated primrose silk.

Andrew helped her to her seat in the phaeton after she had greeted the groom with her warm smile and inquired after his health. Michaels was fast becoming not so much resigned to Miss Carrington and her peculiar ways, as approving of the lady. She always had a smile for him and a bit of conversation, not like some of them highborn ladies, the old groom thought to himself as he let the horses go at the marquess's command and jumped onto his perch behind. No, they act like I'm not even 'ere. It was not the correct thing to make so much of a servant, but he found himself warming to the young lady more and more. And she did look mighty pretty this afternoon, too.

On the seat in front of him, Claire ignored Andrew's continued silence as she settled back in her seat and adjusted her parasol. Whatever can be wrong with him? she wondered. Have I done something that bad? She searched her memory but could think of nothing that would produce such a distracted air, and at last she said, her tones injured, "If I were Miss Greeley, Andrew, you would find me sporting a massive pout. Not only have you not admired my ensemble for the prescribed five minutes, you have barely spoken to me. I shall think I am boring you indeed, and we did promise to tell each other of that fault when we made our pact, did we not?"

Thus admonished, the marquess put his problem from his mind and smiled down at her. They had reached Grosvenor Place by now, and as if coming to a sudden decision, he turned the team away from the direction of the park.

"If you should not dislike it, Claire, I would prefer a run in the country this afternoon. Of course, if you are too disappointed that you cannot show off your most becoming finery to all the *ton*, I shall turn back at once."

"The *ton* can see my finery anytime, and a ride out of town would be delightful," she was quick to agree. "I only pray I do not lose my new hat!"

At this sally, she thought his face brightened a little, and she continued to chat, telling him of something droll the general had said that morning, that his wife had completely failed to fathom.

As he turned the team onto the bustle of the King's Road, they all heard the bells of a fire engine some distance away to their left. Claire noticed that Andrew slowed the pace of the team, and he kept looking in that direction, his glance both searching and anxious.

By the time they had passed through Sloane Square, Claire could see heavy black smoke billowing into the sky beyond the buildings that lined the King's Road, and remarked on it.

"I pray no one will be hurt and that the firemen can control the blaze before it spreads. The tenements in that district are crowded so close together, Andrew, as you will remember from your trip to Dilke Street, which is not far distant."

Surprisingly, the marquess had no comment, but the groom spoke up and said, "M'lord! If that fire's not in Multon Street, it is so near as to make no never-mind!"

Claire was astounded, for never before had the groom intruded on their conversation, and she half-expected the marquess to give him a setdown for his temerity. To her surprise, Andrew only nodded grimly and turned the team at the next intersection to head in that direction.

The fire was indeed in Multon Street, about halfway down the block, and he was forced, by the crush of people and carts and drays, to pull up several houses away.

Michaels ran to the horses' heads, and as Andrew jumped down, he gave him a few terse orders before he turned briefly and called to Claire, "Wait here! I must see how bad it is."

Claire sat for a moment in astonishment as he ran down the street, pushing his way past the curious come to see the conflagration, and then she called to the groom, "What is it, Michaels? And why is Andrew so concerned?"

To another lady, Michaels would have lied without a qualm, but to Miss Carrington he said, "M'lord owns property there, miss, and then, there are the children to see to."

"What children?" Claire inquired, even as she gathered her skirts and climbed down into the street, leaving her parasol and reticule behind her.

"M'lord's orphans, miss," Michaels said as she gained his side. He was having trouble keeping the team quiet now, she noticed, for they could smell the smoke and they were still fresh. Taking advantage of his preoccupation, she lifted her skirts and ran after the marquess.

" 'Ere, miss, don't you go down there! It's dangerous!" Michaels called, but Claire ignored him. The crowds that had gathered had grown in size, and she had trouble pushing her way through them. When she reached the building that was on fire, she saw the marquess shouting orders as he carried out a small, crying child who was coughing badly. Without hesitation she threaded her way through the hoses the firemen were holding, and the dirty puddles, to reach his side.

"Give him to me," she ordered, and without a word Andrew transferred the weeping child to her arms and ran back inside.

Claire looked around and saw a small group of women

116

across the street, all dressed alike in navy gowns and white aprons and caps. They were tending more children, some of them not much more than infants, and she carried her choking burden there, sitting him down gently on the cobbles and kneeling beside him. His face and hands were dirty with soot, and as he gasped for breath, the tears made clean white tracks down his freckled face. She pounded him on the back, not at all sure she was doing the right thing. In a moment he began to catch his breath, and seemed easier. Claire wished she had a handkerchief, and turned to one of the women to ask if she had any cloth.

The nurse shook her head, her wondering eyes staring at Claire's fashionable gown and chip straw hat. When she saw Claire lift that gown so she might tear off some of the bottom of her petticoat, her eyes widened even more.

Ordering the boy to blow his nose, she patted him on the shoulder, and then she got up to run back to the doorway where Andrew had disappeared. There were no flames that she could see, but the smoke was so heavy she could not be positive.

Surely the fire marshal will order us farther away if there is any danger of falling timbers, she told herself, as Andrew appeared once more. This time he had two small babies in his arms. Behind him, Claire was glad to see others entering the building, to return in a moment with more children. She reached out for the babies the marquess held, and he stopped long enough to smile at her and say, "They have almost put the fire out, and we have rescued most of the children. It won't be long now."

But it seemed to Claire, in the frantic moments that followed, that it took an age before some thirty babies and small children, none more than five or six, were gathered safely across the street, being watched over by the nurses and herself. She was sitting on the curb, rocking a screaming infant and trying to comfort it, when she saw the marquess come out of the building for the last time. He stopped to speak to the firemen and then he shook the hands of those men who had helped him before he came across the road.

The oldest nurse went to meet him, wringing her hands. "Oh, your lordship, thank heaven you came! Are all safe?"

The marquess took her arm and helped her back to her charges. "They are indeed, Mrs. Hollins. How did the fire start, do you know?"

"It was the kitchen chimney, m'lord. Being washday, the girls had been heating water for most of the morning, and just when the cook began the dinner soup, something must have caught in the flue. How . . . how bad is it, sir? We must get these little ones under cover and changed. They have all had a shock."

"Too bad for any of you to return tonight, or even for some time to come," the marquess said. The woman burst into tears and threw her apron up over her face in her distress, and he added, "Come, now, Matron! That will not help, and you know how I rely on you. I have already sent a lad to the home on Treadle Street, and they will take you in. It will be crowded, but I am sure it will suffice for a few days, until I can make other arrangements. Then too, if the children who live there cannot help with the infants, they can play with the older ones and take that burden from all your shoulders. Please go and explain to everyone. I am sure the children will enjoy a wagon ride, will they not?"

As he spoke, he smiled down at the first boy Claire had seen him rescue. He had edged closer to the marquess, his blue eyes wide with admiration, still clutching the piece of petticoat Claire had given him. Now the marquess said as he spotted it, "Where did you get that lacy handkerchief, Bert? I shall have to look to my laurels: you'll be a better toff than I am, with such an elegant nosecheat!"

The boy giggled as the matron bustled away and Andrew ruffled his sandy hair.

"Well? I can't believe the fire has frightened you so much that you've lost your tongue. Not the Bert I know."

Claire crouched on the curb, the crying baby forgotten as the boy smiled and leaned his head against the marquess's thigh. "Nah, guv, it ain't mine. It's the leddy's! She give it to me."

Andrew turned then and saw Claire, and his eyebrows rose. "I do not think either you or I should ask how she came by it," he said, his lips twitching. He gave the boy a little push and told him to go and help Matron, for, being such a big boy, he was one of his best helpers. Bert ran off, still smiling.

The marquess held out his hand, and Claire took it and rose from the curb. "Miss Ames, take this baby, if you would be so good," he said, and one of the younger nurses, smiling shyly at Claire as she did so, relieved her of her burden.

Claire wondered why she could feel the color rising in her face as Andrew inspected her. His dark blue eyes were keen, and his face serious. "You are all right, my dear?" he asked, his soft voice urgent.

"Of course. But what of you, Andrew? You were the one who took the risk, going into the building as you did. Why, look there, your coat is burned on the sleeve."

She noticed he had lost his high-crowned beaver, and his blond hair was disarranged, one lock falling over his forehead, and she clenched her hands together to keep from smoothing it back in place.

The marquess did not even bother to inspect the charred material, as his white grin split his lean, handsome face. "You are a fine pot to be calling the kettle black, Claire. Do take a look at yourself."

Claire looked down, and then she started to laugh. The elegant primrose muslin was limp and bedraggled where little hands had clutched it. It was also dirty at the knees where she had knelt in the street. She saw that the hem was dripping with dirty water and had attracted some of the debris from the gutter, and that her sandals were soaked and stained. She could not see that her new hat was covered with ashes, nor that she had a wide streak of soot across her cheek and nose, but Andrew was sure that even that knowledge would not bother her.

As he stared at her, listening to that lilting trill he knew meant she was completely amused, Andrew felt a lump in his throat. How magnificent she is, he thought, and even more beautiful right now in all her dirt and disarray than when she had been dressed for the ball. He started toward her, for there was nothing that he wanted more in the world just then than to kiss her and hold her tight and tell her how much he adored her. He forgot the children, the interested onlookers, and the noise and smoke and dirt of their surroundings. At that moment there was only Claire and himself. He saw her eyes widening, and one small hand go out to him, and his heart pounded in his breast.

Before he could reach her and take her in his arms, the fire marshal interrupted by stepping in front of him to ask what M'lord wished to do about what he called "the proppity." He went on and on, and Andrew forced his thoughts to the problem at hand, although his brain was reeling.

It seemed the roof was badly damaged near the chimney

and would need extensive repairs, and some of the interior walls were scorched. When he had made some decisions and arranged to have the place boarded up until the builders could begin restoration, he turned back to Claire. She had gone back to the nurses to help with the children again. The marquess stared at her, his dark blue eyes cool and contained now, and then the wagons he had sent one of the loiterers for arrived. For several minutes everyone was busy lifting the children to their places.

When Claire would have climbed in too, he stopped her by grasping her arm. "It is not necessary. Let me take you back to the phaeton."

He spoke briefly to the matron, telling her they would precede the wagons to Treadle Street, and then he came and held out his arm. Claire laid her hand on it, and wondered at the way his muscles tensed at her touch. Suddenly she remembered that intent, searing glance he had given her a few moments before as he strode toward her.

As they walked back to where Michaels was patiently watching the team, he seemed lost in reverie, and somehow she did not like to break the spell. Then he said, "Allow me to thank you, Claire. I never expected you to ruin your finery in such a way."

"You cannot be serious, Andrew! What is a gown, after all, compared to little babies?" she asked, her voice incredulous at his compliment.

He smiled, but he did not answer. Claire noticed how the ordinary people in the street made way for them, some of the women smiling shyly as they curtsied and called him "m'lord," their voices deferential. The men too, ill-dressed and dirty though most of them were, tugged their forelocks and fell back to give them passage. Claire was sure Lord Blagdon could walk this neighborhood at midnight, dripping jewels and gold fobs, and be as safe as he would be in his own drawing room. It was very strange, for she was sure Multon Street housed just as many thugs and pickpockets as Dilke Street did.

When they reached the phaeton, she did not hear Michaels's exclamations of distress at her appearance, nor his muttered apologies to the marquess for letting Miss leave his protection. She was thinking hard. As Andrew settled into the seat beside her and expertly backed the horses, she stole a glance at his lean profile. How well-loved he must be by these poor, humble people! She had seen it in their faces and heard it in

their respectful tones. And the children too, especially yo[...]
Bert, whose clinging to his hero made his admiration obviou[...]

She recalled herself to the present as Andrew spoke. "Would
it disturb you too much if we went to Treadle Street before I
take you home, Claire? I would like to be sure that the
children are settled and well, and I must have a word with the
matron, too."

Claire shook her head. "Of course not. Please do not
regard me. Besides, I am very interested in seeing the home
there, for I do not think I saw the one on Multon Street at its
best."

The marquess smiled down at her, his eyes warm, and she
lowered her own eyes to her dirty gloves. She wondered why
she felt so shy, and why her breath was catching in her
throat, and her heart beating so fast. This was only her friend
Andrew, she reminded herself. She did not understand why
she was behaving in such a silly way.

It was after five before matters at the Treadle Street home
had been arranged to the marquess's satisfaction. The babies
had calmed down at last, and when Andrew had assembled
the older children and asked them to help, he made the whole
affair sound like an adventure. Claire saw the children smile
and nod, and the eager way they all crowded around him. She
was surprised to see how patient he was with them, how
warm his smile was, and how intently he listened to their
prattle. At last he told them he would be back in the morning,
and then he came toward Claire. His face was expressionless
now, the gentle smile he had had for the children completely
gone. Claire wished there was some way she could summon
it back.

For a few moments they drove in silence, and then the
marquess said, "Thank you again for all your help, Claire. I
never expected you to run down Multon Street into all that
danger and confusion. However, I must tell you I am glad
you did. When the men saw that you were unafraid, they
came forward too."

Claire noticed that his eyes were intent on the street ahead
of them and that his voice was formal. She waved his compliment away.

"Tell me, Andrew, how long have you maintained these
homes? And how many do you support? To think that you are
such a benefactor, and I never suspected it!"

Her voice was warm with interest, and encouraged, the

told her of his philanthropy in a few brief words.

almost reached Belgrave Square now, and he wanted

home before anyone could see how disheveled and
she was and wonder at it.

Claire ignored the singular picture she made in the smart, shining rig, she was so intent on his story. "But why have you never mentioned it before?" she prodded. "You have let me go on and on about my art, but this work you do must be important to you, and time-consuming as well. I am disappointed you have not confided in me, when I thought us friends."

Andrew sent her a smiling glance. "No one knows. Well, no one but Paul Venables. I have the greatest dislike of notoriety, and not many of the *ton* would understand. In fact, most of them would consider such a topic of conversation a dead bore. You remember how I strive never to be a bore, Claire!"

Her brows came together in a frown as she ignored his jest. "And so you go on letting them think you as worthless and frivolous as they are? Why, Andrew, you are worth a dozen of them—it will not do!"

She sounded determined to change the world's opinion of Lord Blagdon herself, and he was alarmed. "Here, now, Claire, not a word to anyone! Give me your promise!"

Claire failed to see why this was so important to him, but she nodded. "Very well, if you insist on hiding your light under a bushel too, my friend. But we must speak further of this, for there is much I do not understand, much I want to learn."

Lord Blagdon assured her he would be only too willing to tell her of the venture at some future date, as he tooled the team smartly around the last corner of Belgrave Square and drew up before the general's house. Michaels was quick to run to the horses' heads as Andrew put a restraining hand on Claire's arm. For some reason that was unknown to her, she waited there on the perch until he came around to lift her down. As she felt his strong hands encircling her waist to swing her lightly to the flags, she felt the heat rising in her face. Had she waited just so she could be close to him, to feel the warmth of his hands through the thin muslin of her gown? And knowing how agile she was, had he come to help her for the same reasons, or was he merely being polite?

She raised her face to his, her huge gray eyes searching his

122

dark blue ones, and then she heard someone exclaim and
out.

Turning away, she saw Miss Boothby going by in an open
landau, accompanied by three other ladies. Her expression
was comical in her astonishment, her eyes bulging with shock
while her mouth fell open as she pointed to the pair on the
sidewalk with a trembling, accusatory finger.

The marquess released Claire at once, and she waved and
smiled. She was completely unconscious still of the startling
picture she made with her dirty face and damp, creased
gown. Andrew was all too aware of it, and his own disheveled
appearance as well, and he wished that London's premier tattlemonger had not passed through the square at just
that moment. It was not so much that he himself would be an
object of gossip as it was a deep regret that Claire's name
would be bandied about one more time. He realized with
some surprise that he was feeling strongly protective and that
his feeling had nothing to do with his mother's possible
reaction when she should hear of the escapade.

As the landau rolled past, and he offered his arm to Claire
to escort her up the steps, he wondered at the amusement he
could see sparkling in her eyes, and the way her soft lips
quivered as she tried to contain her laughter. Didn't she realize
how unfortunate it was that Miss Boothby had seen them both
looking like this?

He did not know that Claire was wondering at what precise
moment early the following morning Miss Elizabeth Boothby
would enter Lady Banks's morning room to demand an
explanation. She made a wager with herself that if it were a
moment past ten, she would eat her ruined bonnet, knowing
all too well that there was little chance of her having to make
such an unappetizing meal.

Chapter Nine

Now that the damage was done, the marquess lingered on the doorstep, insisting that they must both agree on the story they would tell. Again he stressed that Claire was not to say anything about his orphanages. When she asked how she was to explain her appearance in that case, he told her that he intended to say that during their drive they had seen a tenement on fire, and when they heard children calling, had both gone to help them. This explanation was so close to the truth it would be easy to remember. Although such behavior was sure to be considered extremely odd, if they both told the exact same story and did not deviate from it in any way, it would have to be accepted.

The marquess put from his mind the conjectures of the *ton* that already he could imagine so well. Why, for example, people would ask, had he not sent his groom to the rescue? Surely that would have been more seemly! And what on earth had he been thinking of to allow Miss Carrington to fall into such danger, all for the sake of a few brats who were sure to turn into London's future criminals? He seemed to see Sir Reggie's sneer, that he had bothered to soil his gloves and burn his coat in such an unworthy cause.

And then, as Claire nodded and agreed, the pale green veiling of her hat fell against her dirty cheek, and Andrew could not resist reaching out to smooth it back with one strong finger. As he did so, Claire's eyes went quickly to his face, and she caught her breath at the dangerous light she saw in his eyes. In some confusion, she lowered her long black lashes to her cheeks, biting her lower lip.

The marquess was quick to take her hand in farewell, for he did not dare to stay longer. "I shall call on you tomorrow at three, Claire. By that time we should have some indication of what all London is saying about us," he told her, trying for a light tone.

"I am so sorry, Andrew, but that will not be possible. I a[m] engaged to drive with the duke then." At the sudden coldnes[s] in his face at her pronouncement, she hastened to add, "Do [] you go to Mrs. Eberley's *soirée* tomorrow evening? We can [] compare notes there."

The marquess was forced to accept this alternative plan, and then he sounded the knocker for her and ran lightly down the steps to his phaeton.

He was so abstracted on the drive home that Michaels had to remind him of the turning into Upper Brooks Street. The old groom credited this heavy concentration to his concern for the children, and forbore to comment. Of all Lord Blagdon's servants, he was the only one who knew of the homes, and although he had been strong in his objection to such charity at first, now he knew what a good work his master did. He was not above talking to some of the older boys when the marquess went to visit the homes, telling them of stable work and the marquess's teams, and bragging about how bang up to the knocker they were. Since he allowed the bigger boys to hold the teams or polish a bit of brasswork, he was almost as popular as the marquess.

Since Lady Banks was out, Claire escaped her scandalized reaction. She explained to the horrified butler that there had been a slight accident but that she had not been injured, and she adjured him not to alarm his mistress.

The maid she summoned to bring bathwater was another matter, however, and it seemed to take forever before she could shut the door on her exclamations of horror as she took away the ruined clothes.

Claire had ordered tea, and now, dressed in an old wrapper, she was glad to sit down in the wing chair near the window after she had had her bath and washed her hair. As she sipped the hot, sweet brew, she stared down into the square. How very unusual this afternoon had been; she could recall nothing like it ever happening to her before. Of utmost importance was the discovery that Andrew was not just a Bond Street spark, interested only in his own amusements, his clothes, horses, and consequence. Of course I have always thought him a sensible man, she told herself, but I had no idea of the good he was doing. She did not wonder that he kept it a secret. She herself would have acted exactly the same way, so it did not surprise her that Andrew shunned the limelight. Or was it because he did not wish to appear odd? For a

n to bother with destitute slum children would be
ed eccentricity of the highest order. Claire frowned a
She did not like to think that Andrew was concerned
what others thought of him. No, it must be that he did
want his good works known. She promised herself that
e would keep his charity as secret as he had her artwork.

As Claire poured herself another cup of tea and nibbled a
macaroon, she was struck anew by how differently they had
both behaved this afternoon. Even before the fire, Andrew
had been abstracted and reticent. Perhaps there was something bothering him that she did not know? And then there
was the way he had looked at her after all the children were
safe, that sudden blaze in his dark blue eyes, and the way he
had come toward her, his arms open as if to embrace her and
hold her close.

She wondered what would have happened if the fire marshal had not interrupted them, and smiled at her fancies. But
then she thought of her own reactions, how breathless she had
become, and how her heart had pounded when he stared at
her, and more than once, too. It was all so uncomfortable and
completely inexplicable. She moved a little in her chair as she
gazed with unseeing eyes into her teacup. She and Andrew
were good friends, nothing more, she reminded herself. They
had a pact, didn't they? And of course Andrew was not
falling in love with her or anything silly like that! Of course
not! He had just been grateful for her help and she had
misinterpreted his glances and behavior and was reading too
much into them. How her friend would laugh at her if he
knew what she had been imagining. It was too absurd, especially after she had made such a firm condition that love was
to play no part in their masquerade. She could not help a
small pang when she remembered how quick he had been to
agree with her.

Tomorrow, she told herself, when they met at the Eberley
soirée, she would ask him straight out about his growing
abstraction and the worry she sometimes saw in his eyes.
Perhaps she could help him with some problem. After all,
that is what friends are for, is it not? she asked herself as she
put her teacup down on the tray with a snap. She stood up
and went to her dressing table, determined on this sensible
course as she sat down to brush her black curls until they
shone. Her stroke was so hard that her eyes began to water,

126

and finally she rose with a great air of resolution and took up her sketchbook to begin work on her new painting.

Claire found that she was not required to eat her hat the next morning. She had told Lady Banks and the general at dinner the story she and Andrew had concocted, making light of the adventure, and so when Miss Boothby was announced at the ridiculous hour of nine-thirty-five, she knew she could leave it to her hostess to explain.

Lady Banks had been suitably horrified to learn that Claire and the marquess had been so rash as to assist in a rescue from a burning tenement, but since she had not seen her young relative in all her dirt and disarray, she was able to instruct her butler to admit Miss Boothby to the breakfast room with an easy mind.

Claire had risen from the table as the lady was announced, for she was due at the *atélier* that morning, and she was looking forward to showing her sketches of the Hyde Park scene to Monsieur Duprés. And so she was almost absent-minded in her greeting when Miss Boothby swept in, clad in a gown of puce figured muslin worn with an ornate turban that sported several large ostrich plumes. The lady recalled her to her surroundings in short order by putting both hands over her heart and exclaiming, "Thank God!" in ringing tones.

All at once, Lady Banks looked uneasy, and she was not left in the dark about the reason for this fervent exclamation for long. As Claire smiled and bade their guest be seated and join them in a cup of coffee, Miss Boothby barely nodded before she burst into hurried speech.

"How relieved I am to see you well, Claire. I cannot tell you the severe palpitations you gave me yesterday when I saw you and the Marquess of Blagdon here in the square. I almost was overcome, and if Eugenie Shipley-Brown had not had her vinaigrette handy, I must surely have fainted and perhaps even fallen out of the landau. Naughty girl, to give me such a fright!" she added in a scolding tone, her eyes searching Claire's face for any sign of guilt or self-consciousness.

Claire smiled again as she apologized. "I am sorry to have distressed you, Miss Boothby, but although I realize that both the marquess and I were not togged out in the first style of elegance at that time, there was nothing for anyone to be concerned about."

At Miss Boothby's disbelieving stare, she added, "But must run away now, for I am late for an appointment. Dea Cousin Martha will tell you all about it—not that what hap pened was of any great moment, I assure you."

She kissed Lady Banks's cheek, and ignoring the plea i her eyes that she remain and help satisfy Miss Boothby' curiosity, went away to fetch her cloak and reticule. Jeremy was sure to have walked his team twice around the square by this time.

Miss Boothby did not leave for over an hour. Although Lady Banks told her all she knew of the incident severa times over, it was plain that her story was not believed.

"I have never heard such flummery, Martha!" Miss Boothby exclaimed, fixing her hostess with a stern eye. "Going into burning tenement to rescue slum children—do you think me lobcock? Why were they not driving in the park, tell me that And if, as you claim, they were going for a drive in th country, what were they doing in a slum neighborhood? Th whole thing is too smoky by half, my dear."

Neither lady acknowledged this unintentional pun as Lady Banks was forced to admit she did not know, for Claire had not mentioned their destination. When she tried to gain Miss Boothby's approbation for such a selfless act of Christian concern, she was rewarded by the lady's most scornful disbelieving sniff.

Claire spent a long morning in Dilke Street. Monsieur Duprés was delighted with her new subject, and had severa suggestions as to how she might accomplish her preliminary drawings, from working on the background in the early morning when no one was about, to making thumbnail sketches when she should be driven there in the afternoons by her friend the marquess. He would not allow her to touch her painting of *The Judgment of Paris*, claiming that there was nothing more that she could do to add to its beauty, and beaming and winking at her as he said so. Claire did no notice, for she was trying to appraise the work with impartia eyes, where it stood drying on an easel. She was inclined to agree with her teacher. It was finished; to add a stroke here an embellishment there, would most likely detract rather than add to its power.

She turned her back on it then, and set to work with her charcoal, trying to draw from memory the posturing of the *beau monde* as they strolled in the park.

But that morning her work did not go smoothly, and at last she threw down her charcoal and stared with unseeing eyes at her sketchbook. Andrew had said he would return to the home in Treadle Street this morning. She wondered what he was doing right now, and wished she could be with him. Suddenly her art seemed a frivolous activity compared to the work that he was engaged in. While she spent so much time indulging herself perfecting a talent that was of no importance to anyone but herself, he had been working for the benefit of others. How unselfish he was! She picked up her stick of charcoal and began to draw aimlessly. Somehow she was not surprised a few minutes later to discover that she had drawn his face, with emphasis on his expressive eyes.

Time dragged by at a slow pace, and for the first time she was glad when the lesson was over and she could run down the stairs to her hackney and escape.

By the time the Duke of Severn called that afternoon, she was so restless she could not imagine what was wrong with her. She had changed her mind twice about the gown she would wear, and had driven the maid, Peggy, to distraction by changing her bonnet not once but three times. When she finally left the room, Peggy raised her eyes to heaven. It 'ad to be love, she told herself as she picked up the discarded clothes. Coo! And a duke, no less, mind you! 'Ooever would 'ave thought it possible of the strange Miss Carrington?

William Fairhaven, the Duke of Severn, was quick to admire her final effort, remarking that the deep rose muslin was a perfect complement to her dark curls. As his phaeton pulled away from the Bankses' town house, he ignored the tiger who was clinging to the back to remark, "How delighted I am to see that you are dry and . . . er, tidy today, Miss Carrington. You would not believe the stories I have been hearing about what you consider proper attire for an afternoon drive."

Claire opened her parasol and tilted it over her shoulder at a defiant angle. "I can well imagine, Your Grace. It seems to me that the *beau monde* likes nothing better than to talk about their fellows, and in the telling, embellish a simple happening out of all recognition."

The duke nodded, his dark eyes gleaming with amusement at her stern tone of disapproval for society's foibles. Miss Carrington was a delight, from her conversation and ideas to her unusual escapades; he could not remember when he had spent a more interesting Season.

They drove toward the park in silence, but after the gates had been passed, he said, "How unkind you are, Miss Carrington!"

"I, sir?" she asked, turning a little in her seat so she could see his face. "How can this be?"

"But surely you must realize that I am sitting here all impatience to hear the *real* story of your afternoon jaunt with Lord Blagdon. Yet you persist in reticence. I shall have to think the account I was told is correct after all."

His voice was dry and Claire could not keep asking, "And what did you hear, Your Grace?"

"There were several versions, needless to say, each wilder than the next. My favorite, however, was that in some secluded sylvan spot, while defending your virtue, you stumbled over an embankment into a ditch full of dirty water, pulling the marquess with you."

To his surprise and delight, Claire laughed out loud, completely amused. When she could speak again, she asked, "And did the person relating the story say I had been successful?"

"The implication was that it was a very near thing, and those gentlemen present were left to draw their own conclusions."

Claire frowned now. "In that case, I wonder you care to be seen with me. But how did this person know what had happened? Was he there, hidden behind a tree? I am sure any gentleman of the meanest intelligence, which the marquess is not, would be sure to pick a more secluded spot for such antics if he were so inclined. Bah!"

The duke quirked a black eyebrow as he stared down into her indignant face. "You must not let the quizzes bother you, my dear," he remarked in a steady voice. "As for me, I do what I please, and believe me, it pleases me to be in your company. Besides, everyone who knows him realizes that such an adventure is not at all Andrew's style, nor, if I may say so, does it appear to be yours. But stay! Perhaps another version that I heard was more accurate? I was told by a gentleman who claimed to be very sure of his facts, that you and the marquess went to the rescue of some children endangered in a fire. How noble of you if it should be true, and yet, how surprising."

"Why do you say so, Your Grace? That is essentially what happened."

"I find that story almost as difficult to accept, my child. That Lord Blagdon would be so rash, taking the risk of your injuring yourself, or perhaps being trapped and burned, is not to be considered. No gentleman would be so careless of a lady in his care. No, I insist you tell me the *true* story."

Claire stared at her rose kid slippers. "The marquess was not careless. I did not enter the building. I merely took the children Andrew brought out across the road to safety. There were many others doing the same thing. Besides, I fail to see that my being female has any bearing at all. Women can do a great many things men can do, and just as well, if not better. The convention of treating the so-called weaker sex like delicate flowers is ridiculous and degrading. The only purpose it serves is to keep us firmly in our subservient places."

Her voice was indignant, and the duke smiled. "Ah, yes, I had forgotten you have made a study of the Amazons. Forgive me."

He nodded to Lady Jersey and her escorts as their carriages drew abreast and passed. Claire could see the lively interest in the lady's face when she spotted her sitting beside the duke, and the way she began to speak rapidly to her companions, waving a hand in their direction as she did so.

Claire put up her chin in defiance, her soft lips tightening, and for a while they drove on in silence. Then the duke remarked, "I have heard another astonishing story about the marquess, and this one is from an unimpeachable source."

Although William Fairhaven was not inclined to another marriage himself, he scented a romance in the offing between Miss Carrington and Andrew Tyson. He could not resist a little prying, and so, when Claire only raised her brows, he went on, "Lord Peakes told me that the dowager marchioness has issued a rather surprising ultimatum, but I am sure I do not tell you anything you do not already know."

"An ultimatum?" Claire asked in confusion. "I know of no ultimatum, Your Grace. Whatever do you mean?"

"Indeed? Allow me to enlighten you. It seems the lady is not at all pleased that her son is *épris* with a certain . . . er, unusual heiress. She has ordered him to break the connection or she will never speak to him again."

"But . . . but she doesn't even know me!" Claire exclaimed, and now her gray eyes darkened with anger. "How cruel of her! She must be very cold to banish her only son for such a reason."

"I completely agree with you," the duke said calmly. "In fact I think her behavior enough to drive any man of spirit into proposing to the lady at once."

"The marquess has no intention of proposing to me, Your Grace, nor have I any intention of accepting if he should be so silly. I told you before, we have an understanding and that I have no interest in marrying him or . . . or anybody."

"If that is so, my dear Miss Carrington, why does he continue to see you, or you him? If he has no desire to make you his wife, why does he go to these lengths and estrange his mother? And why do you encourage him? I find the whole situation most incomprehensible."

"Perhaps the marquess dislikes being ordered about like a little boy not out of the nursery, and that is why he persists," Claire said, as much to herself as to her escort. She sounded puzzled, and when the duke did not comment, felt she must explain further. "We are friends, you see, very good friends. Just as I know Andrew will come to no harm at my hands, so too I know I am safe with him. We can depend on each other, tell each other anything in the world, and know the other will help, no matter what the problem. I really had no idea the dowager disapproved of our friendship. I wonder if I should see her and set her mind at ease . . ."

Her voice died away, and the duke had a sudden picture of her standing before the throne chair in the dowager's drawing room, explaining the circumstances of her platonic relationship with the lady's son, and his mouth twisted in a grin.

"May I suggest you do not attempt it? You say you do not know the lady, but I do. She is the most formal, correct *grande dame* in society, and by far the iciest. You would never gain admittance to her presence, and if you accosted her in public would be treated to a most severe setdown. No, no, Miss Carrington, it is not to be thought of!"

He glanced sideways at Claire's troubled face. "She would never accept your explanation that you and the marquess are friends, and friends only, in any case. Why, even I do not believe it."

He was still observing Claire out of the corner of his eye, and he saw her sudden start and the way her wide eyes grew indignant, and he added, "Men and women can never be friends like that. There must always be between them a

132

perception of their different sex. A tension that they have no control over, if you will. Why, even though we are only acquaintances and have no interest in each other romantically, that tension exists between us. Can you deny it?''

Claire looked thoughtful, but after a moment she shook her head. She knew she was only too aware of the duke—his dark good looks, his height and strength. When he danced with her or smiled and took her hand, she could not help contrasting his maleness to her own femininity. Now she stared at his aristocratic profile and shivered a little as he continued, "No, Miss Carrington. Between men and women there can be desire, admiration, and sometimes, love. There cannot be the pure friendship that you speak of, except possibly in old age, when all the fires of the body are banked. And even then I am not sure," he mused.

For the first time in her life, Claire was conscious of the servant clinging to the perch behind and hearing every word of this extraordinary conversation. She could not help casting an uneasy glance over her shoulder. The duke noticed at once.

"Do not worry about my tiger, my dear. I chose him especially, for you see, he is dumb. He cannot speak, and more important, he cannot write either, for I have never allowed him to learn."

As Claire looked horrified, he added, "And so he cannot tell anyone what he overhears. Such a blessing and a bonus in a personal servant, don't you think?''

Fortunately for their rapport, he went on before she could reply. "Allow me to give you some advice, my child, for I have been about the world a good many more years than you have. In spite of the fact that you are four-and-twenty, and even with your liberal education and world traveling, you are the epitome of innocence. How Lady Dawson's detractors would stare if they knew! It is true that you know a great many things that most young ladies would consider bold and unseemly, but in human relationships you are very green indeed. You have said you have no desire to marry, but on what experience do you base your decision? I know you have never known a man and I doubt seriously that you have even kissed one.''

He paused and looked straight into her stunned face, and then he laughed, a soft laugh full of amusement. "It seems to me that before you renounce something so vehemently, it would be better to know exactly what you are giving up. I suggest you think of it seriously, my dear. In your case, spinsterhood would be such a waste!''

''Of course I thank you for your concern, Your Grace, but my mind is quite made up,'' Claire said through stiff lips, finding her voice at last. "Oh, there is Sir Reginald waving to us. Shall you pull up?''

''On no account. The man is a bore. I wish you would send him about his business. But I take your point, Miss Carrington. We will now discuss the current Season, the latest plays, or the vagaries of the royal family. Tell me, what do you think of Princess Caroline's latest start?''

Claire returned a disjointed answer, and the duke conducted a gentle monologue for a few moments to allow her to regain her composure. He had given her a great deal to think about, he knew. As he drove out of the park, he hoped Andrew Tyson would be properly appreciative of the help he had been given today.

He would have been surprised if he had known that far from considering her romantic feelings for the marquess, Claire was still struck by the way he had discussed his groom, and the ugly reasons he had chosen him. Even if the boy could not speak, he could hear. It was cruel to mock his infirmity within his hearing—indeed, cruel to mock it at all. She decided she did not like the Duke of Severn anywhere near as much as she had thought. There had been in his voice the calm assumption of superiority that came from generations of privilege. It was plain that he considered himself not only of exalted rank, but an exalted personage as well, almost as if he were a god, and lesser men like his servant were of a different species entirely. Why, Andrew's caring and generosity to those less fortunate than himself was thrown into bold relief in comparison. He was a warmhearted man and the duke was cold and uncaring and proud. Thank heaven there was no chance she would ever become involved with him except in the most casual way.

At the general's door she made certain to smile kindly at the tiger where he stood clinging to the horses' bridles. He stared at her for a moment, a slight figure with sandy hair and a homely face, before he lowered his eyes, his hurt and resignation showing clearly.

Claire was very quiet for the remainder of the day, for she was thinking hard. She did not consider the gossip she had heard about her outing with the marquess, nor what society was imagining about their relationship. What disturbed her was the fact that Andrew was in danger of his mother's banishment if he continued to see her. Was that why he looked worried and seemed preoccupied of late? Why hadn't he told her about it? And, more important, why hadn't he confessed to the dowager the lack of any romantic involvement? Surely if his mother knew they were only friends, she would relent.

But it appeared Andrew had not told her. Claire knew she must confront him tonight and find out the truth. If what the duke had told her was true, she would insist that the pact she and Andrew had made must be abandoned.

As she was dressing for the *soirée* that evening, she remembered the duke's bland assumption that she and Andrew were in love and the way he had doubted her intention never to marry. Well, he would see, Claire thought as she stared into her looking glass, where the maid was arranging her hair. Yes, he would see that men and women could be friends, and only friends.

As Peggy lowered the leaf-green silk over her head and began to hook it up, she suddenly recalled the way she had grown breathless near Andrew, and how her heart had leapt when he bent that searing dark blue glance her way, and she felt the color rising in her face. For a second she wondered if the duke was right after all, and then she shook her head. All this drivel about men and women and tension! She would not regard it.

Tonight she was wearing Aunt Flora's emeralds. As the maid fastened the clasps, she studied herself in the mirror. The heavy gold choker blazed with sparkling green stones, and the matching bracelets, in the shape of twisted serpents with emerald eyes, were placed on her upper arms exactly opposite the dark green sash of her empire gown. She was pleased with the effect and she wondered if Andrew would approve. And then she gathered up her gloves and the gauze stole embroidered all over with gold thread and left the room impatiently. What did it matter how she looked? As she knew only too well, all women's vanity was nothing but silly affectation, a lure set to trap unwary males. If Andrew had not set such great store by it, she would have had none of it.

When she and Lady Banks joined the other guests in Mrs. Eberley's double drawing room, she was quick to look about.

She saw Sir Reginald, and over on the other side of the room, Wilfred Wilson. He was talking with great animation to a very young lady with soft brown hair and a slight figure who did not look a day over sixteen. Pamela Greeley was surrounded by her usual court of smitten admirers, and standing somewhat apart from the rest was the Duke of Severn. He smiled at her, one eyebrow quirked, before he snapped his fingers for a servant to take his champagne glass and made his way to her side. Lady Banks saw him coming and was quick to excuse herself, leaving Claire to stand alone.

The duke bowed slightly and took her hand. "Miss Carrington," he said, his voice meaningful, as if he were remembering the remarkable conversation they had only a few hours ago. "How lovely you look tonight! I must compliment you on your jewels. Another . . . er, grateful African chieftain?"

Claire put up her chin, her eyes flashing. "No, my aunt was quite taken with the jewelry of the Indians of South America, and had this set made up in Brazil."

The duke smiled down at her, and she withdrew her hand from his with more haste than usual. Again that mocking eyebrow rose, and then he reached out for her dance card.

"How pleasant that I am the first," he remarked as he wrote his name in two places. Claire was indignant that he took the first waltz, but she tried to look pleased. She had just spotted Andrew coming in with Lord and Lady Peakes, but then the orchestra began to play, and the duke was holding out his arms.

"My dance, Miss Carrington?" he asked with calm authority, and she had to go into his arms.

Claire was forced to put off her meeting with the marquess for some time, for after the Duke of Severn's dance, Sir Reginald was there, and Paul Venables as well. Andrew had come to sign her card, but since she had been surrounded by other guests at that time, they had not been able to exchange any private words.

While she was dancing with Sir Reginald, she noticed that Wilfred Wilson was speaking to the marquess at great length. She was surprised at it, even as she wondered why her childhood friend did not come and beg her for a dance as he always did. Of Lady Wilson there was no sign; perhaps the lady was indisposed.

At last Andrew came to claim his dance. She smiled at

him, trying to keep the concern from her face, and was stunned to see amusement dancing in his eyes. Somehow she had expected him to look grim and preoccupied.

"Shall you mind sitting out our dance, Claire?" he asked. "There is something of import I have to relate to you."

"What is it?" she asked as he took her arm and led her to a small sofa set against the wall, some distance from the crowd. "Why do you look so?"

"You will never believe what I am about to tell you, dear Claire," he said as soon as they sat down. "Alas, I hope it does not ruin your enjoyment in the evening."

He sighed, and for a moment she thought he meant to tell her of his mother, before she realized that if that were to be his topic, it would hardly call for this barely concealed merriment.

"Yes, it my sad duty to inform you, my dear Miss Carrington, that your most faithful suitor has deserted you," he went on. "And, I might point out, there appears to be nothing you can do to win back his esteem."

"Andrew, be serious! What faithful suitor?"

"Why, Lord Wilson, of course. He was good enough to come up to me a few moments ago to tell me that he would not be my rival for your hand any longer. I could hardly preserve a sober countenance, Claire, for he was so earnest in his belief that he was behaving in a magnanimous way in leaving the field to me."

"You have had too much champagne, my friend," Claire scoffed.

Andrew laughed out loud. "No such thing! No, Wilfred then waxed lyrical for some minutes about the new young lady he has chosen to honor with his addresses. I am sorry to have to be the one to break it to you, Claire, but it appears that a Miss Pringle has captured his heart, and in an instant, if the man is to be believed. They met two days ago in the British Museum, and although I consider that an unlikely place for Cupid's darts to fly, according to Wilfred they had only to look at each other before they were both smitten."

Claire smiled, wondering what Wilfred's mama had had to say about love at first sight. For her old friend's sake, she hoped Miss Pringle was a considerable heiress.

"How fickle we men are," the marquess observed in sorrowful tones, his eyes still dancing. "If it should not distress you too much, you may observe him dancing with his

137

adored one right now. Here, perhaps you had better take my handkerchief in case you feel the need to weep copiously in your disappointment.''

Claire searched the dance floor and saw Wilfred beaming down at the slender young girl she had seen him with earlier. Suddenly an unwelcome thought intruded in her mind and she forgot the lovers at once.

"If this is indeed the case, Andrew, what a shame that Pamela Greeley has not fallen in love as well, for then we would be free to go our separate ways, and our pact could be disregarded.''

The marquess turned toward her abruptly, all signs of amusement gone from his suddenly frowning face. "What? What nonsense is this, Claire?''

Claire would not meet his eyes, and looked down at her tightly clasped hands instead. "I have heard that our friendship is bringing you nothing but trouble, Andrew. I wonder that you did not tell me of your mother's ultimatum. You know I would never have held you to our agreement, certainly not if it meant you must lose her regard.''

The marquess grasped her arm. "And whom did you have that from, Claire? I'd like to call out the backbiter that told you!''

His voice was bitter, and Claire glanced at him and was astounded at the fury in his eyes. "It does not signify,'' she hastened to say. "It will be common knowledge before long, I am sure, especially if you persist in seeing me.''

The marquess stood up and drew her to her feet. "Come with me! I have something to say to you, my girl, and I think it would be better if we were in a less public place when I do so.''

As he put her hand in his arm, Claire glanced around to see not only the Duke of Severn observing them carefully, but Lady Peakes as well. At that, she did not try to demur, but went meekly with him out the doors to the terrace.

There were other couples there, strolling up and down and enjoying the warm spring evening, and Andrew took her down the steps to the garden. He did not speak until they were out of sight behind a boxwood hedge. The light from the drawing-room windows lit the path, and as they passed through the rectangles of light and shadow, Claire could see how set his face was, the lean planes of it taut with emotion.

She wondered at such anger, and felt a small quiver of apprehension.

Suddenly he stopped in a patch of light and turned her toward him, his strong hands grasping her arms. One of the serpent bracelets bit deeply into her skin from the pressure, but she hardly felt it as she searched his face, her eyes troubled.

"Listen to me!" he ordered, his voice harsh. "My mother has no say in my life. I cannot imagine how you found out about her ridiculous demands . . . Oh, I am sure it was my dear brother-in-law who let the cat out of the bag, for he has a tongue that runs at both ends, and this juicy tidbit would be too much for him to keep to himself—but never mind that. I choose my friends, I alone. And, Claire, I choose you, far and above any misguided maternal commands."

He bent his head closer so he could look into her eyes, and shook her a little. "We will have no more foolishness about this, nor any more discussion, and we will continue to see each other as before. Do you understand?"

"But we must discuss it," Claire persisted. "I could not bear to be the cause of dissension and such a rift in your family."

The marquess snorted and she hurried on, "Why didn't you tell her that we were only friends, Andrew? I am sure if she knew that there is no thought of marriage on either side, she would be more at ease. I do not understand you at all, to be letting her think there is any romantic involvement between us."

Abruptly the marquess dropped her arms and moved away a little into the dark. All at once Claire felt the ache where the bracelet had pinched her skin, and she reached up to rub it, never taking her eyes from Andrew's tall, lean figure.

"I did it to teach her a lesson. Perhaps she will be less busy about my affairs in the future," he snarled at last. Then he came back to her and took her hands in his, shaking his head impatiently. "No, that is not the truth, and I would not lie to you of all persons, my dear. I wondered why I held my tongue myself, for it would have been a simple matter to calm her fears. Of course she would have been horrified by our agreement, but that is not why I did not tell her."

He stared down into Claire's clear gray eyes and for a moment there was silence between them. Very faintly Claire could hear the sounds of a carriage going by outside the garden wall, and a man calling for a hackney. The soft breeze rustled the leaves of the hedge behind her, and somewhere nearby a sleepy bird chirped briefly in complaint.

"Why didn't you tell her, then?" she asked, her voice stiff.

The marquess just stood there, his eyes intent on her face as if he were lost in some reverie and was pondering his answer. And then he straightened up and said simply, "Because I was not at all sure I would not be telling her a lie."

Claire caught her breath. His voice was quiet now, and determined, as if he had solved some great problem that had been bothering him for a long time.

"Oh, no, Andrew, that cannot be," she whispered. He shook his head as if to clear it, and a lock of golden hair fell over his forehead, and then he drew her into his arms and held her close. Claire felt powerless to resist. Not for a second did either of them take their eyes from the other's face as he reached out to tilt up her chin. It seemed an eternity that his dark blue eyes blazed into hers, searching deep, before he lowered his head and kissed her. Claire closed her eyes at last. She had never imagined she could feel like this, as if she were drowning in a whirlpool of sensations that was taking her deeper and deeper and farther away from safety. She could not fight it, she did not even want to try. As his warm lips became even more urgent and demanding, she responded eagerly.

She felt his caressing hands on her back, those hands that held a restless team so easily, or gently soothed a crying child, and she felt tears starting up in her own eyes. She could not help but feel safe and protected, sheltered in those strong arms close to his heart. Her own arms went around his neck, as if she wished to draw closer still.

Reluctantly he raised his head at last, and looked down into her face. Those soft lips were trembling now, and when she opened her eyes, the incipient tears sparkled as brightly as the jewels she wore. "Claire, my darling," he murmured, his voice husky with emotion as he bent his head to kiss her again.

As if his voice broke some magic spell, she began to struggle in his arms.

"No, let me go!" she panted, and he released her at once.

"What is it, Claire?" he asked, his voice bewildered.

"This must not happen. Oh, how could we?" she moaned, backing away from him down the path.

"Because we love each other, my dear," he said as he followed her.

"No! There was to be no love, no . . . no lovemaking! You promised!" she cried, her breathless words quick and hurried. "We agreed to that, Andrew. I *cannot*, I *will* not love you!"

Suddenly she found herself backed against the garden wall and looked around for some way to escape. The marquess put both hands on either side of her on the bricks, imprisoning her as completely as if he still held her in his arms, although he was careful not to touch her. The tears that had come when he kissed her now spilled over her long dark lashes and ran down her cheeks.

"Do not cry, I beg you, love," he pleaded. "I have startled you, but you'll see, my *worldly* innocent." His voice was full of tender amusement, and then he added, "What we have just shared is only the beginning for us, and when we are married . . ."

She shook her head. "No! Let me go—please let me go! I cannot speak of it anymore."

Andrew released her, and taking out his handkerchief, in earnest this time, he dried her cheeks as if she were no older than one of his orphans. Claire swallowed and tried to control herself. At last he stepped back and bowed to her.

"Very well—for now. I shall leave you here so you might have a few moments to compose yourself. You cannot show that woebegone face to the world, love. Do not worry—when you rejoin the party I won't be there, for I would not distress you further."

"Thank you," Claire whispered, her eyes lowered to the gravel of the path.

"I shall call on you tomorrow, however. After you have had some time for reflection, I know you will come to agree with me."

Claire's eyes flew to his face, and when she saw how determined and purposeful he looked, her heart missed a beat.

He made to leave her then, but after two steps he paused and turned back. "I love you with all my heart, Claire. Remember it."

He was gone without another word, but it was some time

141

before Claire felt able to return to the town house. As she made her way up the broad terrace steps, she wished there were some way she could leave without being seen. She was sure that all the emotions of the past few minutes were written plain on her face for all the world to see.

"There you are at last," she heard the Duke of Severn say from where he stood near the balustrade, calmly smoking a cigar. "Now, what forfeit shall I demand, Miss Carrington, of a lady who forgot our dance?"

He threw his cigar away to take her hand and stare down into her face. Claire tried to smile as she apologized.

"Never mind, my child, I understand," he said in quite the kindest voice she had ever heard him use. Then he chuckled. "You see, just a little while ago I saw your . . . er, your *friend* leave the garden."

Chapter Ten

Claire overslept the following morning, for she had spent an almost sleepless night, going over and over the situation with Andrew. By the time she fell into an uneasy slumber, a gray dawn was breaking, but by that time she had come to what she believed to be the only possible solution. It was going to be extremely hard to carry out, and she would have to play the liar's role, but she was determined on her course, no matter how difficult or unpleasant it turned out to be.

When she finally woke, it was after nine. She did not think the marquess would wait very long before he made an appearance, and so she dressed hurriedly in one of her old gowns and pulled a comb through her curls without summoning her maid. She knew Lady Banks had gone to visit a sick friend, so she would be spared any tedious explanations in that quarter, and she only hoped that Miss Boothby would for once refrain from making a morning call.

She had a cup of coffee for breakfast, for it was all that she could swallow, and then she spoke to the butler before she went to wait in Lady Banks's morning room.

At exactly ten, she heard the knocker bang on the front door, and she closed her eyes in a silent prayer. A moment later, the butler announced the Marquess of Blagdon, and she rose and took a deep breath, clasping her hands together before her to steady herself.

Andrew strode into the room, his expression eager, and then he stopped short at the sight of her cool face and waited until the butler had reluctantly bowed himself away.

"Good morning, m'lord," Claire said, glad to hear that her voice did not tremble. "Somehow I knew you would be here early. Won't you be seated?"

She motioned him to a chair, and the marquess, who had started toward her even before the butler had closed the double doors, frowned and stared at her, his expression unreadable. Her voice was even and cold, as if they were mere acquaintances and the events of the previous evening had never taken place.

Claire ignored both the frown and the stare as she took a seat on one side of the fireplace, and Andrew was forced to follow suit. She schooled her expression to one of polite indifference.

"Now, what is all this, Claire? Why do you look at me like that?" Andrew asked.

She allowed her eyebrows to rise in surprise at his words. "I suppose it is because I am so disillusioned, m'lord. What happened between us last night was a shock to me and a very unpleasant surprise. I thought us friends, you see, good friends, and I expected you to keep the pact we had made. You will remember that there was to be no lovemaking between us, yet still you broke your promise. I am disappointed."

The marquess leaned forward the better to see her, and a stray sunbeam streaming through the windows lit up his blond hair and turned it to pure gold. Claire did not think she could stand the ache in her heart at the sight of him. He was dressed with his usual elegance in a coat of dark blue superfine that matched his eyes, tight fawn breeches, and gleaming boots. Above the artistic cascade of his cravat, his lean, handsome face was perplexed, and at the same time, impatient.

"What nonsense you speak, Claire! Is this some kind of joke?" he asked, as if he could not believe his ears.

"It is no joke. I am glad you have called, for it gives me the opportunity to terminate our relationship without further delay."

Andrew jumped to his feet with an oath and started toward her. Her heart beating fast, Claire picked up the bell that rested on the table beside her. "Sit down, sir! I would dislike having to call the butler to come to my assistance, but you may believe I shall do so without hesitation if you come any closer."

She waited until he took his seat again before she lowered the bell to the shining mahogany surface. She saw that he was leaning back now, completely at his ease as he crossed both arms over his chest, but his dark blue eyes never left her face. "Very well. Do go on," he said, his voice harsh and as cold as hers had been. "You were saying you were disappointed?"

Claire nodded and then she paused for a moment before she continued, "I am sorry, of course, that the end of our agreement will leave you to the mercies of Miss Greeley and her mama once again, m'lord. Also, I would not like you to think that it is Lord Wilson's defection that prompts me to this decision, and being safe now myself, I choose to abandon you to your fate. No, it was your behavior in the garden and your words to me that decided the issue."

She paused, but he had no comment, and so she added, "I made up my mind about how I was going to live my life some time ago, and I have no intention of changing it. I will never marry; my art is much too important to me. Perhaps men can have a family life as well as their profession, but for women that is not possible. If I am to be the serious artist I intend, I cannot be distracted by a husband and children, with houses to manage and estates to run."

She noticed one booted leg begin to swing gently, and she hurried on, "You must admit, m'lord, that my determination can come as no surprise to you, for you were warned at the outset of my purpose."

There was silence for a moment and then the marquess inclined his head. "Are you quite through, Claire?" he asked, his voice only mildly interested. Stunned, she nodded.

"Very well. Now that you have finished spouting that ridiculous nonsense, for whatever insane reason you have chosen, allow me to destroy all your arguments. What happened between us last evening cannot be dismissed so easily. I may have kissed you and made love to you, but you cannot deny that you returned it. Yet now you would have me believe that you are prepared to set our love aside in preference for your art. It is impossible for me to put any faith in the truthfulness of your words—not after I felt you surrender in my arms, and reveled in the eagerness with which you returned my kiss."

Claire felt her face paling, and hoped he would not notice it. She rose to go to the window to stare out into the back garden. "I do not attempt to deny it, Andrew," she said quietly. She turned, but she was able to look into his eyes for only a fleeting moment. "I know I surrendered. That is why we must not see each other again."

"You would have me believe that it is because you return my love that you would send me away?" he asked, his voice incredulous. "No, no, I know you better than that! Be honest, Claire! Admit it is the thought of my mother's disapproval that makes you say these things."

"I will admit that her dislike of me has only reinforced my decision, but she was not the primary reason I decided that our friendship must be at an end." She took a deep breath and turned to face him squarely now, her gray eyes steady and serious. "I know you do not understand how important my art is to me, but I have worked so hard all my life to perfect my skill, I cannot give it up. You must believe me!"

"But I would not ask you to give it up," the marquess interrupted. "You would still be able to study, to paint, as much as you like. Did you really think me the kind of man who wants his wife's attention every waking moment? The kind that thinks that nothing but himself and his concerns should be of any interest to her? Claire, Claire! It is your talent, your strong purpose, your uniqueness that has made me love you. If I wanted a silly widgeon to wife, I would have asked Pamela Greeley."

Claire had not taken her eyes from his face. Dear God, but this was harder than she had thought it would be!

"You say that now, Andrew, but as time passes you will revert to the common mold, wanting only a wife you can be sure will not cause any turmoil in the *ton*; a quiet, gentle, agreeable wife who will be a suitable mother to your children. And because I care for you, I will try to be that wife, sacrificing my talent and ambition. In time I will come to resent you, perhaps even hate you. I know this well, for Aunt Flora told me many times of men's expectations and unreasonable demands."

"I wish I had your dear Aunt Flora here right now," the marquess muttered, running a hand through his hair in his agitation, his blue eyes glinting with his anger. "The woman should have been whipped for putting such nonsense into your head."

Claire could not summon up even a ghost of a smile at his vehemence. "No, my mind is made up. There can be no marriage between us. In fact I am sure it is better if we cease to cry friends as well. Being so constantly in each other's company can only bring pain to both of us."

The marquess, who had risen when she did, came and stood close before her. Claire was aware that in moving toward the window she had left the safety of the bell she could use to summon the butler. Now Andrew stood blocking her return to it. She put up her chin and did not let her gaze falter as he inspected her face, searching deep in her eyes.

146

She was a little surprised when he did not touch her, and as if he read her thoughts, he said, "You know I have only to take you in my arms and kiss you, here and now, for you to admit you are wrong."

His voice was soft, but there was a steely determination in it, and as he began to do just that, she put her hands against his chest.

"I beg you will not, Andrew," she whispered. "Yes, I admit I am weak, but as long as you do not touch me, I can be strong enough. And is that how you want me, kissed into an agreement that when I have had time for introspection I will despise?"

He stepped back, his face stern and unmoving except for one muscle beside his mouth that clenched involuntarily. "You know I do not. I want you to come to me freely of your own volition, because you cannot bear to live without me, as I cannot bear to live without you."

"You must accept the fact that I will never do so. Please, Andrew, go away and forget me. I am not the wife for you."

"Nor the good friend I thought I could trust," he could not help adding bitterly. "Your pardon, ma'am. I will not trouble you further."

He bowed then, and went swiftly to the door, closing it softly behind him.

"You are wrong, my dear," she whispered through the painful ache that filled her heart. "In sending you away, I am a better friend than you have ever known. But, oh, Andrew, how it hurts!"

She sank down on a sofa nearby and lowered her face into her hands, making no effort to stem the hot tears that began to fall. She felt as if her heart were breaking. She had done the only thing she had been able to think of that would make him draw back, and it had worked, all too successfully. He will never know how much I love him, she mourned. I can only take comfort in the knowledge that by giving him up, I have restored him to his family.

She cried bitterly for a long time, stifling her sobs with her fists, and then at last she leaned back exhausted. She stared at Lady Banks's workbasket and tambour frame on a table nearby with unseeing eyes. I know that what I have done is right, she told herself, for how can Andrew know what pain it would bring to be estranged forever from those he loves?

But I know, oh yes, I know. It is true that I had Aunt Flora and that I loved her dearly, but that was not the same as having my own mother and father close to me. And Aunt Flora was so busy, so involved with her own pursuits and studies, that I was often lonely, without a sympathetic ear or a warm hug for my troubles. How sad it is that I cannot remember my parents, that I do not even have a miniature of them to keep by me. Sometimes, she remembered, when she had been a little girl, just before falling asleep, she had been able to summon a picture to her mind of a pair of smiling gray eyes, and the faint scent of lavender, and she had pretended that she was held close in her mother's soft arms, being sung to sleep. Of her father there were no memories at all, and yet Aunt Flora had said he had both spoiled her and adored her. What a shame it was that they had died before she ever really knew them, or they her. She knew she would miss them all her life.

But now Andrew would never have to suffer that loss. For that reason alone she had lied to him without a qualm. Yes, even the things she claimed Flora Dawson had told her had been a lie. True, her aunt had never failed to malign any man she felt took advantage of women, as well as the system that had made their sex the mindless slaves of men that they were, but even so she had been quick to point out that all men were not so blind. And it was at her insistence that Claire had come to London for the Season. She remembered how she had pleaded to stay home, and her aunt's tiny smile as she lay in the bed she would never leave again and spoke almost the same words the duke had used.

"Do stop arguing, Claire. You cannot relinquish what you have never known. You say you want to be like me; do you think I have always been happy in my single state? Indeed, I have not. And if I had not had you, my child, I would have become a bitter, solitary woman, the eccentric the world claims I am. You have kept me young and alive. But even though it was not my fate to meet the man who might have understood my hunger for more than just hearth and home and husband, I pray you will be more fortunate. Human beings must love, or they die, and not just the love of their work and learning or the beauty of earth and sky. They must love other human beings to be complete and fulfilled."

Here she had paused, exhausted, and Claire had wiped her brow with a cool cloth.

"No, if only for my sake you will go to London and take

your place in society for one year at least. Then if you still continue adamant, why, then come home to Dawson Hall and take up the life I chose. In my heart I do not think you will. You are too warm, too caring. You are not like me, wanting my independence so badly I was willing to pay the price of loneliness and rejection. Perhaps someday, in a better-ordered world, it will be possible for a woman to have both a family and her work. In this day and age you must choose one or the other. Promise me you will consider both sides before you do, dear Claire.''

Claire remembered how she had given her word, and how she had pondered her aunt's statements many times in the weeks that followed. She had rarely seen Flora Dawson without such a zest for life and all its mysteries, such absorption in her studies and interests, that it was hard to imagine her ever feeling the lack of a husband or children to love. She was sure it was only her aunt's illness that was making her so melancholy.

Now, as she made her way slowly up to her room, Claire realized that her aunt had been right. Notwithstanding her commitment to her painting, if she had been able to choose freely, she would have given her hand as well as her heart to Andrew without a backward glance of regret. She would have let her future success as an artist go, for it did not matter anymore. How much she had changed, and in such a short time, too! But instead, she had been forced to follow in her aunt's footsteps. The irony of it did not escape her as she rang the bell for the maid.

When Peggy came in, she told her she was going back to bed for she was not feeling well, and asked her to make her excuses to Lady Banks. The maid would have stayed to help her undress, but Claire sent her away. After she had pulled the draperies shut, she climbed into bed and fell into an exhausted slumber almost at once.

In the following days, Claire Carrington was not to be seen at any of the *ton*'s festivities. The duke called to inquire for her, and on being told Miss Carrington was feeling a little pulled, sent her flowers and teasing notes. Claire did not respond for several days. Finally, at the end of the week, the butler brought her another note as she sat in the breakfast room listlessly stirring her coffee.

She began to read it without much interest, but then Lady Banks saw her straighten up in her chair, her face becoming animated and her eyes glittering. Lady Banks was relieved. There was something very seriously wrong, and she would wager her best tippet that it was not that Claire was overtired as she claimed. Not Claire, who was as healthy as a horse! Lady Banks had noticed that the marquess was not one of the girl's callers anymore, but Miss Boothby had told her he had gone out of town, so she did not connect Claire's low spirits with his defection.

Now, not for the first time, she wished the girl would confess what was bothering her, so she could help her if it were at all possible. Claire folded her note and rose from the table.

"Excuse me, Cousin Martha. I must reply to the duke at once."

Lady Banks thought she sounded both annoyed and determined as she left the room, and she wondered what the duke had said.

Unlike Lady Banks, William Fairhaven had a very good idea what had happened. It was obvious that Miss Carrington had been thoroughly kissed in the garden at the Eberley *soirée*, for he had seen how upset she was himself. And he had observed the Marquess of Blagdon looking as black as a thunderhead the following afternoon, and noted how abruptly he had retired to his estates only a day later. Since Miss Carrington was absent from every party from that precise moment on, he was able to put two and two together. Aha, he thought, the path of true love is not running smooth!

In his note, he twitted her for her cowardice and told her that since he had deduced the reason for her absences, it would soon be common knowledge throughout the *ton*.

"I do not know what has occurred between you and your 'friend' the marquess, my dear Claire," he wrote, "but to hide and cower alone can only give rise to the kind of speculation I know that you despise. Besides, I miss you. With your permission, I shall call for you this afternoon, driving my high-perch phaeton. That equipage will ensure the most visibility on our turns around the park. Wear something stunning and do not disappoint me. Severn."

Although the duke tried every ploy at his command, including some outright demands that she owed it to him to confess, Claire would not confide in him as they drove around the park that afternoon.

"But this is too bad of you, my dear Miss Carrington," he

150

chided her. "You consign me to theoretical imaginings, and like most people, I am prepared to think the worst. An unfortunate trait of mankind, is it not? What did happen in the garden at the Eberleys'? Did the marquess try seduction after all? Were you less than kind? Did you refuse? That must have been a first for Andrew—he is generally a great favorite with the ladies."

Claire waved to Lord Wilson and his mother, both of whom were escorting Miss Pringle. She noticed Lady Wilson looked resigned to, if not overjoyed by, her son's choice of bride, not that either Wilfred or his fiancée paid her much heed.

"I cannot tell you, Your Grace. What happened between myself and Andrew is private," she said, recalled to present company by the duke's sharp sideways glance. "And it is not kind of you to be so persistent."

"But my dear Miss Carrington, I am never kind. Kindness is a characteristic of weaker men. However, I am interested in the problems of my fellow mortals. Have you ever thought that perhaps my views on the subject might be of help to you? Has the affair deteriorated to the point where there is no chance of reconciliation? I assure you I would be glad to be of assistance, if only to repay you for the pleasure you have given me with your company this Season."

"Thank you, but there is nothing to discuss," Claire said through stiff lips, her face bleak.

The duke sighed. "Very well. You are a stubborn piece, are you not? But rest assured I will discover the problem. I could not in good conscience let two such great 'friends' continue alienated. Besides, I am positive that Andrew Tyson is the very gentleman I once told you about."

At Claire's puzzled look, he added, "The one you would eventually honor with your first curtsy, my dear."

"I do not understand you and I do not see why all of this is of such interest to you, sir," Claire replied, looking him straight in the eye. "Is your life so boring and of so little account that you must pry into others' lives for vicarious amusement?"

For a moment she thought she had gone too far, but she did not care. She did not think she could stand much more of his sarcastic probing. The duke's dark eyes flashed fire, and his heavy brows contracted in a frown. And then, to her surprise, he laughed.

"Well said, if not, perhaps . . . er, the height of tact, my child. Yes, life can be boring, especially when you reach my age and have seen everything time without number. I admit it amuses me to observe the follies of others. When you yourself have been through as many Seasons as I have, you will come to agree with me."

"There will never be another Season for me, Your Grace," Claire said, her voice firm. "I am here in London only because my aunt made me promise I would come before she died. As soon as the Prince Regent leaves for Brighton, I shall go home to Dawson Hall to stay."

"And never leave it again?" the duke inquired. "But you have told me you have no family there. How lonely you will be, year after year. Once again, I do not believe you, my dear, for I have never known a woman who could resist the giddy pleasures of town, the new gowns and fripperies, the plays and concerts and operas, and especially the balls. Ah, the balls and the opportunity they present to flirt and carry on, ensnaring some helpless man in one's coils. No, Miss Carrington, you will be back."

"You do not know me at all, Your Grace, and it is obvious you never met Lady Flora Dawson," Claire pointed out, amused in spite of herself. "Is that what you really think all women are like? For shame!"

"I will grant you yourself a small degree of singularity, my dear Claire. You are well-read and well-traveled, and wonder of wonders, you can converse in an intelligent and witty manner. But regardless of all these marvelous traits, you are still a woman with all the failings of that . . . er, delicious sex. What shall we wager on your prompt arrival next spring, if indeed you can bear to remain in the countryside through the Little Season next fall?"

Claire's eyes were flashing now, and her cheeks were glowing with her anger. The duke thought her very handsome in her indignation.

"You would lose a king's ransom, sir, for I know I should win. And how insulting you are to be talking about the 'failings' of my sex! I have observed some very serious failings in yours, but because I have had a very good mentor, I shall refrain from enumerating them. Besides, it would take too long."

Delighted, the duke laughed and would have continued, but Claire fell into reverie just then, remembering her mentor and wondering what he was doing in Blagdon. She missed Andrew so much she was sure the ache under her heart had become a permanent feature, and no matter how she told herself she would not think of him, he came into her mind with painful regularity.

Seeing her abstraction, the duke changed the subject. "Do you plan to see the new exhibit at the Royal Academy, Miss Carrington? Perhaps you would allow me to escort you there."

"Thank you, I would be delighted. I am particularly acquainted with one of the exhibitors and I would not miss it for the world."

Claire paused, afraid she had revealed too much, but in this instance the duke was not at all curious and only asked whether she wished to go in the morning or the afternoon. A time was agreed on for opening day the following week. Claire knew there was little chance she would be able to study the various works in any detail that day, for there was sure to be a sad crush of all the fashionable world. They would talk and exclaim and praise and condemn, even the most unknowledgeable amongst them, but she knew she could return another day for a quiet perusal.

She was suddenly reminded that she had been most remiss in her attendance at Monsieur Duprés's *atélier*, and as if her drive with the duke signaled the start of a new period in her life, she resolved to go there the following morning. She had indulged herself in useless brooding for too long; it was time to take up her life again. And since it now appeared that painting was to be her life, it behooved her to get on with her studies.

She had no engagements that evening, so she went early to bed after sending a message to Jeremy to have the hackney in Belgrave Square at nine in the morning.

When she entered the studio, she was pleased at how warmly she was greeted by the others. Mr. Stokes, the eldest student, who rarely had much to say for himself, and Roger Tompkins both gave her a smile and a pleasant greeting. Frederick Peckham was full of the new commission he had received to paint the three children of a Mr. Watkins, and how he had obtained it. Monsieur Duprés kissed her on both cheeks with true Gallic enthusiasm and Mimi sent her a wave and saucy smile from behind the tea tray.

Claire took a deep breath, inhaling the pungent smell of oil paints and turpentine that was so reassuring and familiar. As she donned her paint-stained smock and mobcap, she told herself she was happy to be back. What she needed was work; hard, taxing work.

Monsieur Duprés had set up an interesting still life of fruit and wine on a table under the skylight, and Claire walked around it, trying to decide on the best angle. She was already pondering how she could capture the light coming through the bottle and the glasses and contrast it to the white cloth and colorful fruit.

During one of the breaks, she noticed that her painting, *The Judgment of Paris*, was missing from the easel where she had left it to dry. Monsieur Duprés smiled at her when she inquired for it, saying that he himself had sent it to the framemaker's in her absence. Since it was difficult for her to carry large paintings down the five flights from the loft, he had done this for her many times before, and Claire did not question him further.

Then she remembered how eagerly she had been looking forward to showing the finished work to Andrew and she felt that familiar stab. She turned away and went to Frederick Peckham's easel to discuss the still life, determined to put the marquess from her mind.

Chapter Eleven

Claire made herself go to the studio every morning, and sometimes, on rainy days, in the afternoon as well. She accepted all the duke's invitations, and to keep busy was much more tolerant of Sir Reginald's attentions too. This gentleman was feeling daily more confident now that the Marquess of Blagdon had left town. He knew the duke did not contemplate remarriage, and so he did not fear any competition from that quarter. He was quick to intensify his efforts to win Miss Carrington's hand. He made up a party for the theater one evening that concluded with a delicious supper at Grillon's Hotel, he suggested that Claire might enjoy a trip to Epsom when the races started, and he tried to get her to promise to spend the summer in Brighton after the Season's end.

His confidence and happy expression did not escape notice, and the odds in the clubs were shortening for his success with the lady. One morning, on the strength of discovering at White's that it was now considered almost a sure thing that he would capture his unusual heiress, he went out and ordered several new coats at Weston's and a pair of boots at Hobey's. He even had a look in at Tattersall's to make plans for the acquisition of the team he would purchase the moment the young lady succumbed to his considerable charms and said yes at last.

The Duke of Severn watched and waited, much amused. Miss Carrington had let slip the extent of her indifference to Sir Reginald and he wondered why she did not discourage the red-headed peer's pretensions. It was most unlike her to be unkind and lead the young man on, the duke thought, somewhat surprised.

The truth was that Claire did not even notice him. She moved through the days in a fog of numbed emotion. What Sir Reginald took for a serious evaluation of his person and accomplishments was in reality complete indifference, for she was looking right through him.

Claire often wondered what she would do when she came face to face with Andrew again. She knew she could not count on his remaining in the country for the rest of the Season, but even as she longed to see him, she dreaded the encounter. At every dance, every concert and reception, the first thing she did was to search the assembled guests with a keen eye, holding her breath as she did so. When she had made certain he was not there, she would sigh with relief, although any enjoyment she might have had in the party disappeared at once.

Paul Venables almost always came up to speak to her, but he never mentioned his friend the marquess, and Claire could not ask, no matter how she longed to have news of him.

Paul was aware that Andrew had proposed and Miss Carrington had refused him, for that much the marquess had let slip before he left for Blagdon. What he did not know was why Miss Carrington had done so, for she had seemed to like Andrew to the exclusion of all others. When he saw the misery on his friend's face, his first reaction was to think the young lady a cruel flirt. But then he saw how unhappy she looked herself when she was not schooling her expression in company, and how quiet and withdrawn she had become, and he changed his mind.

One evening, as he was chatting with Claire, he could not help introducing the marquess into the conversation. He saw her start a little at his name, one hand going to her throat for a moment before she quickly controlled herself.

"It is most unusual for Drew to stay away so long," he remarked. "I look for him daily, for his estates are so well-run, I cannot imagine that there is any problem of such magnitude as to claim all this time."

"I am sure you miss him, sir," Miss Carrington said politely, her voice stiff, and then she changed the subject.

Venables thought of writing to Andrew and telling him how unhappy Miss Carrington seemed, but then he noticed how often she was in the Duke of Severn's company, and how Sir Reginald hovered around, and he wondered if he had been mistaken after all. Perhaps she was seeking bigger game and only seemed quiet because she was making plans to become a duchess? Finally he told himself that if Miss Carrington was in love with Drew, she would not encourage the attentions of other men, and decided to leave well enough alone.

The duke had arranged to pick Claire up in Belgrave

Square at three the afternoon the exhibition opened. She was wearing a very smart gown of pearl gray, cut severely in the new French style and worn under a matching half-coat. The ensemble was trimmed with narrow bands of charcoal satin and on her head she wore a large-brimmed bonnet decorated with a cockade of satin ribbons. With her big gray eyes and the shining black curls just peeping from under the brim of her hat, she looked stunning and the duke was quick to tell her so. She waved a gloved hand in thanks as she settled her skirts in the carriage.

"Now, whatever will you do with that handsome outfit at Dawson Hall, I wonder, my dear Claire?" the duke asked, taking his place beside her. "Go walking in a muddy country lane? Make a grand entrance at evensong in the village church? No, now I know we will see you in London again, for such elegance would be wasted on the rustics. And when I think of such as you burying yourself in the country, I shudder."

Claire smiled at him. She was becoming used to his teasing ways and his almost constant sarcasm. She knew he considered the country a dead bore, for he had told her he never spent a moment longer there than he had to. She had not been able to resist remarking on how unfair this was to his hopeful family, and at her criticism, the duke's eyes opened wide and his black eyebrows soared.

"But, my dear child, you cannot have thought! Only consider that my heir is at Eton with other grubby schoolboys, and the youngest, the twin girls, are only seven. The others are at equally unappealing ages. What on earth would I do with them? No, no, my dear Claire! They are better left to the care of their tutors and governesses and nannies until such time as they can comport themselves with grace and adult dignity." He thought for a moment and then added glumly, "If that time ever arrives."

He had told her then of a time when both twins, in being constrained to kiss him hello on one of his infrequent appearances at the ancestral acres, had become so nervous of the honor that one of them had broken into tears and wailing, and the other had stuttered and giggled until they both had to be removed. The revulsion with which he told this story made it impossible for Claire to point out that if he spent more time with his children such things would not happen. Instead of being frightened of a stranger, they would probably adore him, as she herself would have adored her father if she had had the chance.

Now, as his coachman drove them to the Royal Academy, he began to tell her of some of the exhibitions he had seen in the past, and some of the artists who had been collected by past Dukes of Severn and were now hung in a spacious north-lit gallery. He was knowledgeable, and Claire forgot to be cautious as she joined in a lively discussion of art.

"I admit to pride in our collection," the duke said. "It is made up of only English artists, you see. Besides two Hilliards and several Coopers, there are many Dobson miniatures. Such jewels they are! Most of the older works are portraits, of course. One wonders why some of my uglier ancestors bothered . . . but let that go. Every man has his pride. There are some excellent studies of horseflesh by George Stubbs as well, and just recently I acquired what I consider a prime example of the English landscape genre in a painting by Samuel Scott."

Claire remarked that the collection at Severn was most comprehensive and she was glad that the duke continued the family tradition of supporting the arts.

"I consider it an act of charity. Artists, poor devils, rarely become wealthy. Most of them lead a precarious existence. Sometimes I wonder why they persevere."

"Because they must," Claire said, and at his sudden stare for her vehemence, she added quickly, "I mean, I am sure they are driven by their talent, don't you agree?"

The duke nodded, and to Claire's relief referred again to his own collection, concluding by saying, "Perhaps someday you will see my gallery. I can assure you it is better hung and lighted than the one we are going to see today."

Claire smiled. "It would have to be, Your Grace. That huge room, crowded with paintings from top to bottom, sometimes six high, makes it impossible to appreciate any of the works."

"And if you are an artist who is not in the good graces of the academy, you are apt to find your canvas hung two stories away, next to those high windows near the ceiling," the duke agreed. "I make it a practice to note only the names of artists I admire, and then I go to their studios if I wish to study their work further."

Claire asked if he were acquainted with the work of Turner.

"Indeed I am. His seascapes are especially fine. What a

shame the man himself is such an abomination, so uncultured and slovenly."

"And so prejudiced against women," Claire said tartly.

"Now, how would you know that, Miss Carrington?" he asked idly, but Claire was not forced to invent an occasion, for just then the carriage halted before the academy.

A footman was quick to let down the steps. He helped first Claire and then the duke to alight, while the other footman cleared a path for them through the crowds so they could enter the courtyard.

When they reached the main exhibition hall, it was just as crammed full as Claire had known it would be, not only with paintings but also with all the fashionable world come for the opening day.

As she looked around, the duke murmured in her ear, "And there is the Dowager Marchioness of Blagdon, my dear. Now you can see with your own eyes Andrew's gentle mother. She is being accompanied by Lady Peakes."

Claire followed his gaze to where a thin elderly woman was standing, somewhat apart from the crush, and looking very severe and disapproving as she did so, with her pinched nose in the air. Claire studied her carefully. For some reason their paths had never crossed until now. She did not think the lady looked at all kind or loving, for the cold expression in her icy blue eyes, her haughty arched eyebrows, and her narrow forehead and pursed lips all showed her disdain for the majority of her fellow human beings.

Lady Peakes inclined her head an inch when she saw Claire looking their way and whispered to her mother. The dowager's eyes swept over the duke and the lady in pearl gray as if they were invisible, and then she turned away to study the paintings on the wall nearest her.

"Brrr!" The duke shivered in mock alarm. "Now you see how right I was, Miss Carrington. She always makes me feel as if I were a pane of glass, for she refuses to acknowledge me. I do not live up to her . . . er, rigid standards for the nobility. But I wonder why she has taken you in such aversion?"

"I have no idea," Claire replied, although she found herself becoming angry. "From her expression, I gather there are few people that she can tolerate. But come, shall we walk about and at least try to see the exhibition?"

Putting the dowager from her mind, she began to search for

Frederick Peckham's landscape. She hoped her fellow student was not hung too high or in a dim corner, for she wanted to call the duke's attention to his talent.

They passed quite close to the dowager marchioness, although she had her back turned to them now as she studied the paintings before her. And then, as so often happens in a crowd where everyone is talking at once, a sudden silence fell, and Claire heard her cold, piercing voice exclaim, "Andrew! There is my son!"

Claire turned back, sure she was to be brought face to face with the marquess at last and unable to still the rapid beating of her heart. She saw the dowager grasp her daughter by the shoulder and heard her demand, "What is Andrew doing in that *disgusting* painting, Marion? Why, he is *unclothed*!"

Confused, Claire looked to where the dowager was pointing with a long bony finger, and she gasped. There before her, and hung very prominently in only the second tier of works, was her painting, *The Judgment of Paris*.

She was not aware that the duke was staring intently at her, or of the other members of the *ton* who crowded closer for a better look. Without taking her eyes from her painting, she reached out and took the duke's arm in both hands, crushing the fabric of his coat in her utter surprise. Her gray eyes were wide with shock and her mouth fell open as she stared. Of course! Paris was as much Andrew as if he had sat for his portrait. Why had she never noticed it before?

The dowager suddenly moaned and crumpled to the floor. Dimly Claire was aware of Lady Peakes's exclaiming, and the excited voices of the other visitors, but she never took her eyes from the face of Paris—no, the face of Andrew Tyson, she told herself bitterly. How could she have done such a thing, even unintentionally?

Two gentlemen lifted the dowager and bore her away to an anteroom, still in her deep swoon. She was followed by her daughter, already searching her reticule for her salts and vinaigrette. The buzz of voices finally penetrated Claire's consciousness.

"Are you all right, Miss Carrington?" the duke asked as he bent toward her in concern. "I pray that you will not faint too."

Claire swallowed. "Of course I shall not, Your Grace. Why on earth should I?" she asked in what she hoped was a normal voice.

"I only ask because you are crushing not only my sleeve but also my arm—indeed, I shall not be at all surprised to discover a dark bruise when I remove my coat," he said meekly. Stung, she dropped his arm as she would have a hot poker.

"Lady Blagdon startled me. I am so sorry," Claire said, and then her eyes went back to her painting as if it might have disappeared into thin air. In a way, she wished it would. Why was it here? How had it been entered in the exhibition without her knowledge, and how had it come to be accepted?

The duke took her arm in his, and patting her hand, moved forward. Such was his air of assurance that other, lesser members of the *ton* fell back and allowed him to take her right up to the painting. As Claire continued to stare at it, fascinated, the duke raised his quizzing glass.

"Yes, the Dowager Marchioness of Blagdon was right," he remarked to all and sundry. "That is Andrew Tyson to the life. How very extraordinary."

"But surely it is a coincidence that he appears, Your Grace," Lady Warner said, peering around Claire for a better look at this startling near-nude portrayal of a member of one of England's oldest families. The excitement in her voice was obvious to everyone.

"I cannot imagine him posing for it. Why, that fellow's clad only in a flimsy drapery. Egad!" Lord Grant exclaimed, and then he coughed, his face growing red.

"No, no, it cannot be" . . . "I am sure he did not" . . . "Impossible!" . . . "How very upsetting for his mother, no wonder she fainted . . ." several others chimed in, but Claire heard their barely concealed exultation and knew that soon all London would buzz with this delicious story. She wished she could sink into the floor in her shame.

"It is very well done," the duke continued, stepping back slightly so he might study the canvas as a whole. "Yes, most excellent. The muscular figure of Paris, for example, those clouds, this nymph's draperies—and do observe the authoritative use of light and shadow. Obviously it was painted by a talented artist."

At any other time, Claire's heart would have warmed at such lavish praise, but now she only waited in dread for what she was sure would come next. She was not disappointed.

"But who is the artist, Your Grace? Who could have hated Andrew Tyson so much that he made him appear such a fool?'' Lady Jersey asked in her quick, breathless voice. "Can you read the signature?''

The duke stepped close again. He was so tall, his head was on a level with the bottom of the frame, and he had no difficulty seeing those bold initials. Claire found herself holding her breath.

"I do not think it is signed,'' he said after what seemed an hour to her. There was a murmur of disappointment, and he added, "I can make out no name, only what appears to be a letter or two, and I am not sure they are not just part of the design. Certainly there is no signature.''

Regretful but still intrigued, the *ton* crowded closer to see for themselves, and the duke came back to Claire's side. She had not moved all the time he was inspecting the canvas, and now, as he took her arm and led her away, neither of them said a word. They had reached the other side of the room and a quiet corner before the duke leaned down and whispered, "You may thank me later, Claire. I suppose I should not have been so surprised, for you did say you were particularly acquainted with one of the exhibitors, did you not? I myself would have put it more strongly than that. I should have said '*intimately* acquainted,' my dear Miss 'C. C.' ''

"Whatever do you mean . . .?'' Claire began, but the duke raised a deterring hand.

"Acquit me of slow wit, if you please, my dear *artiste*. If the initials do not stand for Claire Carrington, why didn't Charles C. or Cedric C. or even Cecil C. sign his name? No artist who was hopeful of gaining fame and fortune would be so reticent and retiring. No, only a woman would sign her paintings that way, for otherwise her work would stand no chance of being judged, never mind exhibited.''

Claire tried a light laugh. "And now I discover that in addition to your other attributes, you also possess a vivid imagination, sir.''

She looked back to where people were still crowded in front of her painting, and knew her only chance to remain anonymous was to convince the duke he was mistaken. "Indeed I am flattered, and of course your reasoning is sound. Perhaps it is a woman artist. Why should that be so unusual? I believe a woman can wield a brush as well as a man if she has been trained to it. But that woman is not I. Surely there are others in the world with my initials.''

The duke shrugged. "I do wish you would trust me, my

dear, but no matter. It is useless for you to deny it. Your conversation on the way here, so knowledgeable and professional, your remark about Turner—and, of course, your great friendship with the marquess, to say nothing of the way you were educated. Why, all clues point to you. And then there was your reaction when you first saw the painting. You were stunned, were you not? Could it be that you did not know it was to be exhibited? Or was it that you did not realize until that moment that you had painted Tyson's face? Even I cannot imagine him posing for you, so you must have painted him from memory, putting his head on another model's body. Come, do confess! I quite long to hear all about it.''

Claire smoothed her gloves, looking down with great concentration as if the tiny wrinkles absorbed her entire attention. "I cannot help what you think, sir, but I beg you not to speculate about it anymore. You must see how disastrous such unfounded suspicions would be for me if they became known.''

The duke glanced around the gallery. "I doubt if it will be necessary for me to air my theories. Others are sure to make the connection sooner or later. And if I am not mistaken, it will be sooner rather than later, for Miss Boothby and Lady Banks have just come in.''

"Oh, no,'' Claire whispered, whirling around to see where he pointed. The two ladies were arm in arm, and when Miss Boothby saw the crowd gathered in front of Claire's painting, she was quick to head that way. Claire found herself breathing a fervent prayer that Lady Banks would not blurt out her name before she thought. "Let us go at once, Your Grace,'' she pleaded.

"Go? But we have not seen the exhibition as yet. My dear Claire, you cannot be thinking. If we tear away now, it will only make it easier for everyone to connect our flight with your guilt. Come, take my arm and we will stroll the room, pausing at such works as merit our attention. And do not continue to look in that direction, if you please. Your face gives the game away.''

Claire straightened her back. He was right, of course. She would just have to brazen it out as best she could. She took his arm and smiled up at him, and he whispered, "Good girl!'' and then pointed to a small oil nearby and asked her what she thought of it.

But all their nonchalance was wasted. In a very few minutes Claire could see incredulous eyes staring at her and hear the busy hum of shocked conversation and barely veiled titters. She knew Lady Banks must somehow have let it slip that she was an artist. She tilted her chin and tried to keep her expression unconcerned. No one could be positive unless she herself admitted it to the world, and she had no intention of doing that.

The duke was now admiring Frederick Peckham's canvas. Warming to him for his support, Claire decided to let him at least in on the secret, for she needed his advice.

"I see that it is useless for me to dissemble, Your Grace, for you are too clever. Yes, I am the artist who painted *The Judgment of Paris*, and a fellow student of Mr. Peckham's as well. We both study at the *atélier* of Emil Duprés."

"Peckham's work is as admirable as yours," the duke replied, his tone of voice casual, as if what she had just revealed was of no great importance. "I am glad you told me, Miss Carrington," he added. "You can be sure I will keep your confidence."

"There will be no need for you to do so, for you were right, sir," she said bitterly. "Look there where Miss Boothby is even now making the rounds of her friends, dragging my poor cousin Martha with her."

The duke smiled. "Lady Banks looks almost frightened, does she not? I do hope she is not about to faint! You are more like your aunt, Flora Dawson, than I had suspected. In her day, didn't she also cause ladies to swoon by her *outré* remarks and behavior?"

"What should I do?" Claire asked bluntly, ignoring this pleasantry. "Should I deny it if anyone asks, or admit it?"

The duke appeared to consider her question seriously. "I think that must be your decision, my dear child. If you refuse to admit it, no one can be positive you are the artist, but either way it will be a scandal. I do warn you, however, that your admission will put paid to any liaison you might have hoped for with Andrew Tyson. No man would stand for being made mock of in such a notorious way."

"I did not do it to mock him," Claire said in some distress, and then she shook her head. "It does not signify in any case. There was no thought of any liaison even before this, sir. I have refused his proposal."

"So that is why he went away. I thought it something like that. But news of his being immortalized will bring him back

164

to town, posthaste. At least being a woman saves you from his challenging you to pistols for two, some misty dawn in the near future."

Claire looked so unhappy that he added sharply, "You must smile! We have spent enough time so that no one can accuse you of beating a hasty retreat. I am going to take you away now, for I see Miss Boothby bearing down on us. We must make our escape without delay. And to tell the truth, I am anxious to hear the whole story as soon as we are private."

As he spoke, he walked leisurely toward the entrance, smiling and nodding to his acquaintance, although he did not pause to speak to anyone. To Claire it seemed the gallery had grown immense; she thought they would never reach the door.

At last they were in the courtyard again, and she closed her eyes for a few moments in relief. She did not notice that the duke spoke quietly to one of his footmen, nor that the servant saluted and went into the building they had just left.

When they were settled in the carriage, the duke ordered his coachman to drive out of town in the direction of Twickenham, and then he settled back beside Claire with the air of someone about to be entertained in royal style.

"Thank you for not deserting me, Your Grace," Claire remembered to say. "I am sure other men would have left me at once when they learned I was so brazen as to take up such an unwomanly occupation."

Her voice was scornful, and the duke laughed. "But I am not like 'other men,' as I have told you before. The Duke of Severn is a law unto himself," he reminded her. "Your talent for painting is . . . er, unusual, to be sure, but then, you have made a practice of being so, have you not, Miss Carrington? When did you discover you had this gift? I assume you have been working hard for some years. There is that about your painting that shows the confidence of an expert. I looked very carefully, and I could see no faltering or hesitation. Your brushwork, your use of color and design—all powerful and most impressive."

"Thank you," Claire said with real gratitude, her deep contralto gruff. For some reason, his praise eased the depression she was feeling. "To answer you, I began when I was in my early teens. Before that, I did only the usual sketching and watercolors. I started my study of music at the same time."

She paused and smiled, albeit a little weakly. "That was soon discarded. You see, I cannot, with the best will in the world, carry a tune."

"That failing does not seem to deter other young ladies from musical performances," the duke said with a grimace. "One can only be grateful that in your case Lady Dawson had a discerning ear. But do go on. . . ."

"My aunt saw how interested I was in art—indeed, she often teased me for preferring a pencil or a stick of charcoal to my other lessons. She was quick to engage a good painting instructor, however. It was at Mr. Briggs's instigation that I tried oils, and I knew I had found my medium at last. There is something jewellike about oils, don't you agree? They are so rich, so glowing, and they have such depth when you work up from the underpainting. I could never get that effect with watercolors or pastels."

She stopped and then said in a contrite voice, "You should not have asked me, Your Grace. When I get on my particular hobbyhorse, it is hard to stop me. I am sure I am boring you."

"I am not in the least bored," he told her. "I think you know me well enough to realize that in the unlikely chance that I should become so, I will be quick to inform you."

He paused, and as Claire chuckled, he added, "But tell me, how did this particular painting come to be in the exhibition?"

"I have no idea," Claire replied, her gray eyes puzzled. She threw out her hands and shrugged. "I must suppose Monsieur Duprés entered it. I noticed it was missing from the *atélier*, and when I asked about it, he told me he had sent it to the framer's. He often does this for me, and so I did not question him further." Her eyes grew stormy. "I shall have something to say to Emil when next I see him!"

"I beg you will not quite shatter him, my dear. I am sure he did it for only the best of reasons."

When Claire looked askance, he added, "Because, of course, it was of such excellence that he wanted the world to see it."

"And now all the world has seen it, and look at the trouble I am in," Claire could not help saying.

The duke laughed. "Perhaps not all the world, but all the world that matters to you and to Lord Blagdon, I suppose. You said you did not put his face in the painting to mock him. Why, then, did you do so?"

Claire stared out of the carriage window for a moment, but

the duke was sure she was not seeing anything there. "I do not know if you will believe me, Your Grace—indeed, I find it hard to believe myself. I had no idea I had done so until the dowager pointed it out. Frederick Peckham posed for Paris; I remember he remarked I had not made the face at all like his."

She paused and a slight color tinged her cheeks. The duke waited, but when she did not continue, he prodded, "And what did you reply to Mr. Peckham?"

"I told him I was painting a god, not a man," Claire whispered.

"And of course now you are wondering why you chose the marquess's face as your ideal, are you not?" the duke asked. Then he took her hands and gently unclenched the fingers she had curled into her palms. "My dear, you are very naive. Shall I tell you why you did so?"

His voice was kind, but more than a little amused, and stung, Claire answered, "It will not be necessary, sir. You must acquit me of slow wit, too. I did it because I am in love with him. I know that."

The duke nodded, as if to a bright child who had come up with the correct answer. For a moment they rode in silence, and then he asked, "But in that case, my dear Claire, why did you refuse him when he asked you to marry him?"

"Because his mother had told him he would be dead to her forever if he continued to see me. I could not have that on my conscience, you see. Besides, even though Andrew thinks her banishment would not matter, I know it would. I never really knew my parents: they died when I was three. But not a day passes that I do not miss them."

"And having seen his gentle, loving mother, you still feel the same way?" the duke asked, his voice sarcastic. Claire winced.

"It is true that she does not appear to be very warm, or . . . or caring, but perhaps that is only her public face. In private she is sure to show her concern, her love."

The duke snorted. "And *I* am sure she is a horrid old woman at any time. But let us forget her. Tell me instead why Andrew accepted your refusal. Surely he did not agree that he would rather have his mother's approval than your love?"

"I did not tell him that was my reason. Instead, I pretended that my art was of such importance to me that I could

167

never give it up, that I had worked too hard to sacrifice it for any man.''

"And he did not convince you that any such sacrifice on your part would be unnecessary? Come, Claire! No intelligent man would believe such nonsense!"

"I told him he would change his mind, that he would end up wanting a conformable wife, no matter how he said I could continue my studies," Claire explained, and then she looked right at the duke and added, "And I said that because I loved him, I would give up my work for him, and perhaps in time, come to hate him.''

The duke's eyes were keen. "My sincere apologies, Miss Carrington. You are not as naive as I thought."

Claire nodded bleakly, and they rode on in silence, each deep in his own thoughts.

"Of course, now there is no question of marriage, nor any need to hide what Andrew calls my 'light under a bushel,' " Claire said finally. "The truth is out; everyone will know I painted that canvas.''

"Not if you continue to deny it," the duke reminded her. "Andrew will know, of course, but I think we can assume he will keep your secret. My, my. I wonder what he will make of it? I myself would be very elated and encouraged if I were in his place."

Ignoring Claire's surprised look, he continued, "But not before I fell into a towering rage and gave you a setdown you would never forget. I very much doubt I would be able to keep my whip from your sides. I do beg you, Miss Carrington, for the sake of our friendship, not to put my face in any of your canvases. I might not be the noble duke that Lady Blagdon considers proper, but I really do think I would take exception to that."

When Claire seemed about to speak, he added, "But then, there is no danger of that, is there? I am not a god to you—not your ideal."

If Claire had been listening more carefully, she would have heard the slightly rueful tone he used, as if somehow he regretted that this was not the case, but her thoughts had taken another direction. "But why shouldn't I admit it, Your Grace?" she asked. "I am not ashamed of my art, nor of my talent. And since art is to be all my life from now on, perhaps I should take advantage of this gossip as the windfall it is. Why, everyone in the *ton* is sure to clamor for a Carrington landscape or portrait now. My reputation has been made.''

The duke, listening more carefully than she had done, heard the bitterness in her voice and he took her face in his hands, turning her to face him squarely. ''Will you take my advice, my dear?'' he asked, his sarcastic voice for once curiously gentle.

He waited until she nodded, and then he said, ''I beg you to keep your own counsel, at least for a while. You see, I am not as sure as you are that your art is to be your entire life from this time on. Come, promise me that you will do as I ask. What can a small delay matter, after all? Continue to deny you are the artist, laugh at such a wild idea if you can manage it, and I will do all I can to disabuse society that you are the culprit. On no account are you to retreat from the social world. I expect to see you at every ball, every reception, every tea and masquerade that you receive an invitation to. We will sound the advance, my dear Claire, and under no conditions will we retreat.''

Claire was puzzled, but since she shrank from the scorn and abuse she knew was to be her potion, in spite of her brave words about being proud of her skill, she was quick to agree.

The duke pounded his cane on the carriage roof, and when the coachman pulled up and opened the trap, he ordered him to return to town.

He then gave Claire a great many orders. She was to buy several stunning new gowns, she was to accompany him on a walk, not a drive, in the park tomorrow afternoon, and she was to save him two dances at Mrs. Acton's waltz breakfast in four days' time. Furthermore, although she was under no circumstances to return to the *atélier*, as soon as she reached home she was to write to Monsieur Duprés and demand his silence, and that of her fellow students as well.

Claire listened and nodded, wondering why the duke was taking up her cause. Perhaps it was the challenge of rescuing her from this imbroglio, she told herself sadly, not that it mattered to her at all. She knew it was only for Andrew's sake that she agreed. To be painted half-nude by a male artist was bad enough, and sure to cause a seven-day wonder, but to be thought to have posed that way for a woman would stir up such a scandal broth he would never live it down.

Chapter Twelve

It was a beautiful early June in the English countryside. Day after day dawned sunny and mild, and those occasional showers that did fall only lingered long enough to bring a fresh, tender green to the grass and fields and cause the apple blossoms and early flowers to open in bursts of scented splendor.

It might just as well have been dank and gloomy, for then the weather would have been the perfect foil for Andrew Tyson's present mood. He was sorry now that he had left town in such a precipitate way. At least there he had things to do, parties to attend and friends to see, and his orphanages to manage as well. In Blagdon, he had entirely too much time to spend alone, with no one to distract him from his thoughts.

Sometimes he still could not believe that he had lost Claire—and right after discovering how much he loved her. In his mind he went over and over their interview that last morning, trying to find some sign to encourage him. Finally he had to admit that what she had told him had put paid to any hopes he might have had of winning her hand. True, she had been honest enough to admit she loved him, but after only one brief surge of elation at her confession, he had been plunged into depths of depression. Because she cared for him, she would try to be the kind of conventional wife he deserved. In vain had he tried to tell her that he would not change, that he didn't want a conformable wife.

Now he added to himself that if any children they might have demanded such a namby-pamby mother, he would disown them at once. Ruefully his mouth twisted at this savagery. Perhaps it runs in the family, he thought, recalling his mother's ultimatum.

In walking through the grounds in the soft dusk of early evening, he often thought of their only kiss, that night in the Eberleys' garden. How soft and giving her lips had been in her surrender! And how pliant and yielding her slender body had felt as he held her in his arms, the lovely curves of her breasts crushed against his chest and fast-beating heart. He groaned.

He remembered that it had been in another garden that she had refused Lord Wilson the first night he met her, and some of her words as she had done so. She had said husbands were "demanding," "restricting," and "completely unnecessary." And she had said that if falling in love was anywhere near as painful and all-consuming as it appeared to be from her reading of it, she would do very well without it.

Ah, Claire, Andrew thought as he ran his hands through his blond hair in frustration, how could you be so wise, my worldly innocent? It is indeed painful and all-consuming, as now I am only too well aware, to my sorrow.

But it was obvious that he was to be no more to her than Lord Wilson, in spite of her love for him. How could she walk away after she admitted that? Surely she had been lying to him! It was not her art that worried her at all, it was his mother's hatred and threats. When he thought of this, his spirits rose, and he almost ordered his valet to start packing for an immediate return to town. But then he would recall her cold, set face as she stood in Lady Banks's morning room and told him she would never marry him or any other man.

He groaned again. He had not really thought he had lost her until he heard her say that if he touched her she would surrender, but she would hate herself for her weakness later. That had convinced him she was in deadly earnest. He knew he could have kissed her into blushing compliance—Lord, how he had ached to do so!—but what he had told her was true. He did not want her that way. No, if she came to him it must be with all her heart and open arms, with no reservations on her part to mar their future. And since she had no intention of doing that, she was lost to him forever.

He was not sleeping well, in spite of the country air and the days he crowded full of hard physical activity. Jennings, his butler, was concerned at his master's weary, unsmiling face, its lean planes set in stern lines, and he wondered what the matter was. The Marquess of Blagdon was generally the sunniest of men, good-tempered and of even disposition. The housekeeper claimed that it was as plain as the nose on your face that a woman was behind it, and Jennings was inclined to agree with her.

He always brought the early post directly to the breakfast room, and one morning, after the marquess had been in residence for over two weeks, he carried in a silver salver piled high.

Andrew was staring into space, ignoring his breakfast, but at Jennings' apologetic cough he recalled himself and motioned the butler to put the salver by his plate. His blond eyebrows rose at the amount of mail he had received.

"More coffee, m'lord?" Jennings asked as he watched him turn his letters over.

"Thank you. It appears I shall need it if I am to wade through all of this," the marquess said, still looking astounded. As the butler refilled his cup, he heard him mutter, "Marion . . . Paul . . . Mrs. Venables . . . my mother . . . Miss Boothby . . . Lady Banks . . . Good heavens! Even a volume from the Duke of Severn! Now what's to do?"

Jennings put the cup down and stood waiting for further orders. The marquess was holding the last bulky envelope and staring at it. When the butler asked if there would be anything further required, he waved his hand in dismissal and then took up his fruit knife and broke the blob of red wax with which the letter was sealed.

Andrew did not hear his butler go softly out the door and close it, for he was already reading the first of several sheets that were covered with closely written lines. His brows contracted in a frown as he did so.

My dear Lord Blagdon,

I would wager any amount you like, sir, that your post is very heavy today. However, I do pray you will read my letter first, for it will do a great deal to make the hysterical ravings of the others intelligible to you.

To be as brief as possible, I had the pleasure of escorting Miss C_____ to the opening of the new exhibition at the Royal Academy only a few hours ago. Imagine my surprise on entering the main hall to hear your mother call out your name—your *given* name, and in public, mind, dear boy—while looking at one of the paintings. She then fell into a deep swoon.

On closer examination, I easily established that the central figure of this mythological scene was none other than yourself, clad only in an abbreviated toga or robe.

Allow me to assure you that *The Judgment of Paris* is an excellent piece of work, and most faithfully portrays your face. But even though I have often observed you stripped to your breeches in Jackson's Boxing Salon, I cannot be sure the figure is also yours. . . . No matter.

The canvas was signed only with two initials. Is it at all necessary for me to mention that they were both the letter C?

Now, my dear fellow, kindly do not throw these sheets to the floor, utter a great many foolish oaths, and bellow that your fastest horse must be saddled at once! Read on, I beg you. All will be made plain.

Miss C_____ was also in some distress when she saw the canvas. I fully expected her to faint as well, but she managed to control herself, although the look of shocked surprise on her face more than convinced me that she had no idea her painting was to be exhibited.

All might have passed off with only the usual wild speculations if Miss Bo_____ and Lady Ba_____ had not come in. I do not know what was said, for I had taken Miss C_____ away to the other side of the room, but from the stares and whispers directed toward the young lady, one can safely assume that her elderly cousin let slip some pertinent and damaging fact. Some women, my dear Lord Blagdon, as I am sure you will agree, should be strangled at birth.

I took Miss C_____ for a drive in my carriage after we quit the hall, and she was persuaded to confide in me. It is obvious that her teacher entered the painting in the competition without her knowledge. What was really surprising, and I am sure of great import to you, was that until your mother's outburst, Miss C_____ had no idea that she had portrayed you. You ask how this could be possible? A Mr. P_____, one of her fellow students, posed for the figure of Paris. He noticed Miss C_____ had not used his face, and on asking her why, was told she was painting a god, not a man. Interesting, is it not? She admitted to me very freely that she must have done so unconsciously, out of her love for you, for you were ever in her thoughts. I wonder if you have any idea, my dear boy, how fortunate you are, but let that go.

I have managed to convince the lady that admitting

she is the artist will serve no good purpose at all, and she has promised to deny it to all and sundry, at least for a while. Of course this denial in itself would never be believed, except I have taken the liberty of purchasing the work and having it removed from the exhibition this very same afternoon. Without it to stare and snicker at, and compare to the original, we might be able to convince the *ton* that they were mistaken, and that what they saw for a few brief minutes was not at all what they supposed. There are other handsome blond men in England still, I believe.

One other point about the painting that might interest you: the figure of Paris stands a little right of center, surrounded by his three attendant nymphs. Two of them are looking down or away, their expressions simpering and coy, but the dark-haired lady he is about to choose is looking right at him. She is smiling, as he is, and one of her hands is a little extended as if to draw him closer. It is most touching. I will be proud to add it to my collection.

You may trust me to handle the entire matter with the utmost discretion. I have it in mind to escort Miss C———— about with diligence, not permitting her to retire to the country as she has expressed a wish to do. What there is that is so fascinating about rural locations in times of stress escapes me. It is the last place I would think of taking refuge.

Now, my dear Lord Blagdon, perhaps you should read your other letters before you decide what your course should be from this point on. I do not see that your self-imposed exile can do much good anymore; indeed, it might do a great deal of harm. Besides, I know you are not a coward. If you return to town and are seen to be perfectly at ease in company with Miss C————, it might help to stifle the rumors. I beg you not to regard the tattlemongering as any great matter. You know how the *ton* loves to talk.

Are you asking yourself why I have set myself the tedious task of rescuing Miss C————, and, incidentally, yourself as well? I do it because she is unique, a talented woman it is a rare privilege to know, and a joy as well. I know you agree.

Allow me to extend to you my sincere hope that there

will be a successful conclusion to your quest. I shall try to contain my envy, dear boy.

Severn

Andrew read the bold signature on the last sheet and dropped the papers to the table. His dark blue eyes were hooded, for he was thinking hard.

His first feelings of great rage had disappeared by the time he reached the end of the duke's amazing letter, and in its place had come a stab of elation that grew even as he continued to sit there. Claire had put him in her painting; she had admitted to Severn that she loved him. He would go to town this very day, and he would not rest until he had her promise to marry him.

But stay! Why would this new tangle change her mind? Would she not become even more adamant that she would make him a disgraceful wife after what had just happened? And perhaps the delight of knowing that her work was good enough to be accepted by those august judges at the Royal Academy might strengthen her ambitions to remain a serious artist.

Andrew pushed back his chair to stride up and down the room at this disturbing thought. Finally he shook his head. Be that as it may, right now she needed him by her side to defuse the gossip. He admitted to himself that there was no place he would rather be. And while they were together again, even in circumstances such as these, he would do everything he could to make her see that his love for her was powerful enough to overcome every obstacle.

His face was determined as he took his seat again to read his other letters as quickly as he could. From his friend Paul Venables he had a report much like the duke's, which at the end urged him to come to town as soon as he could. Mrs. Venables and Miss Boothby wrote in coy hints and half-veiled conjectures predicting imminent disaster, all heavily underlined. When she took up her pen, Lady Banks had obviously been so distraught to be the catalyst of this farce that her letter was almost unintelligible. At her third abject apology he crumpled the letter in disgust.

He was glad to hear from Marion that his mother had taken no permanent damage from her swoon. His sister also urged him to return to town with all speed.

"I beg you to come at once, Drew," she wrote. "Mother

has already contacted her solicitor with an eye to bringing the artist to book. However, I was able to get her to abandon such a notorious move by pointing out that for a Tyson to appear in court would be unthinkable. However, her desire for revenge on Miss C‗‗‗‗‗ is still great. She will not appear in company, and she is ranting about leaving the country. Do come and help me calm her."

Marion had signed the letter with her love, and then, crossing her lines, had added a postscript. "Did she really paint it, Drew? It is so excellent, I cannot believe it."

Andrew saved his mother's letter for last, and his eyes grew cold as he read the few lines it contained.

> M'lord [it began abruptly],
> I assume you have had other communications that make the matter of your disastrous liaison with that woman's niece clear to you. Now you must admit I was right in my assessment of her, although even I had no idea of the depths of her depravity. You see what your willfulness, beginning with your father's death, has brought on our old and honored name. I shall never be able to hold my head up in society again, and so I am making plans to leave England forever and live abroad.
> Do not communicate with me or try to see me again. I cannot bear to look into the face of such a traitor. I have no son from this day forward.

She had not bothered to sign it. How typical, he thought as he crushed it in his hands, and in his rage got up to throw it on the burning coals in the fireplace. As if Claire was not worth a dozen of her, that silly, prejudiced old woman, so proud of a name that she had not even been born to! A name that she put before love, and talent, and happiness, a name that made her think herself exalted and far above the rest of mankind. Let her go. He would not miss her.

He gathered up his other letters and left the breakfast room, calling for his butler and valet as he did so, he was so anxious to be on his way back to Claire.

In London, Lady Banks took to her bed as soon as she returned from the Royal Academy and had written to the Marquess of Blagdon. She refused to see even Miss Boothby when she called, for she was so mortified at what she had revealed to the *ton*. In vain did Claire point out that it was not as bad as she thought, for even though the lady had let slip that Claire was an artist, she had not said she had painted that particular painting, and no one could prove differently.

Lady Banks moaned and waved her away from her darkened bedroom, where she lay surrounded by pills and potions and pastilles.

It was left to Claire to deal with Miss Boothby, and somehow, for Andrew's sake, she found herself eager to pick up the gauntlet that had been thrown down. Miss Boothby arrived at ten the morning following the opening, supposedly to inquire for Lady Banks. She began by bemoaning her illness and saying how much she prayed it would not result in an immediate demise, or at the least, a sad decline.

"I am sure you exaggerate, my dear ma'am. She will be well directly some new gossip engages everyone's attention," Claire said with a smile, passing her guest a plate of muffins. For once, Miss Boothby declined the treat.

"I am sure I hope you are right, Claire, but with everyone talking about you this way from one end of Mayfair to the other, I am afraid it will not answer."

"Perhaps it would help if you would not do so quite so diligently, ma'am?" Claire asked sweetly. At Miss Boothby's astonished stare, she added, "If instead you were to say that the whole thing is just the stupid mistake that it is, and that Cousin Martha is only laid down on her bed with shock that her words could have been so misinterpreted, I know the situation would improve. And it would be such a kindness to us all to have you on our side, and such a Christian act too."

Miss Boothby swallowed a biting retort. "But those initials, Claire! So . . . so damning, are they not? And then there is the fact that until Andrew Tyson went out of town, you were forever in his company."

Claire tried to keep her expression calm. Would she always feel her heart jump at the mention of his name?

"We certainly had some enjoyable jaunts and parties together, that is true." She paused for a moment, and decided to try a new tactic.

"In a way it is flattering that the *ton* thinks me capable of such a distinguished work of art. How the Duke of Severn and I laughed when we heard! If you could see some of my daubs, my dear Miss Boothby, you would be in whoops as well. I am no more than the veriest amateur."

Miss Boothby leaned forward, nodding her head. "Of

course you are right. I myself had the hardest time believing any gentlewoman could have painted it. Why . . . why, the figgers were as good as naked!''

As she whispered the last word, she blushed bright red and hid her face in her handkerchief. Claire hid a smile.

"Indeed, that is what makes it so ridiculous that *I* or any woman should be accused. You mark my words, it will turn out to be a man. I do wish he had been named Ferdinand Von Hopple, though, if he felt he had to use his initials.''

Miss Boothby appeared to be much struck by this, and Claire sipped her tea to allow her the slow process of serious thought.

"Did you hear that the painting was removed from the wall only moments after you left the hall, dear?'' Miss Boothby asked next, her little round eyes avid at this bit of news. "Now, why was that done, do you suppose?''

Claire had had a brief note from the duke early that morning and so she was more than ready for this barb.

"I don't suppose—I know. The Duke of Severn purchased it for his collection. If anyone can find out the artist's name, I am sure it will be he. Perhaps you should apply to him for information.''

Miss Boothby ruffled up like an indignant peahen. "Why, Claire! I am sure it is none of my business—''

"No, it isn't, is it?'' Claire was quick to agree. Miss Boothby's several chins quivered as her hostess went on, "It is no one's business except mine, and that only because I find myself in such a scandal broth. Primarily, of course, it is Lord Blagdon's concern. Perhaps when he returns to town he will be able to find the impersonator.''

"The impersonator? Whatever can you mean?''

"But surely, my dear Miss Boothby, you cannot have thought that *he* posed for the painting? Not the Marquess of Blagdon! So therefore it follows that someone is playing a sad prank on him, and perhaps on me as well.'' She shook her head and tried to look severe. "It is a shame that members of the *ton* lend themselves to this kind of thing, a prank worthy only of a silly undergraduate.''

"I do not understand. What prank?'' Miss Boothby complained, her heavy face puzzled.

"But it is really very simple. Surely one of Lord Blagdon's more irrepressible friends commissioned the work as a joke.

Or perhaps it is the result of a wager. As you know, most gentlemen will bet on anything.''

"That is so," Miss Boothby said, nodding her head and pleased to be able to add a mite to the conversation. "Young Lord Trumbull wagered a vast sum only last week that he could teach a chicken to communicate with him by tapping its bill once for yes and twice for no. I wonder if he can?'' she mused.

"I wonder," Claire said, counting to ten slowly. Patiently she brought Miss Boothby back to the matter at hand. "But do consider, dear ma'am, that perhaps this unknown out-and-outer used my initials to make an even greater scandal, since he knew the marquess and I were such good friends. It is too bad!''

She noticed that Miss Boothby put down her cup with such a vacant look as she digested this information that it almost fell to the floor. As she caught it and restored it to the table, Claire added, "It appears to be a case for the law, but that of course will be up to the marquess. He is the more severely injured party.''

Just then Lady Banks's butler knocked and entered to present Claire with Sir Reginald Randolph's card. Although she had no desire to see him, she could not help but be glad of his timely interruption. Miss Boothby was good for another hour at least, ruminating over all the things Claire had said, and endlessly suggesting other possibilities. Claire found she had the beginnings of a headache.

She rose and held out her hand. "It was good of you to stop by, ma'am. You may be sure I will tell Cousin Martha of your concern, but now I must beg to be excused. Here is Sir Reginald to see me, and then I have a luncheon engagement.'' She waved toward the shawl and reticule that she had the foresight to bring downstairs with her before she added, "I am also engaged to walk in the park with the Duke of Severn this afternoon. Perhaps we shall see you there and you can inquire if he has made any progress discovering the identity of the mysterious artist.''

"But, Claire! There were so many other things I meant to ask—''

"How kind you are, but I would not dream of detaining you further. I know you have a great many more calls to make today. I only pray you will not be worn to a thread and afflicted with hoarseness by teatime.''

She held out her hand, and Miss Boothby was forced to take it before she gathered up her belongings. Only remembering the new information she had garnered in Belgrave Square allowed her to accept her dismissal with anything like her usual complacency. Perhaps she could just stop by Lady Wilson's before she called on Mrs. Venables, she mused as Claire walked with her to the door.

Sir Reginald was exchanging greetings in the hall with an impatient General Banks, who had been about to leave the house when he was admitted. As Miss Boothby neared them, she clasped her shawl and reticule to her heart and breathed, "How touching, sir! I am quite overcome by your faithfulness when all the world is pointing an accusatory finger. But I shall spare your noble blushes and say no more—"

"That will be the day," General Banks observed with a snort. "Bosh, bunk, and tommyrot, Lizzie! All the world are silly widgeons with nothin' but maggots in their heads. I never regard 'em."

"Just so, sir," Sir Reginald muttered as he bowed to an indignant Miss Boothby and waited for her to take herself off. As she seemed prepared to remain indefinitely, General Banks solved the problem by taking her arm and moving her briskly toward the door.

"Come away, Lizzie, do, and stop your nattering," he said impatiently. "I'm on my way to Brooks's and I'll drop you off if you are going my way."

As the butler closed the door behind them, Claire turned to Sir Reginald. "Won't you come into the morning room, sir? I was not expecting your visit and can spare you but a few minutes. I have an appointment."

Sir Reginald saw that her expression was serious and her voice impatient, and he wondered at it. He had expected to be greeted with smiles and gratitude for his goodness in attending her. After all, he had heard the rumors and the gossip, and that was enough to make most men cut the connection at once. But it had not taken a great deal of thought on the previous evening before he had decided that Miss Carrington's fortune made such social niceties as regarding her with antipathy impossible. No, he would continue her suitor come what may. Surely such devotion would turn the tide in his favor, and the lady would be delighted to fall into his arms without further ado.

Now, as she waved him to a seat, he caught her glancing at

the Cartel clock on the mantelpiece as if to time his visit. She did not appear to be overcome with gratitude for his constancy; perhaps with his measured courtship he had not made it plain that matrimony was his object? It appeared that more direct action was required. And so, instead of taking the chair she indicated, he strode forward and caught her up tightly in his arms. Claire was so astounded that for a moment she did not protest.

"My darling girl, you must not be afraid, nor look so pale," he exclaimed in fervent, ringing tones. "I am beside you, and when we are married, no one will say a word to your discredit, or they shall answer to me. My word on it!"

He moved away then, unable to resist striking a pose, and Claire was quick to retreat behind Cousin Martha's worktable. "Whatever do you mean?" she asked. "We are not going to be married."

"Oh, but we are, radiant creature! Forgive me if I have startled you with my impetuous declaration, but I have spent a sleepless night worrying about you. I came as soon as possible this morning to reassure you that I shall not fail you, no matter how the world reviles you. I shall not regard the scandal that now attaches to your person. No, I shall remain true, and in my arms you shall be safe."

He started toward her, those selfsame arms outstretched as if offering her sanctuary. His face wore such an expression of pleased smugness at his noble generosity that Claire could barely suppress her laughter.

"Stop!" she ordered in a shaking voice. "I fear you go too fast, sir. I have no intention of marrying anyone. Furthermore—"

"My pretty innocent! This is no time to play the coquette," he interrupted, shaking a playful finger at her where she sheltered behind the table. "We must make haste—the day for lingering wooing is past. You must say you will be mine at once so you will have the protection of my name. Can it be that you do not realize the amount of noise that is going around about you and that dreadful painting? Of course it is all tommyrot, as General Banks maintains. I know you could not have painted it."

"Indeed?" Claire asked, stiffening a little. "Why not?"

"Little temptress! So, you want conversation instead of kisses, do you? Very well, I shall indulge you, sweet, and instruct you as well. No woman could have done it. Ladies

181

do not paint such subjects, and in oils, too. Besides, it was too well-executed and much too professional, and therefore beyond any female's small talent and limited intelligence. But you must not fear, dear lady. I shall proclaim your innocence to the world, and as my affianced wife, no one will dare to malign you further."

Claire was now in a towering rage, and forgetting the duke's lectures on the benefits of silence, she said in a passion, "How very noble of you! And yet I think I shall refuse the treat. You silly, ignorant man! How dare you tell me that my intelligence is less than yours—yours, which is almost nonexistent? How dare you say that women have limited talent? You insult my sex, sir!"

Sir Reginald barely heard her, for he was admiring the way her gray eyes were flashing and how very handsome she looked with the color that had come into her cheeks. Dimly he was aware that perhaps he had gone too far with the unusual Miss Carrington, and so must mend his fences.

"But you are teasing me," he said, laughing, as he came toward her again. Claire put the table in his path, but Sir Reginald was not to be denied. He wrested it from her hands and set it to one side. Before she could escape, he had her in his arms again. Claire was strong, but she was no match for his wiry strength. He held her captive easily as he said, "I would not insult you for the world, my darling girl. Come, you must admit the superiority of men in all worldly matters. It is a well-known fact that women are not capable of logical thought. It is not their fault, poor things, it is just that their brains are not as well developed as a man's."

Still struggling to escape him, Claire started to refute this pompous masculine viewpoint, but he stopped trying to instruct her and began to kiss her instead. Gasping, she swung her head this way and that to counter him so that most of his kisses fell on her hair and forehead. At last she managed to get one hand free, and she made a fist and hit him as hard as she could in the eye.

Stunned and in pain, Sir Reginald howled and fell back, causing the table holding Lady Banks's workbasket and embroidery to crash to the floor. The contents of the basket, including several spools of thread, spilled out and rolled around the floor.

Furious now, Claire forgot to be frightened, and she advanced on him, both hands clenched in tight fists. Through the one green eye that was not covered by his hands, Sir Reginald watched them uneasily.

"How dare you prate to me of male superiority?" Claire demanded. "How dare you touch me? Leave this house at once, sir, and never let me see you again. I do not need your consequence and limited intelligence to protect me, and even if I did, I would not marry you for all the tea in China!"

Flashing through his mind's eye was the huge pile of unpaid bills crammed into his writing table, his ramshackle mortgaged estate, and the team of blacks at Tattersall's that now he would never possess, and Sir Reginald lost his temper too.

Reaching out, he grasped her arms in a tight grip, and then he said thickly, "And I do not want to marry you, shrew! It was only your money that tempted me to tie myself to such an oddity. I would even go so far as to say that perhaps the gossip is right after all. No doubt you are a painter; heaven knows you are not a gentle, feminine creature worthy of your sex."

Claire kicked him as hard as she could, but Sir Reginald was wearing his new top boots, and she hurt herself more than she hurt him. Tears of pain and rage came to her eyes as he sneered down at her, furious at her insults. "And everyone knows artists have the loosest of morals, do they not? All that 'free love' they practice, and standing about staring at naked models. I wonder I did not think of it before, and take advantage of your character, ma'am."

One hand came up to pull at the neck of her gown and fondle her breasts, and Claire, frightened now by his superior strength, called loudly for the butler. Sir Reginald stopped her by kissing her. His thin lips ground against hers, and he forced her mouth open with his tongue. For a moment the world swung and she was aware of a growing darkness, and then she remembered the pistol. It was behind her in her reticule on the sofa with her shawl.

With a strength she did not know she possessed, she tore away from his clutching hands to snatch up her bag and remove the pistol. She was trembling so much she needed both hands to cock and aim it, but something in her face stopped Sir Reginald in his tracks. He beat a hasty retreat backward, never taking his eyes from the shining gun that was pointed at his heart.

The door opened to a suddenly silent room. Claire turned

toward it gratefully, but instead of the butler she had summoned, the Duke of Severn stood there. Slowly he removed his high-crowned beaver and kid gloves as he surveyed the scene, and then he handed them and his cane to the interested servant she had expected to see. Behind the butler, a footman craned for a better look over his shoulder. The duke closed the door in their astonished faces.

As he did so, Sir Reginald's cautious retreat brought him into contact with two of the spools of thread he had spilled, and he went sprawling with a loud crash.

The duke eyed him with distaste as he did so. "Well, at least that saves me the trouble of knocking you senseless, sir," he remarked in a bored voice. "How fortunate I do not have to soil my hands on such as you."

He walked over to Claire. "Good morning, Miss Carrington. You have been having an exciting time of it this morning, have you not?"

He tilted her chin, observing the murderous look in her eyes, her uneven breathing, and her disarranged gown. "Yes, I quite agree, but you cannot shoot him, my dear, no matter how much he deserves it. Not in Lady Banks's morning room, in any case. Put the gun away. I hope you shall tell me all about it presently. I am anxious to know if you always carry a firearm to cool unwanted ardor. May I suggest we retire to another room? This one is in such a state of disorder it is unworthy of us."

He stared down at Sir Reginald, who was cowering behind a wing chair, and frowned. "I am sure the servants will be able to restore it to its usual tidy state—after they have removed the . . . er, the debris, that is. Come."

Claire put her pistol away before she picked up her shawl and reticule and took his arm. He led her to the door and then turned back and said in a tight, cold voice, "If any whisper of this gets out amongst the *ton*, Sir Reginald, you shall answer to me. But I do not think we should have any fear of that, my dear Claire. How detrimental to a gentleman's reputation to be named an attempted rapist. Why, I daresay the scandal that would result would force such a man to flee the country and make it impossible for him ever to return."

The duke opened the door then and surprised the butler and footman, both of whom fell back, looking sheepish.

"I am sorry to have to interrupt your eavesdropping, but I must ask you to bring some brandy to the library for Miss

Carrington at once. Then you may remove the man who is sullying Lady Banks's carpet. Come to think of it, you had better take him a tot of brandy, too. I am sure he is in dire need of it.''

As he led Claire in the direction of the general's bookroom, the butler heard him say, his voice quivering with amusement, ''My congratulations, Madam Amazon! Remind me never to annoy you, not even in the most infinitesimal way.''

Chapter Thirteen

For three days the *ton* was treated to the sight of a casual, composed Miss Carrington, who was in the company of an attentive Duke of Severn more often than not. No one remarked Sir Reginald Randolph's hasty departure from town. The suspected artist who was the duke's latest flirt, and the continued seclusion of the Dowager Marchioness of Blagdon, were much more fascinating to discuss than the whereabouts of the red-headed peer who had wooed Miss Carrington with such eagerness just a short time ago.

Claire walked or drove with the duke every afternoon and attended all the parties she had been invited to. She found she had ample opportunity to practice holding her head high as if she didn't have a care in the world. When the boldest of the *ton* asked her outright about her painting, she laughed in disbelief, wondering aloud what people would find to say about her next. She was often heard to remark that she found the gossip so diverting.

There were those who snubbed her, of course, and those who sympathized with the dowager marchioness, but they were in the minority. The *ton* watched and whispered and waited, unsure of the facts, and the scandal showed no signs of abating.

Claire attended the Actons' waltzing breakfast dressed in a new white muslin gown trimmed with silver ribbons. She danced twice with the duke. It was remarked that she did not sit out a single dance and that several of his intimate cronies formed a most admiring court.

Watching from her seat handy to the buffet table, Miss Boothby began to wonder if perhaps William Fairhaven might not be about to take the matrimonial plunge yet again. His constant attendance on Miss Carrington certainly made it appear likely. She exchanged pregnant glances with Mrs.

Venables, who was seated nearby, and both ladies raised their brows.

Halfway through the festivities, the duke led Claire to a sofa and snapped his fingers for a footman.

"I am proud of you, Miss Carrington," he said as he took two glasses of champagne punch from the tray and gave one to her. "You are a consummate actress. Why, even the most astute among the *beau monde* are beginning to doubt that you are the artist, for surely you could not appear so unmoved if you were."

"That, no doubt, is due to your prompt removal of the painting from the exhibit, Your Grace. It answered beautifully," Claire replied as she waved her silver fan before her flushed face. The June day was almost sultry, and she wondered that so many in society would care to waste a morning twirling around a crowded, overheated room, all in the name of enjoyment. For a moment she felt a pang that she was not standing before her easel in Monsieur Duprés's studio, working hard on a new canvas, but true to her promise to the duke, she had abandoned her studies for the present time.

"Or perhaps it was my speculations about a shy and retiring Charles, Cedric, or Cecil. And only yesterday afternoon I overheard two men arguing about whether the principal figure in the canvas had straight brown or curly blond hair. We progress, my dear Miss Carrington, we progress," the duke said, interrupting her musings. Claire sat up straighter as he continued, "I almost forgot to tell you. I expect the Marquess of Blagdon to call on me this afternoon. I wrote to him, you know, telling him everything and begging his quick return."

"You did what?" Claire asked, dropping her fan to her lap.

The duke returned it, and pressed her fingers around the sticks as he did so. "My dear, how can you be so shocked? Of course he must come back to town and try to discover the name of the scoundrel who so maligned him. If he did not do so, his identity as the model would be established without a doubt."

Claire nodded reluctantly, her heart beating faster at the thought that Andrew was only a few streets away at this very moment. How can I face him? she thought wildly. Whatever can I say to explain it to him, and beg his forgiveness? Will he be angry with me? Will he expose me and denounce me? And even if he does not do that, how great his disgust for me must be to be made such a laughingstock. I know how he shuns notoriety and I do not think I can bear it."

She squirmed a little in her fashionable gown, and the duke coughed, recalling her to her surroundings. "I am sure that being treated as if I were of no more importance than a bootboy is a salutary lesson for me, but I cannot like it, Miss Carrington," he said, his voice sharp. "It is not at all what I am used to."

With difficulty Claire put Andrew from her mind. Studying the duke's haughty, aristocratic face, she asked with real interest, "Why do you bother with all this, sir? I have often wondered at your involvement, for surely just duping the *ton* cannot be all that amusing."

The duke shrugged. "The *ton* interests me not at all. No, it was for your sake, and your sake alone, that I took a hand."

"There are some women who would misinterpret that remark, Your Grace," she pointed out, her voice steady.

"But they are not the clever Claire Carrington, are they? Who knows? Perhaps it is because you please me—your talent, your conversation, your gallantry. Besides, even if I were trying to fix your interest, it would do no good, and well I know it. I shall always regret that our paths in life crossed so late, but I know your heart has been given. I cannot change your mind."

His dark eyes blazed into hers as he bent nearer. "Could I, Claire?" he asked softly.

She shook her head, unable to speak, and he raised her hand and kissed it, which caused Miss Boothby's and Mrs. Venables's eyebrows to soar again.

"Do not question the goodness of my motives, if you please. I might be tempted to return to my earlier indifference. But let us go back to the marquess. I shall tell him everything that has been occurring in his absence, and where he might meet you next. There must be no awkwardness—at least not any more than might be expected from the innocent victims of the painting scandal. And when he is seen at your side as often as he ever was, and you appear pleased and easy, the gossip is as good as gone. The only question is, can you do it?"

Claire looked down to twist a silver bracelet on her wrist. "I shall certainly try," she whispered. "Do not think me a coward when I tell you I would so much rather not, however."

The duke smiled. "You will come through with all flags flying, I am sure of it."

"Tell me, Your Grace, is it true that Andrew's mother refuses to appear in public anymore? I have heard she is ill, and I cannot tell you how upsetting that is to me. To think it was all my doing!"

The duke snorted. "She is not ill, she is only furious. Do not waste your time sympathizing with the woman, for she is impossible. For years she has lorded it over society, cutting anyone who did not meet her cold, rigid standards. I daresay there are only half a dozen people in the *ton* that she considers at all worthy of her attention, and probably she even has some severe reservations about them. However, now that she finds her exalted self talked about and laughed at, the butt of jokes and conjectures, she cannot bear it. Leave her to her fury—she is not worth your pity."

Claire nodded, but her big gray eyes were troubled. "If only I did not feel such a charlatan," she mourned. "Every time I am forced to dissemble, I wish I could die, and I *hate* having to pretend I cannot paint!"

"Come, now, none of that! If you did not lie, it would be much, much worse, not only for you but for the marquess as well. I am sure you would do anything to protect him, would you not?"

Claire looked straight into his eyes. "Yes, I would. Anything."

The musicians were tuning up for another piece, and the duke rose and held out his hand. "I do hope Andrew appreciates you, my dear. You are indeed unique," he said, his voice admiring, and then he added, "But for now, let us forget the deceit. We will scandalize society and waltz again. That will give them something new to chew over."

Claire looked puzzled for a moment as she went into his arms, but then she shook her head at him. "You are too bad, sir! I know a gentleman is allowed only two dances, for Andrew told me so. To waltz with me again is a sign of such distinguished attention that everyone will be looking for an interesting announcement."

"And I am sure they will have one," the duke said smoothly. As he bent his dark head close to hers, he whispered, "Alas, that my name will not appear in it next to yours."

"Nor anyone else's name, Your Grace," Claire was quick to add, but the duke would only laugh and murmur, "We shall see."

When the morning's entertainment was over, he escorted

189

her to Lady Banks's carriage, making an appointment for a walk with her that afternoon. Claire waited for him to mention the possibility of Andrew joining them, and was more than a little disappointed when he did not do so. She barely saw the crowded streets or heard the din of traffic and all those loudly calling their wares as she was being driven back to Belgrave Square. She was wondering what she should wear, just in case he did come. The pearl gray was stunning, of course, but perhaps the new peach silk was prettier?

Attired in the peach and a wide-brimmed white bonnet with matching peach roses tucked under the brim, Claire walked the paths of Hyde Park that afternoon with the duke. She knew she looked well and that her gown and peach parasol were the envy of many, and so she was able to smile and nod to those people who paused in their own promenade to greet them. Nevertheless, she felt breathless and impatient. In her head a little voice whispered, "Soon . . . soon!" She wanted to ask the duke if the marquess had come indeed, but he did not introduce the subject, not with so many others in earshot. She could not help wishing they would all disappear like magic.

And then she saw Andrew striding toward them, his lean figure and long legs covering the ground easily, and everyone else did disappear. His dark blue eyes devoured her face as he came. Involuntarily Claire's hand tightened on the duke's arm.

The duke muttered an oath and then he whispered, "Steady, Claire, I beg you!"

She nodded and took a deep breath. She had not looked away from Andrew, but now she had made herself turn. She saw Miss Boothby and her friend Miss Shipley-Brown in a passing landau. London's premier gossip was in danger of falling to the roadway for certain this time, she was leaning forward so precariously. Her little eyes were wide in her avid face, she was so interested in the scene that was about to take place. Claire remembered to smile and wave to her. When she turned back, suddenly Andrew was there, removing his beaver and sweeping them a bow. His blond hair gleamed golden in the sunlight, and in the taut planes of that face she knew and loved so well, a muscle moved for a moment beside his mouth. He did not smile or speak, and Claire knew she was incapable of doing so either. It was left to the Duke of Severn to try to redeem this potentially dangerous situation.

"My dear Lord Blagdon!" he exclaimed, bowing in return, and then he hissed as he straightened, "Smile, *mes enfants!*" In a normal voice he continued, "How pleasant to see you safely returned to town, my dear fellow. I trust you left the country in its usual state of somnolence?"

"Your Grace," Andrew said, his deep voice stiff as his eyes continued to pierce Claire's face. "I cannot say I really noticed," he added, his voice indifferent. And then he took Claire's hand and raised it to kiss. "Miss Carrington."

"M'lord," Claire managed to get out past the lump in her throat, feeling both hot and cold at the same time from the shivers that ran along her spine at the touch of his lips. Beside her she heard the duke sigh in exasperation.

"Won't you join us, my dear boy? I am sure you and Miss Carrington have so many things to catch up on, being such great 'friends,' do you not? Do give the marquess your other arm, my dear, and we will stroll on. I fear we are blocking others' passage."

Obediently Claire took Andrew's arm. She felt the muscles tighten under her trembling hand and hoped it was not too noticeable. On her other side, she could hear the duke conducting a rambling monologue, and since she did not dare to look up at the handsome profile now so close beside her, she turned her head toward William Fairhaven, trying to calm her fluttering heart.

". . . glorious day, don't you agree? . . . Ah, good afternoon, Mrs. Sanford, sir . . . yes, as I was saying, can there be anything more delightful than a stroll with friends in pleasant weather? You must tell us about your journey to town, Andrew. You notice I do not ask about the country? Just so. I abhor the country . . . Lady Pearson, servant, ma'am . . . and, dear boy, you will never believe the exciting news we have to tell you . . . Lord Roland, m'lady. Miss Roland, you should never wear anything but that particular shade of blue. Devastating! . . ."

Claire smiled at the Roland family and took a deep breath. Everyone would remark it if their silence continued much longer, and although it was very good of the duke to bear the major part, it was not at all fair to him. "Indeed, what the duke says is true, m'lord," she said, staring straight before her. "But perhaps you have heard the ridiculous story that all London is buzzing about? What a shame that we cannot be the first to tell you of it, since it involves you and me so closely." She tried a light laugh, and although it was a poor imitation of her usual lilting trill, it seemed to break the spell Andrew had been cast under.

"Alas, there were several before you, Miss Carrington," he said. "But of course I am anxious to hear *your* version."

"That is better," the duke remarked under his breath. "Shall we take this side path, my dears? I am sure Miss Carrington would wish to see the Serpentine on such a day as this. Besides, it will be much less crowded," he added under his breath again.

The side path was narrow, and the marquess had to step back and allow the others to go ahead. Now that his disturbing presence was not so close to her, Claire tried to get her tumbling thoughts in order, although she could feel his dark blue eyes boring into her back.

The duke led her to a rustic bench under an elm some distance from the ornamental water. There was no one close by, and he nodded his satisfaction before he rounded on the marquess and demanded, "Now, why the devil did you come, m'lord? I thought we were agreed that it would be better for you to call on Claire in Belgrave Square before you attempted a public meeting."

"I could not help myself," the marquess said absently as he continued to stare into Claire's face.

The duke sighed. "I see that there will not be an iota of sense to be had from either one of you until you have had a chance to converse privately. I shall leave you, therefore, and go and commune with nature, much as it pains me to do so. Hopefully, no one will come by and observe you in your *tête-à-tête*. I shall come back in fifteen minutes and then we will return to the main promenade. I trust that a more equitable conversation will be possible at that time."

His bow was ironic before he walked away toward the water. Andrew took the seat beside Claire, neither one of them noticing that the duke had left them.

"Oh, Andrew, how you must hate me, how you must regret the day you ever met me!" she whispered. "But, please, please let me explain, or try to. Believe me, I am so very sorry! I never meant to . . . indeed, I did not even realize I had done it . . . I have been so miserable to think that I brought you this notoriety and pain, my dear friend, . . . oh, I wish I had never painted it, never even learned to paint . . ."

The harsh planes of his face relaxed and he picked up her hand and held it in both of his. His eyes glowed and she caught her breath at the fervent light she saw there. "Shhh, love. Yes, I have been miserable too, but not because of your canvas. It is an excellent, powerful work. You must never regret painting it."

"You have seen it?" she asked, her voice wondering.

"The duke showed it to me when I called on him earlier. How well you caught me! There can be no doubt who the hero of the piece is. No wonder my mother fainted when she saw it."

Claire thought he sounded rueful, and she shivered. "Now she has as much reason to hate me as you do. I am so ashamed!"

"Claire, listen to me! I was angry at first, but only for a little while. I know you did not do it to hurt me. And how could you know your teacher would enter the work, or that it would be hung? No, I am proud of you, and proud you put me in your painting."

"Proud? How can this be? I have ruined your reputation, made you a laughingstock with your friends, and alienated you from your mother. I am surprised you do not take me to court for defamation of character, never mind speak to me."

Her voice was deep and bitter and she lowered her thick black lashes to hide the tears in her eyes. She turned away so the brim of her bonnet concealed her face, but Andrew was having none of that.

His long fingers reached out to grasp her chin, forcing her to face him again. "Claire! Claire! If you knew how encouraged I was when I saw the painting! For the first time I could hope that you loved me as much as I love you. All this silly scandal will pass when we are married. I warn you that I will not take no for an answer this time."

He let go of her chin, but only to grasp her shoulders and caress them. Claire felt a fierce elation, even as she realized that nothing had changed.

"You are not thinking clearly, Andrew," she made herself say. "I can never marry you now. At the moment, Monsieur Duprés has promised to keep my identity a secret, as have the other students, but it is sure to become known sooner or later. And then I will be reviled and considered a weird eccentric. Why, even Sir Reginald . . ."

She stopped abruptly, but the marquess ignored her last

words. "Who cares?" he asked quickly. "For myself I would like to proclaim your brilliance to the world. But I think you are evading your real reason still. Are you not still holding back because of my mother's ultimatum? If that is the case, you may be easy. After she saw the painting, and without even waiting to question me about it, she wrote to tell me that she had no son anymore. You need not fear, you see, that our marriage will cause her to cast me off, for she has already done so. And only for the crime of getting myself talked about, mind you. She will not concern us, love, for she is about to leave England, never to return."

"But, Andrew," Claire exclaimed, her eyes wide with shock, "you must be mistaken! No, I am sure it is just that she is so distraught and upset at this particular time. If you continue to deny that you had anything to do with the canvas—and that is surely the truth—and we are not seen together anymore, she will relent in time. I know she will; why, she is your mother!"

Andrew's mouth twisted in a grimace of distaste which Claire mistook for agony. She pressed his hands gently. "I am right, I know it."

The marquess stared at the Serpentine for a moment and then he said quietly, "Listen to me, my dearest, and believe me! I am not lying to you. I do not care if my mother does leave the country or even if she stays and never speaks to me again. There has been no love and very little affection between us all my life. I will not miss her. Furthermore, I do not care what the *ton* says about us, not a single one of them. I never have. I love you as I never thought to love any woman, and I want you for my wife, now and forever."

He paused and then he dropped his hands. Claire could still feel their warm pressure as he added, "Now that you have been accepted by the Royal Academy, you must realize how important it is that you continue your studies. It would be a crime if one as talented as you are stopped painting. I promise you I will not stand in your way. You may paint seven days a week if you choose. I only ask that you allow me the joy of your company at those times you are not working. Say you agree!"

"You are too good," she murmured, her voice stiff with her pain. "But I cannot agree, Andrew, for I am not sure. What you say now, and what you may say in the future, may not be the same . . ."

Her voice died away. She was so tired of lying, first to society about her painting, and now to her only love. What she longed to do was to throw her arms around him and confess that compared to her love for him, her love for her art was a very poor second best. But in spite of his words about his mother, she could not believe him. Surely if she held herself aloof from him, the dowager would relent. And then, when Claire left London, perhaps to travel abroad, he would forget her.

She straightened her back and faced him squarely. "You must give me some time to consider. I am so confused! And I think it would be best if we do not see each other while I am doing so. You have a very disturbing effect on me, my friend."

The marquess bowed his head in disappointment, and it was several seconds before he could control his voice well enough to say, "Very well. You shall have all the time you like. But in the end, you will marry me. My promise on it, Claire."

She shook her head a little at the determination in his voice, and then he leaned toward her as if to take her in his arms. Claire concentrated on not moving toward him as she yearned to do. Then, to both her relief and disappointment, he rose from the bench.

"I shall leave you now. Please make my excuses to the duke. Suddenly I cannot bear the thought of wandering through the park, the cynosure of all eyes, while the three of us chat of nonsense. Since you ask it of me, I will not call on you either. When we do chance to meet in public, I hope you will receive me as your friend."

He paused until she said, "Of course I will," and then he added, "I never thought to have my best friend and dearest love all in the same person, but understand this, Claire. Having found you, I do not intend to lose you. No, I will ask you again and again until finally you relent and come to me at last, admitting your love as honestly as I have admitted mine. I live for that day."

Suddenly he was striding away across the grass as if he did not dare to stay longer. Claire watched him until the tears she had not shed before him blurred her vision.

When the duke came back a few minutes later, he found her alone. Her face was pale, but it was composed, and there was no trace of her recent tears. She answered all his questions in an even voice, but he noticed that when he told her in exasperation at last that he wished he might beat her for her stubbornness, she did not even try to smile.

Although Andrew often found himself bowing to Claire at a party or meeting her in a country dance the following days, true to his word, he did not try to seek her out. Claire found herself living for those few seconds she could touch his hand or look into his questioning eyes. When he did not find the answer he sought in her own clear gray ones, his own eyes grew cold and distant again.

Not only the duke, but all society watched their every meeting. Aware of the intense interest, Claire remained cool and composed, but she was not sleeping well and she felt listless and tired.

Lady Banks had risen from her bed at last when it appeared that neither Claire nor the marquess had come to any permanent harm after her outburst at the academy. She saw Miss Boothby and heard the latest gossip, glad the duke continued to show an interest in Claire. The absence of the marquess, she accepted without question, although it saddened her. Of course he would no longer court her young guest—not now.

The duke began to squire Claire to other, more sophisticated parties. Claire suspected that it was because she was seldom asked to the more elevated *ton* parties anymore. Too many of London's hostesses had never cared for her frank conversation and unconventional ways, and the current scandal gave them the perfect excuse to cut her from their guest lists. It did not matter to Claire, for she was beginning to make plans to go home to Dawson Hall. June was well advanced now, and soon the Regent would leave for Brighton and she would be free of her promise to her aunt. She had had her Season; that it had ruined her life was something even Aunt Flora could never have foreseen.

Chapter Fourteen

To say the Duke of Severn was becoming impatient would be to understate the situation to a considerable degree. He knew why Claire continued to be stubborn, and although he thought her foolish beyond permission, he had to honor her for her scruples. If only the dowager marchioness was worthy of such a sacrifice, he thought, remembering the lady's icy eye and haughty pride. He had fully expected that Andrew Tyson, on his arrival back in town, would soon put paid to any of Claire's objections and sweep all before him in triumph. After, that is, he swept the lady into his arms and silenced all her objections with as many passionate embraces as it took to gain her ecstatic surrender.

But the Marquess of Blagdon did not sweep. He not only did not make love to her, he never even tried to see her alone anymore. Puzzled, the duke watched them whenever they chanced to meet. In his view, they both behaved like the merest of acquaintances. And at the rate they are going, he thought, that is all they will ever be.

Why didn't the marquess continue to pursue her? Why did he accept her refusal when he was so deeply in love with her? What the devil was the matter with the man? Since he did not know Lord Blagdon well enough to question him outright on such a delicate matter, and Claire refused to discuss it, the duke remained in the dark.

He decided he would have to take a hand. The end of the Season was almost upon them, and if Claire disappeared to the country or journeyed abroad as she had once or twice mentioned she might do, the chances of Andrew Tyson making her his bride were slight indeed.

Besides, the gay companion who had enlivened so many hours for him that spring, and of whom he was so fond, had disappeared. True, Claire still conversed with wit, but the sparkle he had come to admire in her and the audacity of her outspoken comments had dimmed. She would never be boring, but there was no gainsaying that she was not the delightful crony she had been before. The duke wanted very badly to shake her.

Having determined on his course, William Fairhaven wasted no time. The very next afternoon, he called for Claire in his phaeton to take her for an afternoon drive.

Claire was dressed in a new gown of violet muslin, for the afternoon was warm. The duke's tiger gave her a shy smile as the duke lifted her to the perch. She opened her parasol and smiled back in secret conspiracy as the duke came around and climbed up to his seat. Claire's eyebrows rose a little as he called to the tiger, "Let 'em go! And go back to the stables, boy. I shall not need you this afternoon."

The duke glanced sideways into Claire's serene face, as if to gauge her reaction to his command as the tiger did as he was bid. "You are not concerned, Miss Carrington?" he asked as the team sprang into fluid motion. "How brave of you—or how insulting to me. I have not decided which it must be, as yet. But stay! No doubt you have your pistol in that dainty bag you carry, all primed and ready. That salvages my pride!"

His dark eyes glittered with mischief and Claire ignored the devil in his eye. "I am not carrying my pistol this afternoon, Your Grace. I must admit I am puzzled as to why you let the tiger go. Since he cannot speak and you have never hesitated to say whatever outrageous thing came into your mind, why then did you refuse his services this afternoon?"

"Perhaps so you would feel free to say whatever outrageous thing comes into your mind," the duke said coolly. "But come! Aren't you concerned that I might lose my head, ma'am? You are, after all, quite, quite alone with me."

"I wish you would not be so silly, William," she said severely, calling him by his name as if he were no more than two-and-ten. The duke subsided. "With both hands on the reins, how can you possibly attack me? Besides, I know you have no designs on my person. It has to be something else, and no doubt you will tell me about it in your own good time."

"Now I know I have been insulted," the duke murmured as he maneuvered his team around a large accommodation coach and headed for the King's Road. "And here I have been making the most delicious love to you all these weeks. Can it be you did not hear me?"

"I heard you, but I did not believe you," Claire said evenly. "You are not in love with me, and we both know it. You like me, and that is all, primarily because I am unusual and say what is in my mind. Besides, I make you laugh. You find me amusing, but love me you do not."

"How lowering for both of us," the duke remarked, dropping his hands a little as the phaeton reached a more open stretch. Obediently the team settled into a fast trot, and Claire tried not to remember that the last time she had come this way it was with Andrew, the afternoon of the fire in Multon Street.

"You are very sure of your deductions, are you not, Miss Carrington? But what, after all, do you know of a man's passions? Perhaps I have been concealing mine because of your love for the marquess."

Claire stared at him. "May I ask you a personal question, sir?"

As he raised his brows and nodded in surprise, she asked, "Did you love your wife?"

The duke's black eyebrows rose even further. "What a singular thing to ask a man with five children!"

Claire ignored the mockery in his voice. "I believe it is possible to sire any number of children without an ounce of love on either side. It is a biological act that only requires lust."

The duke did not point out how improper this conversation was. His face was somber now with thought. For a while they rode in silence. At last he said slowly, "No, I did not love Anne. I married her because she was pleasant and pretty, because her birth was equal to mine, and because her relatives were not likely to become a charge on my purse. I needed an heir and I married to get one. She understood."

Claire wondered. Perhaps the last duchess had loved her husband. Knowing he did not return that love must have been a constant sadness for her. Claire rather suspected that that must have been the case, for there were those five children she had borne him to account for. Wisely she did not point this out to the duke, for he was frowning now. "You know, I don't believe I have ever loved anyone," he admitted in a wondering voice, as if the failing had just occurred to him. Then he smiled, albeit grimly. "From what I have seen of the state, I should be congratulating myself. It appears to be an uncomfortable, consuming tangle of broken dreams and unfulfilled promises, more painful than rewarding. And even when it is resolved happily at first, it soon molders away into mere habit and convenience. I rather think I have been fortunate to escape it.''

"I said something very like that myself once," Claire mused.

The duke brought them both to order. "Miss Carrington, if you please! I did not drive you out into the country to discuss the paucity of love in my life."

In spite of herself, Claire had to smile. "No, you did not, did you, sir? But then, I have been very clever, have I not?"

"Minx!" he scolded, delighted with her return to wit.

"Someday, however, Your Grace," she continued, "when you do fall deeply in love, you will discover what it is like. I wish you more joy of it than I have had."

The duke took advantage of this slight breach in her defenses to begin his campaign to get her to change her mind about her future with the marquess. Not one of his careful, reasoned arguments had any effect on her at all. After several miles and his ever-more-impassioned pleas to stop being a wet-goose and grasp the happiness that would be hers and Andrew's, the duke gave up. He halted his team on a clear stretch of road and, without a word, turned them and headed back to town at a gallop. Claire clung to the side of the phaeton, holding on to her bonnet. After one glance at the duke's tight lips and his black eyes snapping with frustration, she did not try to converse with him again.

When they reached Belgrave Square a short time later, steam was rising from the wet, heaving flanks of the horses. Claire almost fancied she could see matching steam escaping the duke's arrogantly tilted beaver.

"Can you get down by yourself?" he asked, breaking the silence they had shared. "Without the tiger I cannot leave the team," he added brusquely.

Claire climbed down nimbly and then turned back to say good-bye, thanking him with a smile for the pleasant drive.

"Claire Carrington, you are an impossible woman," the duke informed her coldly through gritted teeth. "You are stubborn, willful, overly sure of your own omnipotence, and shortsighted to boot!"

Claire tilted her head to one side to consider this devastating criticism. "Oh, dear. Does that mean you intend to cut the connection, Your Grace?" she asked, her voice sweet.

"Insolent baggage!" he muttered, and at her gurgle of laughter, he drove off before he was tempted to say more.

The duke did not permit this setback to deter him, and as soon as he reached Severn House in Park Lane, he sent a note to Lady Peakes, ordering his footman to wait for a reply.

Whatever Lady Peakes thought of this communication from a man she hardly knew, she did not refuse his request for an interview, and replied at once, setting a time for the following morning.

When the duke was admitted to her drawing room, he was glad to see that she was alone. He had not liked to ask that her husband be excluded, but he had no desire to air the problem he had brought to the lady with Lord Peakes in attendance. He had long considered the man a muttonheaded idiot, sure to spread the secret far and wide.

Lady Peakes motioned the duke to a chair and instructed her butler to pour them some wine. She studied the duke as she did so. William Fairhaven was only a few years her junior, but their paths had never crossed to any degree. Marion had long and secretly admired him from afar. He was so handsome, so aristocratic with his tall, lean build and sophisticated air, and such a contrast to her husband. She could not restrain a tiny sigh of regret. And then there were his five children as proof of his virility. Percy had not been able to father a single offspring. Life was most definitely not fair.

She was recalled to the drawing room as the butler bowed himself out and closed the doors behind him. The duke sipped his wine and then put his glass on a table near his chair.

"Thank you for seeing me, Lady Peakes. I am sure you are wondering why I am here. Not, of course, that a woman of your beauty ever has to wonder about that," he added, his grin white in his dark face.

Marion felt her heart beating a little faster, although not a muscle moved in her cool face. She nodded her thanks for the compliment. "I do admit to curiosity, Your Grace," she said. "I do not believe you mentioned the purpose of your call in your note."

"I did not care to entrust it to paper. You must forgive me if I seem blunt and overly curious, ma'am, but I am in need of your assistance. Tell me, how do you regard any liaison between your brother and Miss Claire Carrington? Are you of your mother's mind?''

At her wide-eyed stare, he added, ''I trust my plain speaking will not overset you.''

Marion put her wineglass down, for her hand was trembling. ''I am afraid I do not understand why *you* should ask.''

''I am aware that to do so makes me appear as much a busybody as Miss Boothby, does it not? I assure you that is not the case. I am very fond of Claire Carrington and she loves your brother. I might also add that the marquess returns her love and is determined to marry her.''

The duke rose and paced the room for a moment while Marion watched him with startled eyes. ''There is a serious impediment to their union, as I am sure you know. To wit, your esteemed parent. Claire, learning of your mother's dislike of her, has steadfastly refused to marry Andrew. She feels, you see, that if she does not do so, the dowager will relent and not cast off her son.''

''She is wrong,'' Marion interrupted. ''My mother never changes her mind. She is the stubbornest woman alive.''

The duke bowed slightly. ''I suspected that might be the case. But tell me, how do you yourself feel about welcoming Claire as your sister-in-law?''

Marion frowned, and her cold blue eyes grew thoughtful. For a moment the duke was sure he was about to suffer a major defeat.

''A short time ago I agreed with my mother that Miss Carrington was impossible, and certainly not a fit mate for Drew. However, I have had a chance to observe him since his return to town, and I can see he is miserable. My brother is very dear to me; I cannot bear to see him unhappy. If he loves her so much, then I must try to love her too. And now there is no reason for Drew to suffer a marriage of convenience in the name of propriety, as I have had to do.''

Her voice was bitter and she stopped in some confusion. The duke was aware that Lord Peakes came from one of the oldest, most illustrious families in England. He was also aware that his name was his only attribute. No doubt the dowager had forced her daughter to marry him. He sent her a pitying glance of understanding, and Marion hurried into speech again, two red spots burning her cheekbones.

''It really does not matter whom Drew marries. Since the

painting scandal, my mother has refused to acknowledge him as her son. She sails for Bermuda next week, never to return."

The duke hoped that lovely island would manage to survive the dowager's exile, as he remarked, "In that case, the only bar to their marriage is Miss Carrington herself."

"I do not understand," Lady Peakes complained. "Surely, with my mother gone, and Drew's continued wooing, she will change her mind."

"But he is not wooing. Claire has told him she must have time to think, but what she really intends is to disappear. I have tried to explain the situation to her, but she does not believe me. Perhaps, dear Lady Peakes, if you spoke to her . . . ?"

Now it was Marion's turn to rise and take an agitated walk around the room. "I? Surely you are not serious, Your Grace! Why, every feeling must be offended. I could not possibly . . ."

"But if you do not, your brother will be miserable," the duke pointed out, his voice harsh and a little impatient. "Come, come! I am sure you are not such a poor honey as to condemn him to a life of misery only because you did not have the courage to be unconventional."

Marion eyed the duke doubtfully. "Surely Miss Carrington will think me very bold," she whispered. The duke laughed and went to take her hand to lead her back to her chair. He pressed it as she sat down, and smiled at her, using every bit of the charm he was so well aware he possessed, to sway her to his side.

"Miss Carrington is not such a high stickler, believe me. She scorns so many of society's conventions, this little liberty will be as nothing."

Marion twisted her handkerchief, not meeting his eye. "Well, yes. But that is another thing. I am not sure even now that Drew will be happy with such a strange girl. She is so free, so . . . so brazen!"

She kept her eyes on her lap in some confusion, and the duke restrained a sigh. "My dear Lady Peakes, you would be absolutely astounded at the extent of Miss Carrington's innocence."

Her eyes flew to his face, suspecting he was mocking her, as he added, "She may be well-educated, well-traveled, and extremely talented, but she is the veriest child when it comes to men. I am sure you will accept my assessment. You must be aware that I have had some . . . er, slight experience with your sex.''

Again his smile teased her, and with all her heart Lady Peakes wished she were twenty and single again.

The duke took the chair beside her and leaned close. "If you will but go to her and tell her what you have just told me about your mother, I am sure it will answer. And you will have the satisfaction of winning the gratitude of two very unhappy people, to say nothing of mine, my dear lady.''

Marion was not proof against his blandishments. She only wished there was more she could do to earn his approval. "Very well," she said with conviction. "I will do what you ask.''

"Today?'' the duke prompted. "There's no time like the present.''

"Oh, I could not go today," Lady Peakes demurred. "I never call on anyone without making prior arrangements. You see, my mother would never allow—''

"But you do not have to do what she deems proper now, any more than your brother does. Think how wonderful it will be to do something on the spur of the moment, something just a tiny bit . . . er, shameless!''

The duke's black eyes flashed with hidden meaning, and Lady Peakes rose, feeling somewhat breathless. This was going too far! He laughed as he got to his feet, watching her confusion.

"I shall call on Miss Carrington tomorrow, Your Grace,'' she said. "I want to observe Andrew at the Mannerings' ball, and perhaps she will be there as well.''

The duke had to be satisfied with this slight delay. He knew he had won a major victory as he bowed and made his graceful farewells.

As soon as he had gone, Marion sat down and wrote a note to Miss Carrington, asking if she might call the following afternoon at two. A short time later she received a formal reply confirming their appointment.

As she was dressing for the Mannerings' ball that evening, Claire wondered if Andrew's sister was coming to see her in order to beg her to give him up. Claire told herself she was glad to have the opportunity to reassure Lady Peakes that she did not intend to marry her brother. Surely the lady would go to the dowager at once with this good news, and then Andrew would be reunited with his mother. She wondered why this perfect solution to the problem made her want to burst into tears and wail in misery.

The ball was a perfect crush and all the *haut ton* seemed to be there, including the Marquess of Blagdon. His gleaming blond hair was in striking contrast to the black of his perfectly fitting evening clothes. Claire had the greatest difficulty keeping her eyes from that tall, lean figure and handsome face. And every time she looked his way, he seemed to be staring at her, those dark blue eyes stabbing into her heart as if he wished to read what was written there.

Andrew made a sudden decision to ask Claire for a dance. As she had requested, he had kept away from her all this time, but it had been the strongest test of his willpower that he had ever experienced. Tonight, however, she looked so lovely in her gown of pale pink silk with its fashionable overskirt of wispy, floating panels, and the ropes of creamy pearls she wore at her throat, that he could not stay away from her.

The Duke of Severn was about to sit down with her on a small sofa, but at Andrew's entreaty that he be allowed to dance with the lady instead, the duke bowed and gave him her hand. Claire knew she could not make a scene, but her eyes flashed. Both men completely ignored the indignation written there.

As the sounds of a waltz filled the room, Andrew took her in his arms. For a moment neither of them spoke. Claire did not think she could, for the delicious sensation of being so close to him was making her feel warm and helpless and dizzy. As they turned to the music, Andrew bent his blond head close to her black curls and sighed.

"Please forgive me, dearest Claire. You must admit I have been very restrained all this long time, but I could not help breaking my promise tonight. My life has been hell, seeing you and not being able to speak to you. Tell me, are you still of the same mind? Can you give me no hope that you will end this impasse?"

Claire looked up, but only for a brief moment. To continue to hold his gaze was much too dangerous; he was sure to see her love for him in her eyes. She knew now, clearer than she ever had before, that if it had not been for his mother's disapproval, she would have consented to be his wife without a single backward glance. Let her unusual upbringing go, her former opinions about marriage, and all the gossip of the *ton*. Her art, her work, did not mean anything to her without him, for nothing was more important than the love they shared. She would never stop loving him for the rest of her life. How she wished she were free to surrender to him!

As they turned again, she saw his sister watching them carefully, and the condemnation she thought she saw on her cold face stiffened her resolve.

"I cannot, sir," she said, barely above a whisper.

"What? No hope at all? You consign me to purgatory so easily?" he asked, his hand tightening on her waist until she was sure she must cry out.

"Andrew! You are hurting me," she said, and at once he loosened his grasp, although Claire could not make herself move away from him. When he did not speak, she stole a glance at his face from under her thick lashes. She was surprised to see that instead of despair, there was a stern determination written there, as if her words had had no effect on him at all. Could it be possible that he did not believe her even now?

"You must not come near me again," she ordered, and although she knew she should smile as all the others were doing as they danced, she could not make the muscles in her face obey.

"I will come near you every chance I get," he replied evenly. "I will never stop until you admit you love me. Claire, Claire! How can you be so stubborn? How can you let our love go this way? And what good will it do? I shall love you always and I shall never marry another. Can you really banish us both to lives of loneliness?"

Claire looked about desperately. She did not think she could continue to act this part much longer. Never had a waltz seemed so long! She saw the duke watching them, and she murmured, her throat tight with unshed tears, "You exaggerate, my lord. You will not be alone for long. And neither shall I."

No, she added to herself bitterly, I shall have my art as my only companion.

The marquess gasped and stopped to hold her away from him so he could search her face. Fortunately the waltz drew to a close just then and this singular behavior aroused no comment. As the other dancers bowed and curtsied and stopped to chat with their friends as they left the floor, he held her still.

Afraid at what he might blurt out, Claire hastened to say, "You must excuse me, my lord. I am promised for the next dance to the Duke of Severn."

She had never seen the marquess look so wild. He was white with shock and his lips were pale. Every lean plane of his handsome face was taut with such emotion that it was twisted into a mask of agony.

"Claire," he said at last, "are you trying to tell me that you are promised to the duke for more than just the next dance?"

Before she could cry out a denial, Claire made herself try to break away. The marquess became aware of others standing by and watching them curiously, and he took her hand in his arm and led her from the floor. As they neared the duke, he said, "I do not believe you. I *will* not believe you. And if by some cruel twist of fate what you have intimated is true, I shall kill him."

"Andrew," she whispered, her eyes lowered, "please, I beg you . . ."

"He shall not have you. You are mine. And in your heart, Claire, you know you are."

He stopped short of the duke and turned her to face him, putting both hands on her arms and bending close so only she could hear his words. "Once I said that if you found another I would release you from our pledge, but now I am not so noble. You will marry me, my dear, so think well on what you are doing."

Without another word, he led her to the duke and bowed and left them. The duke wanted very much to question her, but one glance at Claire's face told him that such a move might well propel her into hysteria. And so instead he chatted of the ball and the other guests as he signaled to a footman to bring her a glass of wine.

For the remainder of the evening Claire was always conscious of Andrew. Andrew dancing a lively schottische with Pamela Greeley and waltzing with Miss Mannering, Andrew chatting with Lord Alvanley and Lady Jersey, Andrew staring at her as she danced and chatted as well. In spite of her brave words to him, he had all her heart and she longed to follow it across the room and never leave his side again.

She left the ball as early as she dared, pleading a headache as she bade farewell to her hostess. It was not at all a lie.

Lady Peakes watched her go, and then her eyes went to where her brother was standing, and she caught her breath. The naked longing and misery on his unguarded face as he watched Miss Carrington leave made the matter very plain. Beside her the duke whispered, "You see I was right, dear lady."

Marion nodded, unable to speak for a moment, but then she said, "I thank you for coming to see me, Your Grace, and telling me of the situation. I do not know how I could have been so blind! You may trust me to explain everything to Miss Carrington tomorrow. I am positive I can convince her that any noble sacrifice of hers is unnecessary, for her place should be beside my brother."

Chapter Fifteen

Even as determined as she was, Lady Peakes was still a little stiff when she entered the Bankses' drawing room the following afternoon. Her greeting therefore was cold and formal. She thought Miss Carrington seemed ill-at-ease too, although her manner was gracious as she begged her guest to be seated. Marion studied her closely. Her huge dark-lashed eyes were serious in her pale face. She was wearing gray again, and although her ensemble with its slim skirt was stunning, it seemed to match her mood of nunlike severity.

Before she could gather her thoughts and begin, Miss Carrington said, "I am so glad to have this opportunity to speak to you, Lady Peakes. I wanted to tell you that I am aware of your family's distaste for any relationship between myself and Lord Blagdon. Believe me, I . . . I quite understand."

For a moment her soft lips tightened and a more militant expression sparkled in her eyes, but then she clasped her hands more tightly in her lap and continued in a stiff voice, "There is no need for you to be concerned. I have no intention of marrying Andrew. I tell you this at once so you might be easy on that head. And it would be a kindness if you would inform the dowager marchioness of my decision as soon as possible. I have not liked to think that Andrew has been estranged from his mother because of me."

She paused, and Lady Peakes asked, "You love him very much, don't you, Miss Carrington?"

Her voice had softened, and Claire thought it sounded pitying as well, and she had to swallow hard. "My feelings for the marquess have no bearing on our discussion. Suffice to say, whatever I feel for him, I shall not marry him."

"Oh, I do so hope I can convince you to change your mind!" Marion exclaimed. Claire's eyes widened and she looked startled, as if she could not believe what she had just

209

heard. "You see, it would be such a shame if you did not marry him, for then Andrew would be so unhappy. My brother is very dear to me and it is difficult for me to see him suffering because he has lost you."

"But . . . but, his mother! Can it be that she has changed her mind, ma'am?"

Claire was leaning forward eagerly now, her eyes glowing with hope. Marion hated to have to disappoint her, and she hurried into speech. "My mother will never change her mind. She never does, once she has taken a position. However, she is leaving England next week and her wishes need not concern you further."

"But I must be concerned," Claire insisted. "Surely if you were to tell her that I have renounced Andrew, she will stay and mend this rift between them."

Lady Peakes sighed. "I assure you she will not. Originally my mother did tell Andrew that if he married you, she would never acknowledge him again. He was given two weeks to cut the connection. He showed no signs of doing so, but before the time was up there was the scandal at the Royal Academy, and you ceased to matter."

"I ceased to matter?" Claire asked, bewildered. "But I was responsible for the scandal. I do not understand."

"It is hard to understand, I know. You see, it was not so much your painting him, horrible though that was, as it was that by continuing to pursue you in spite of my mother's orders, Drew had in fact caused the painting to be done. He might just as well have commissioned it in her view. And so it was his fault that we were placed in the awful position of being talked about. Don't you see, everyone in society was laughing at us. Imagine! The Tysons to be tittered over just like ordinary mortals! That was what was so intolerable to a woman as proud as my mother. Believe me, she will never forgive him for that. It does not matter whether you marry him now or not. She wrote to Drew the very day she saw the painting to tell him she had no son anymore."

"I cannot believe any mother would be so cruel!" Claire exclaimed before she thought, and then she colored up. "Oh, I do beg your pardon."

Lady Peakes smiled at her, and for a moment she looked so much like Andrew that Claire gasped.

"I see I must tell you the entire story, my dear, unpleasant as it is. Indeed, I came here on purpose to do so. It is not at all common knowledge, but since I hope you will soon be a member of the family, it is time you learned the Tyson secret. To explain why my mother is so proud and cruel, I must go back many years.''

Here Lady Peakes paused and could be seen to be collecting her thoughts. In some confusion, Claire waited quietly for her to begin.

''When Drew was eight years old, my father drowned. I was fourteen then, both of us old enough to have known and loved him very much. He was a wonderful man, my father, warm and caring and always laughing. Andrew looks just like him. I think he is like him in temperament, too, or at least he could be, given half a chance.''

''The late marquess drowned? His death was an accident, then?'' Claire whispered, remembering her own parents' deaths.

Marion nodded, her expression sad. ''Yes. He drowned saving Drew. Although he knew he was not supposed to, Drew had gone out on the river in an old punt. It began to leak, and since he couldn't swim then, he called for help. My father, who was riding along the bank with his agent, jumped in and swam out to him. He grabbed the painter of the boat and towed it back to shore. When he reached the shallows, he threw the painter to the agent. He must have had a heart attack then, for suddenly he gave a loud cry and sank out of sight. The river carried him away before anyone could reach him.''

''How terrible for you all!''

''Yes, it was terrible, but especially so for my brother. Drew blamed himself for a long time, and my mother . . . well, to tell you the truth, I think she still blames him. In her way, she loved my father too. She had never been gay and informal, but it was not until after his death that she became the woman she is today. I used to think if Drew had not grown up to look just like his father, she might have been able to forgive him. Instead, she grew colder and sterner and she treated him more and more severely. He was not allowed to play or have any amusements anymore, and he was only eight, Miss Carrington! Instead, for the rest of his boyhood she set about making him a competent successor to his father, worthy of the title and his exalted heritage.

''There were endless instructions and lessons, and when he rebelled sometimes, as any boy of spirit would have done, she punished him. Sometimes she had him beaten with a

211

leather strap, sometimes she locked him in his room, and sometimes he had to wear a heavy board for days at a time so he could never relax. I tried to stand between them and protect him as much as I could. It was not always possible.''

Here Lady Peakes paused and asked if she might have a glass of water. Horrified at what she was hearing and knowing what it meant for Lady Peakes to speak of such things before a stranger, Claire insisted she have some wine. When she had brought it, Marion sipped it gratefully, and then she went on, more slowly now, as if she were choosing her words with great care.

"I myself was reared just as strictly, for as the sister of the future marquess, I had an exalted position to fill. As a young girl I was afraid of my mother and I never rebelled as Drew did for fear of bringing her wrath down on my head too. Strange, is it not, especially when I am afraid I have grown to be just like her? You see, she has no close friends, for there are so few people she can approve, and she has come to depend on my support and companionship. And by being with her so much, I have absorbed many of her rigid ideas and standards. You must forgive me, Miss Carrington, for agreeing with her at first that you were not a worthy consort for my brother. I . . . I did not understand the depth of Drew's love for you.''

She paused until Claire sent her a shy smile, and then she continued, "Drew did not break under this harsh upbringing, thank God, he survived. But the day he reached his majority, he moved to London and took his own rooms here. He allowed my mother to retain the London mansion in return for leaving Blagdon Hall. She fought the move and threatened him then too, but he was adamant. Drew was always polite to our mother, he still is, but he let her know that there was nothing further she could do to control his life in any way.''

Lady Peakes sipped her wine again. "She never really accepted it, however, and she continued to try to manipulate him. In turn, he ignored her. It is unfortunate that as a female I was not able to do so as well.''

She looked at Claire and was not surprised to see the pity in her eyes, and she tried to smile. "So you see, Miss Carrington, it would be a terrible miscarriage if, loving him as you do, you did not tell Drew that you will marry him. He deserves some happiness in his life, and it is evident that your being by his side is the one thing that will ensure that happiness. I had to marry my mother's choice, without loving Lord Peakes or even feeling any affection for him. I married a noble lineage, not a man, for there was no way that I could defy her. But now I realize that I do not have to accept her standards as well; I can live my life as I choose."

"I am so sorry, Lady Peakes," Claire whispered, and Marion sat up straighter and squared her shoulders.

"I have grown accustomed, my dear, and Percy is not unkind. But allow me to point out from experience that a life spent without love is a terrible burden and an awful waste. In your case and Drew's, it is also unnecessary, don't you agree?"

"Yes, now I do!" Claire cried, and Marion smiled to see how eagerly she jumped up and how her gray eyes shone like stars, transforming her whole face. Marion rose as well, and gathering up her things, came and put her arms around Claire and kissed her.

"I will say good-bye, then, my dear, for now. I shall be waiting, however, for the happy news that I might call you sister very soon."

Claire hugged her and kissed her, the eyes of both women wet, and then she saw her to her carriage. As she reentered the house, her mind was racing. How terrible Andrew's life had been; why, she had no idea. Of course, being the kind of man he was, Andrew had never said a word against his mother, even to use as an argument to convince Claire to marry him.

She ran up to her room to write him a note begging him to come and see her as soon as possible. She had written no more than the salutation before she realized she could not wait even that long.

She ran back to the head of the stairs and called down to the butler to send someone for Jeremy and his hackney. General Banks, about to enter his library for a discreet afternoon nap, harrumphed and looked offended at this noisy irregularity. His bushy white brows rose as Claire laughed out loud and blew him a kiss, but before he could lecture her about her improper behavior, she had gone back to her room in a whirl of skirts.

Until the cab arrived, she was very busy trying to remedy a most neglected part of her education.

At last a footman knocked and told her the cab was at the door, and she tied on her prettiest bonnet and gathered up her reticule and gloves before she flew down the stairs and out to the cab.

"Dilke Street, missus?" Jeremy asked, holding the door and tipping his greasy top hat. He grinned at her, and the gold front tooth he sported that made him look so much like a pirate gleamed.

"No, not Dilke Street today, Jeremy," Claire said, and then she paused, looking stricken. She suddenly realized she had no idea where Andrew might be found.

"Tell me, Jeremy, where would a noble gentleman be likely to be at three-thirty in the afternoon?" she asked.

The burly cabbie stared at her, not sure she was not playing a joke on him. Reassured by the little frown on her serious face, he rubbed his unshaven chin in thought.

"Well," he said slowly, " 'e might be at one o' 'is clubs. There's a deal o' them about, missus. Or 'e might be out ridin' or drivin'. Come to think o' it, 'e might be at Manton's doin' wot the swells call 'culpin' a wafer,' or at Gentleman Jackson's havin' a mill. 'E might be gamblin' or drinkin' or wen . . . er, never mind that. It's possible 'e might be havin' a new toge fitted or buyin' some snuff. Lord, missus, 'e might be anywhere!"

For a second Claire seemed stunned by the magnitude of the problem, but then she smiled and nodded her head. "Take me to Treadle Street, if you please, Jeremy," she ordered, settling back.

"Treadle Street?" Jeremy asked, his voice disbelieving. " 'E won't be there, missus, not if 'e's a real swell like wot you claim."

"Treadle Street," Claire repeated firmly, and shaking his head, the cabbie climbed to his seat and clucked to his old horse. He told himself stoutly that it didn't matter where the missus wanted to go. A fare was a fare. Besides, he liked Miss Carrington, she was a nice gel.

Some minutes later, with Claire sitting impatiently on the edge of her seat now, they drove slowly down Treadle Street, but neither Andrew nor his phaeton was anywhere in sight. Claire made Jeremy inquire at the orphanage, but no one there had seen the marquess, and he was not expected.

After relating this bad news in a mournful voice, Jeremy was surprised to see Miss Carrington still looking cheerful. "Then we'll go on to Multon Street. Quickly now, Jeremy!"

The cabbie peered at her. Multon Street was even worse

than Treadle, and both were only a tiny bit more respectable than Dilke Street. You would hardly find Jeremy frequenting such neighborhoods, never mind the toff the lady was searching for. He shook his head, but he set out as ordered.

When they reached the corner of Multon Street, the way was blocked by a farmer's dray that was tangled with one of the oldest coaches Claire had ever seen. Both drivers were deep in a loud, angry discussion of whose fault the accident had been, and it did not appear that the problem would be solved, or the road cleared, for some time.

Grasping the side of the hood, Claire stood up in the hackney to stare past them down the block. Her heart leapt when she saw Andrew's phaeton and his groom Michaels, surrounded by small boys, standing to the horses' heads.

"There he is!" she exclaimed.

"Mayhaps we'd best go round the other way, missus," Jeremy growled from behind her, now entering fully into the spirit of the chase. Claire was about to agree when she saw Andrew coming down the steps of the orphanage, adjusting his beaver as he came. He paused for a moment to speak to the boys, his hand on the side of his carriage. At the thought that he might drive away before she could reach him, Claire sprang into action.

She jumped down onto the cobbles and pushed her way through the loungers who had gathered to see the accident. Once clear of them, she picked up her narrow skirts almost to her knees and ran as fast as she could down the street.

She did not notice the stunned looks of the passersby, or hear their rude whistles and catcalls, for her eyes were on Andrew, willing him not to leave until she could reach him. As she saw him put one booted foot on the step, she cried out in desperation, "Andrew, Andrew! Wait for me!"

For a moment she thought he had not heard her, and she tried to run even faster, though she was panting now and had a stitch in her side. And then she saw him pause and look back. His eyes widened in amazement as she sped toward him, her beautiful bonnet falling unheeded to the road as she came, and her skirts held high.

"Oh, Andrew, thank heaven," she cried as she reached him and fell breathless against him. He reached out and grasped her arms to steady her while he studied her face, his dark blue eyes searching deep into hers.

"Why, Miss Carrington," he said. "Here you are running

through the streets again. Will you never learn?" His voice was unsteady as he added, "And you have lost your hat."

"Bah! Never mind my hat," she gasped. "Yes, Andrew! Yes, yes, yes!"

For a moment the marquess did not move. He seemed to have turned to stone at her words, and Claire wished she had the strength left to shake him.

"Yes?" he asked, his voice almost emotionless in his determination to keep it even. "Do not think me slow-witted, ma'am, but I must ask you what you mean."

"I mean yes! Yes, I love you . . . yes, I have always loved you . . . yes, I will marry you tomorrow. Yes, Andrew! Now, always, and forever."

He drew in a startled, delighted breath as he took her into his arms and held her tightly. She raised her face and he bent and kissed her, his eager lips warm on hers as they demanded a surrender she was only too delighted to give him. Both of them were completely oblivious of anyone who might be observing them.

On this lovely June afternoon, Multon Street provided any number of interested onlookers. An old-clothes man pushing a heavily laden wheelbarrow gawked at them as he passed, one of Andrew's nurses leaned from an upper window of the orphanage, and three old women with market baskets paused across the street to point out this unusual sight. A gang of obvious thugs muttered to each other and grinned behind their hands, and Multon Street Mary, coming back from the gin shop where she had spent far too much time drinking blue ruin, clung to a lamppost and peered blearily down the street as if she could not believe her eyes.

Neither Claire nor Andrew was aware that anyone else in the world existed, lost in each other's arms as they were. Claire's heart was racing with joy at being so close to him at last, feeling his wonderful mouth possessing hers and his strong hands holding her as if he never wanted to let her go.

After a long time the marquess lifted his head reluctantly to stare down into her face. Her thick dark lashes hid her eyes, but her mouth quivered into a little smile of pure delight.

"I assume this means you will be my friend again, Claire?" Andrew teased, his deep voice warm with happiness as he laid his cheek against her hair.

Claire opened eyes shining with her love and leaned back so she could see his face. "Oh, yes, let us cry friends again, m'lord. Friends, and so much more, for I must confess I have lied to you. You have always had my heart. There is no one else.''

"And so the Duke of Severn is safe from my wrath?'' he asked, shaking her a little.

Her gray eyes danced as she nodded. "He was never in any danger of being called out on my account,'' she confessed. "How could he be? I do not love him, I love you.''

"My darling Claire! I was beginning to think that all was lost, I was so jealous of the duke last evening. Do not tell me just yet why you changed your mind and came to find me, if you please. We can discuss that miracle later. Tell me instead of your love, for I can never hear of it too often. And I will tell you mine, not that there is time enough left for me in the world for all I have to say.''

He bent and kissed her cheek and whispered, "My beautiful, talented, unusual bride! I adore you!''

"And I love you, Andrew, with all my heart,'' she replied.

Andrew could not resist kissing her again very thoroughly at that statement. And then the world intruded.

" 'Ere, now, Mr. Michaels, wot's the marquess doin' with that leddy?'' a small voice piped up.

"He's . . . er, kissing her, son,'' they heard the groom announce in stiff tones behind them.

"But *why* is 'e kissin' 'er?'' the small voice persisted.

"I imagine it's because he wants to marry her. Now, run along, all of you. Go on, now, scoot back inside at once,'' Michaels ordered, to forestall any more questions. His embarrassment was evident in every syllable.

Claire buried her face in Andrew's lapel to stifle her laughter. She felt glad and giddy and glowing all at the same time. "Oh, dear, I am completely shameless,'' she whispered. "And I have shocked your dear old groom yet again.''

"He will have to get used to it, dearest,'' Andrew replied. "I imagine I have shocked him too, but you know, I cannot seem to feel even an iota of remorse. Kiss me again!''

"Does this mean you won't be needin' me any more today, missus?'' a gruff voice called, and Claire made herself turn to see Jeremy and the ancient hackney pulled up beside the marquess's gleaming rig.

Michaels looked astounded that she had been riding in anything so revolting, and his face grew red with his indignation. Claire had to cover her mouth to contain her

217

laughter, for it was obvious from his expression that this type of lower-class vehicle would not do at all for the future Marchioness of Blagdon.

"Oh, Jeremy, there you are," she said airily when she could speak at last. "No, that will be all for today. I shall go with the marquess."

"I think those are the most wonderful words that I have ever heard. Know that you shall go with me always, my love. Always. I will never let you go," Andrew murmured, pulling her close again as his hands caressed her back. Claire was assuring him of her complete acceptance of such a plan when Michaels cleared his throat.

Suddenly Andrew looked around and realized the kind of fascinated attention he and Claire were receiving. He laughed and swung her up into his arms preparatory to tossing her into the phaeton.

"Let us be off at once, my darling. We shall drive to the park and find a secluded spot where we can continue our . . . er, our discussion," he told her, his dark blue eyes alight.

"Wait! Put me down, Andrew," Claire ordered, pounding his chest with her fists until he obeyed. His blond eyebrows rose as she backed away from him, saying, "I almost forgot!"

And there on Multon Street, amidst the slops and dirt and rotting vegetables, and the crowd of interested onlookers, Miss Claire Carrington sank into the deep curtsy she had been practicing earlier. Her head was held high, but her shining gray eyes proclaimed her homage and her love.

For a moment the marquess seemed stunned, and then he grinned, his own eyes crinkling shut in amusement. He swept his shining beaver to one side and placed his other hand over his heart as he returned an elegant bow.

As he took Claire's hand and drew her up and into his arms again, to murmur his love against her black curls, Multon Street Mary began to clap and cheer. "Aye, that's the ticket, me dearies," she called. "And 'ere's to you—'ip, 'ip, 'urray!"

About the Author

BARBARA HAZARD was born, raised, and educated in New England, and although she has lived in New York for the past twenty years, she still considers herself a Yankee. She has studied music for many years, in addition to her formal training in art. Recently, she has had two one-man shows and exhibited in many group shows. She added the writing of Regencies to her many talents in 1978, but her other hobbies include listening to classical music, reading, quilting, cross-country skiing, and paddle tennis. Her previous Regencies, *The Disobedient Daughter*, *A Surfeit of Suitors* and *The Calico Countess*, are also available in Signet editions.

JOIN THE REGENCY READERS' PANEL

Help us bring you more of the books you like by filling out this survey and mailing it in today.

1. Book title:_____

   Book #:_____

2. Using the scale below how would you rate this book on the following features.

Poor		Not so Good			O.K.		Good		Excellent	
0	1	2	3	4	5	6	7	8	9	10

Rating

Overall opinion of book. . . . . _____
Plot/Story . . . . _____
Setting/Location . . . . _____
Writing Style . . . . _____
Character Development . . . . _____
Conclusion/Ending . . . . _____
Scene on Front Cover . . . . _____

3. On average about how many romance books do you buy for yourself each month?_____

4. How would you classify yourself as a reader of Regency romances?
   I am a ( ) light ( ) medium ( ) heavy reader.

5. What is your education?
   ( ) High School (or less)   ( ) 4 yrs. college
   ( ) 2 yrs. college   ( ) Post Graduate

6. Age_____   7. Sex: ( ) Male ( ) Female

Please Print Name_____

Address_____

City_____State_____Zip_____

Phone # (   )_____

Thank you. Please send to New American Library, Research Dept, 1633 Broadway, New York, NY 10019.

SIGNET Regency Romances You'll Enjoy

SIGNET Regency Romances You'll Enjoy

*Prices slightly higher in Canada
†Not available in Canada

Buy them at your local

bookstore or use coupon

on next page for ordering.

Other Regency Romances from SIGNET